Northanger Abbey

Also by Val McDermid

A Place of Execution
Killing the Shadows
The Distant Echo
The Grave Tattoo
A Darker Domain
Trick of the Dark
The Vanishing Point

TONY HILL NOVELS

The Mermaids Singing
The Wire in the Blood
The Last Temptation
The Torment of Others
Beneath the Bleeding
Fever of the Bone
The Retribution
Cross and Burn

KATE BRANNIGAN NOVELS

Dead Beat
Kick Back
Crack Down
Clean Break
Blue Genes
Star Struck

LINDSAY GORDON NOVELS

Report for Murder
Common Murder
Final Edition
Union Jack
Booked for Murder
Hostage to Murder

SHORT STORY COLLECTIONS

The Writing on the Wall
Stranded
Christmas is Murder

NON FICTION

A Suitable Job for a Woman

Northanger Abbey

VAL
McDERMID

THE BOROUGH PRESS

The Borough Press
An imprint of HarperCollins*Publishers*
77–85 Fulham Palace Road,
Hammersmith, London w6 8jb

www.harpercollins.co.uk

Published by HarperCollins*Publishers* 2014

1

A catalogue record for this book
is available from the British Library

isbn: 978 0 00 750424 4

This novel is entirely a work of fiction.
The names, characters and incidents portrayed in it are
the work of the author's imagination. Any resemblance to
actual persons, living or dead, events or localities is
entirely coincidental.

Typeset in Andrade by Palimpsest Book Production Ltd,
Falkirk, Stirlingshire
Typographic design by Lindsay Nash

Printed and bound in Great Britain by
Clays Ltd, St Ives plc

MIX
Paper from
responsible sources
FSC
www.fsc.org
FSC C007454

FSC™ is a non-profit international organisation established to promote
the responsible management of the world's forests. Products carrying the
FSC label are independently certified to assure consumers that they come
from forests that are managed to meet the social, economic and
ecological needs of present and future generations,
and other controlled sources.

Find out more about HarperCollins and the environment at
www.harpercollins.co.uk/green

To Joanna Steven, constant reader, constant friend, who is indirectly responsible for introducing me to the delights of the Piddle Valley.

Acknowledgements

I'd first like to thank Jane Austen, without whom this book could never have come into existence. She's given me countless hours of pleasure, and I'd like to think there's a quantum universe somewhere where she is getting her own back reimagining Tony Hill and Carol Jordan.

My eternal gratitude goes to Julia Wisdom, who had the chutzpah to offer this irresistible assignment to me and who has always believed in my ability to achieve the unlikely.

As usual, I tip my hat to the queen of copy editors, Anne O'Brien, to my agent Jane Gregory and to Kiri Gillespie, who never complains. Thanks also to the team at HarperCollins who have supported The Austen Project with such quiet efficiency.

And thanks finally to my family and friends who never let me down in spite of extreme provocation.

1

It was a source of constant disappointment to Catherine
Morland that her life did not more closely resemble her
books. Or rather, that the books in which she found its
likeness were so unexciting. Plenty of novels were set in small
country villages and towns like the Dorset hamlet where she
lived. Admittedly, they didn't all have such ridiculous names
as the ones in the Piddle Valley where her father's group of
parishes was centred. It would have been hard to make credible
a romantic fiction set in Farleigh Piddle, Middle Piddle, Nether
Piddle and Piddle Dummer. But in every other respect, books
about country life were just like home, only duller, if that were
possible. The books that made her heart beat faster were never
set anywhere she had ever been.

Cat, as she preferred to be known – on the basis that nobody
should emerge from their teens with the name their parents
had chosen – had been disappointed by her life for as long as
she could remember. Her family were, in her eyes, deeply
average and desperately dull. Her father ministered to five
Church of England parishes with good-natured charm and a
gift for sermons that were not quite entertaining but not quite

boring either. Her mother had given up primary school teaching for the unpaid job of vicar's wife, which she accomplished with few complaints and enough imagination to leaven its potential for dreariness. If she'd had an annual performance review, it would have read, 'Annie Morland is a cheerful and hard-working team member who treats problems as challenges. Her hens are, for the third year in a row, the best layers in the Piddle Valley.' Her parents seldom argued, never fought. Between the two of them, there wasn't a single dark secret.

Even their home was a disappointment to Cat. Ten years before her birth, the Church of England had sold the draughty Victorian Gothic vicarage to an advertising executive from London and built a modern executive home with all the aesthetic appeal of a cornflakes packet for the vicar and his family. In spite of its relatively recent construction it had developed just as many draughts as its predecessor with none of the charm. It was not a backdrop that fuelled her imagination one whit.

Cat's tomboy childhood had been a product of her desire to be the heroine of her own adventure. The stories she had first heard and later read for herself had fired her imagination and given her a fantasy world to play with. Her delight at having siblings – older brother James and younger sisters Sarah and Emily – was largely due to the roles she was able to assign them in her elaborate scenarios of battling monsters, rescuing the beleaguered and conquering distant planets.

For most children blessed – or cursed – with so vivid an imagination, the natural outlet is school. But Annie Morland had experienced what she called 'the education factories' at first hand and it had left her with a firm conviction that her children would best thrive under her own instruction. And so

Cat and her siblings were denied exposure to a classroom and playground society that might have subjected them to life's harsher realities. No one ever stole their dinner money or humiliated them in front of a roomful of their peers. Instead, they came under the constant scrutiny of a mother and father who wanted only the best for them.

James, blessed with natural wit and intelligence, would have succeeded whatever educational system had been imposed on him. And Cat, who cared more for narrative than knowledge, would probably have done no better wherever she'd been taught. They would certainly have become wiser in the ways of the world if they'd escaped their mother's apron strings, but had that been the case, their story would be too commonplace to hold much interest for an ardent reader.

Their only significant contact with their peers happened in the small park that had been created from a water meadow donated to the village on the occasion of the Queen's Silver Jubilee. The gift had been made by an international agribusiness keen to catch the eye of the Prince of Wales; and besides, the field had no significant agricultural potential since it lay within an oxbow of the Piddle and so could not be aggregated into one of the prairies so beloved by commercial farming. The park contained a football pitch, a tennis court, an adventure playground and, thanks to an American couple who had moved into the Old Schoolhouse, a rudimentary baseball diamond. Whenever school was out, the field acted as a child magnet. Little was formally organised, but there were always pick-up games of one sort or another into which the junior Morlands were readily absorbed. Cat particularly enjoyed any sort of ball game that included rolling or sliding in the dirt.

Cat progressed from tomboy to teenager without showing any academic or sporting distinction whatsoever. Her enthusiasm seldom lasted long enough to produce any solid results. Often her mother despaired of ever managing to shoehorn a French irregular verb or a simple algebraic equation into her daughter's brain. After a nature walk, Cat would rather sit round the fire telling ghost stories than discussing the flora and fauna they'd seen in the woods and fields. She made notes when her mother insisted, then promptly mislaid them. Whenever she could drag their lesson off track, she did. In a history lesson, Annie would suddenly realise that instead of learning about Tudor foreign policy, her daughter was making the case for Henry VIII's much-married state.

Faced with constant failure, Annie tried to find an explanation. Perhaps Cat was one of those individuals whose right brain dominated, making them creative, musical and imaginative. 'Does that also include being utterly incapable of focusing on anything for more than two minutes at a time?' her husband asked with mild exasperation when she outlined this theory to him one night as they retired to bed. 'Who knows if she's musical or creative? She says she loves music but she never practises the piano. She says she loves stories but she never finishes any of the ones she starts writing. She can't be bothered earning pocket money because there's nothing she wants to spend it on. All she wants are novels, and she can get as many of those as she wants from our bookshelves and the library bus. Honestly, Annie, as far as I can tell, she inhabits an entirely separate universe from the rest of us. She's a completely dozy article.'

'And what kind of future is she going to have?' Annie tried

not to admit pessimism into any area of her life, but where her eldest daughter was concerned, it was hard not to let it sneak in through the slightest crack in her defences.

'One that requires no qualifications other than a good heart,' Richard Morland said, rolling over and punching his pillow into submission. 'Look how good she is with the little ones. Catherine will be fine,' he added with more confidence than his wife thought he had any right to. That, she supposed, was where your faith came in.

Cat meanwhile was sleeping the sleep of the unconcerned, lost in happy dreams of adventure and romance. The details of her future never disturbed her interior life. She was serenely convinced that she would be a heroine. In her mind, all her life had been a preparation for that role. That wasn't to say there wouldn't be obstacles. Anybody who knew anything about adventures knew there would be stumbling blocks aplenty along the way to true love and happiness. Their families would be at war or her beloved would turn out to be a vampire or they would be separated by an ocean or an apparently terminal illness. But she would triumph and conquer every barrier to a satisfactory ending.

The only problem was how these exploits were going to get started. Years of ranging through the back gardens and living rooms of Piddle Wallop under cover of childish games and pastimes had convinced her she knew all there was to know of her neighbours. Of course, she was entirely mistaken in this assumption, but her blissful conviction was unlikely to be over-turned while she paid more attention to the inside of her head than the secrets of those who surrounded her. As far as Cat was concerned, she knew nobody who was likely to provoke

any sort of adventure. If she was going to embark on an esca-
pade, she would first have to escape the narrow confines of the
Piddle Valley. And she couldn't see how she was ever going to
manage that.

She was on the brink of despair when the impossible
happened. In one brief moment, her prospects were transformed. Like Cinderella, it appeared that Cat was going to have
her chance after all. If not at Prince Charming, then at least at
the twenty-first century equivalent of the ball.

Their neighbours, Susie and Andrew Allen, were the culture
vultures of the Piddle Valley. Andrew was the shrewdest of
angels. His eye for theatrical gold had led him to a tidy fortune
through investment in the West End commercial stage. He had
no particular love of the performing arts but he possessed the
knack of knowing what would please the popular taste.

For years, he had spent the summer in Edinburgh for the
Festival, cramming every day to capacity with Fringe performances and Book Festival events that might conceivably inspire
a musical. But a minor heart attack had felled him in the spring
and Susie had insisted that this year must be different. This
year, she would accompany him and he would be permitted to
attend a maximum of two shows a day. 'Because there are plenty
of ways to have a good time in Edinburgh without having to
sit through a one-woman show of *King Lear*, or a comedian
doing Jane Austen's Men,' she'd said to Annie Morland. For
although Susie Allen had herself been an actress, she had a
surprisingly low threshold of attention when it came to
attending the theatre.

But in order for Susie to enjoy those good times, she needed
a companion for the awkward occasions when Andrew insisted

on seeing a show whose description alone made her shudder. She had a very clear idea of the style of companionship she wanted. Someone whose youth would reflect positively on her; someone whose unformed opinions would have insufficient grounding to contradict hers; and someone who would attract interesting company without ever dominating it.

This was not how Susie expressed the matter either to herself or to the Morlands. And thus Cat was to be found one morning at the beginning of August packing her bag for a month in the Athens of the North, excited and delighted in equal measure.

2

No golden coach with white horses was laid on to transport Cat to Edinburgh. Instead, she faced the prospect of spending eight hours confined in the back seat of Susie and Andrew Allen's Volvo estate. But Cat was convinced she'd be fine, even though she'd never been further than Bristol in the Morlands' ancient people carrier. In the car, she'd be able to sleep and to read, those two essential components of her life.

There was no elaborate leave-taking of her parents. It was as if they had exhausted their potential for making a fuss of departing children when James had left four years before for Oxford. Cat had to admit to a twinge of disappointment at the apparent indifference of her family to her imminent absence. True, her mother gave her a smothering hug but it was followed by a brusque reminder to take her vitamins every morning. 'And don't forget you're on a budget. Don't blow the lot in the first few days. What you've got has to last you a month. You can't turn to the bank of mum and dad if you run out of cash,' she'd added sternly. Annie displayed not a sign of concern about what dangers might lurk on the streets of Edinburgh, in spite of having read the crime novels of both Ian Rankin and Kate Atkinson.

Hoping for something a little more affectionate or apprehensive, Cat turned to her sisters. 'I'll text you when I get there,' she said. 'And I'll be on Facebook and Twitter big time.'

Sarah shrugged, either from envy or indifference. 'Whatever,' she mumbled.

'I'll post photos too.'

Emily looked away, apparently fascinated by the contrail left by a fighter jet. 'If you like.'

Cat gave her father a look of appeal, hoping he at least would display some sign of dreading her departure. He slung a companionable arm round her shoulders and drew her away from the driveway towards the ramshackle garage where he indulged his woodworking hobby. 'I've got a little something for you,' he said.

Fearing another of his wooden trinket boxes, Cat let herself be led out of the sight of her mother and sisters. Instead, her father dug into the pocket of his jeans and produced a pair of crumpled twenty-pound notes. 'Here's a little extra spends for you.' He put the money in her palm and folded her fingers over it.

'Have you been robbing the collection plate?' she teased him.

'That's right,' he said. 'There would have been more but the congregation's been down this month. Listen, Cat. This is a great opportunity for you to see a bit of the world outside your window. Make the most of it.'

She threw her arms round his neck and kissed him. 'Thanks, Dad. You always get it. This is the start of an amazing adventure.

All these years, I've been reading about exciting exploits and wild escapades, and now I'm actually going to have one of my own.'

Richard's smile held a touch of sadness. 'I remember reading *Swallows and Amazons* and the Famous Five books and thinking that was how my life was going to be. But it didn't turn out like that, Cat. Don't be disappointed if your trip to Edinburgh doesn't play out like a Harry Potter story.'

Cat snorted. 'Harry Potter? Even little kids don't believe Harry Potter's for real. You can't long for something you know is totally fantasy. It's got to feel real before you can believe it could happen to you.'

Her father rumpled her long curly hair. 'You're talking to the wrong person. I believe in the Bible, remember?'

'Yeah, but you're not one of those crazies who think the Old Testament is history. What I mean is, all that magic and sorcery – nobody could believe that. But when I read about vampires, it could be true. It could be the way things are beneath the surface. Everything fits. It makes sense in a way that Quidditch and silly spells don't.'

Richard laughed. 'Well, I hope you can have an adventure in Edinburgh without being bitten by a vampire.'

Cat rolled her eyes. 'Such a cliché, Dad. That's so not what the undead are all about.'

Before he could respond, they were interrupted by a car horn. 'Your carriage awaits,' Richard said, gently pushing her out of the garage ahead of him.

The journey north was uneventful. In deference to Cat's taste in literature, Susie had downloaded an abridged audio book of

Bram Stoker's *Dracula*. For Cat, schooled only in contemporary vampire romance, it was a curious and unsettling experience. It reminded her of the first time she'd tasted an olive. It was unlike everything that had crossed her palate before; strange and not quite pleasant, yet gilded with the promise of sophistication. This was what she would like when she knew enough of the world, it seemed to say. It was a guarantee that was more than enough to keep her focused on the conflict between the Transylvanian count and Professor Van Helsing.

The book ended and Cat drifted into consciousness of the outside world just as they reached the outskirts of the city centre. She squirmed out of her slouch on the back seat and eagerly scanned the neighbourhood, taking in the imposing symmetry of the grey stone buildings that lined the streets, interspersed with orderly tree-lined gardens enclosed by spiked railings. Although the light was barely fading into dusk, in her imagination it was a dark and foggy evening, when this would become a thrillingly ominous landscape. She had come to Edinburgh to be excited, and even at first sight, the city was living up to her expectations.

Mr Allen liked to live well, and he always took comfortable lodgings for his August pilgrimage. This year, he'd rented a three-bedroomed flat towards the West End of Queen Street which came with that contemporary Edinburgh equivalent of the Holy Grail – a parking permit. By the time they'd found a parking space that matched it, then lugged their bags up several flights of stairs, none of them had appetite or energy for anything more than a good night's sleep.

Cat's room was the smallest of the three bedrooms, but she didn't care. It was painted in shades of yellow and lemon and there was plenty of room for a single bed, a dressing table, a wardrobe and a generous armchair that was perfect for curling up and reading. Best of all, it looked out over Queen Street Gardens. Cat had no difficulty in ignoring the constant traffic below and enjoying the broad canopy of trees. Now twilight had taken hold – and to her astonishment, it was already almost eleven o'clock, when it would be properly dark in Dorset – she could see bats flitting among the leaves. She gave a little shiver of pleasure before she closed the curtains and slipped into sleep.

Breakfast with the Allens was an even more casual affair than at the Morlands. When Cat emerged from the shower, she found Mr Allen in his dressing gown reading the *Independent* by the window, a cup of coffee at his elbow. He glanced up and said, 'The supermarket delivery came. There's fruit and juice and bacon and eggs in the fridge. Croissants in the bread bin and cereals in the cupboard. Help yourself to whatever you fancy.'

Spoiled for choice, Cat poured a glass of mango juice while she considered her options. 'Is Susie still sleeping?' she asked.

Mr Allen grunted. 'Probably.' He made a performance of closing his newspaper and draining his cup. 'I've got a ticket for a show at half past ten at the Pleasance. A sketch comedy group from Birmingham doing a musical version of *Middlemarch*.'

'That doesn't sound very likely.'

He stood up and stretched. 'And that, my dear Cat, is precisely why it might just work.'

Cat realised she still had a lot to learn about contemporary theatre. With luck, she'd know much more by the end of her four weeks in Edinburgh. 'Are we coming with you?'

He chuckled. 'God, no. Susie won't venture anywhere near a cultural event until she's kitted herself out in this season's wardrobe. You two are destined for the shops this morning. I hope you're feeling strong.'

At the time, she'd thought he was exaggerating, as she knew men are inclined to do on the subject of women and shopping. But by the fifth shop, the fifth pile of clothes, the fifth changing room, Cat was beginning to feel amazement at Mr Allen's level of tolerance. Admittedly, she'd had little opportunity to observe married life at close quarters, apart from that of her parents. But although she didn't like herself for the thought, Cat reckoned she had somehow previously missed the realisation that Susie Allen was the most empty-headed woman she'd ever spent time with. What was bewildering about this discovery was that Mr Allen was definitely neither empty-headed nor obsessed with how he looked. It was puzzling. All they seemed to share was curiosity. But while Mr Allen's curiosity was aimed at finding new wonders to bring to the public's attention, Susie Allen seemed interested only in spotting famous faces among the crowds that thronged the shops and the streets of Edinburgh.

'Isn't that the little Scottish woman who's always on the *News Quiz*? Oh, and surely that's Margaret Atwood over there, trying on hats? Oh look, it's that rugby player with the big thighs.' Such was the level of Susie's discourse.

Her one saving grace, at least to a teenager, was her generosity. While she lavished a new wardrobe on herself, Susie was not slow to treat Cat to similar delights. Cat was not by nature greedy, but there was never much to spare in the Morland family budget for the vanity of fashion over practicality. Although Cat knew it was generosity enough to bring her on this trip and that her parents would disapprove of her accepting what they'd regard as unnecessary charity, she couldn't help but be seduced by the stylish trifles Susie thought her due. Even so, by mid-afternoon, Cat was weary of retail therapy and longing to plunge into some cultural life.

Her prayers were answered when they returned to the flat to find Mr Allen sitting by the window with a cup of tea and his iPad. 'I have tickets for you both for a comedy show this evening at the Assembly Rooms,' he announced without stirring. 'I've been invited to a whisky tasting, so I'll meet you in the bar after the show.'

Cat retreated to her room, where she spread her new clothes on the bed and photographed each item with her phone. She posted her favourite shot – a camisole cunningly dyed in gradations of colour from fuchsia to pearly pink – on her Facebook page then sent the others to her sisters. She texted her parents to say she'd spent the day walking around with Susie and they'd be going out to see a show in the evening. Instinctively, she knew what not to tell her parents. Sarah and Emily wouldn't give her away. Not because they were intent on keeping her confidences, but rather because their annoyance at what they were missing out on would manifest itself in blaming their parents.

The pavement under the triple-arched portico of the Assembly Rooms was busy with people milling around, eyes darting all over the place, eager to spot acquaintances or those they would like to become acquainted with. Posters plastered every surface, over-excited fonts trumpeting the attractions within. Everything clamoured for Cat's attention and she clung nervously to Susie's arm as they pushed through the crowds to get inside.

The scrum of people seemed to grow thicker the further they penetrated the building. Mr Allen had spoken of the grace and elegance of the interior, explaining how it had been restored to its eighteenth-century glory. 'They've kept the perfect proportions and returned it to its original style of decoration, right down to the chandeliers and the gold leaf on the ceiling roses,' he'd told them over their early dinner. Cat had been eager to see it for herself, but it was too crowded to form any sense of how it looked. In between the heads and the hoardings she could catch odd glimpses here and there, but it formed a bewildering kaleidoscope of images. The sole impression she had was of hundreds of people determined to see and be seen on their way to and from an assortment of performances.

'I know where we're going.' Susie had to raise her voice to be heard in the throng. She half-led, half-dragged Cat through the crowd until they finally reached their destination. Susie handed over their tickets and they were admitted to the auditorium.

This was not Cat's initiation into live performance. She'd regularly attended performances in the village hall and even, occasionally, at the Arts Centre in Dorchester. She knew what to expect. Rows of seats, a soft mumble of conversation, a curtained proscenium arch.

Instead, she was thrust into a hot humid mass of bodies that filled the space around a small raised dais at one end of the packed room. Through the gloom, she could see some chairs, but they were all taken. What remained was standing room only. Standing room so tightly packed that Cat was convinced if she passed out, nobody would know until they all began to file out and she crumpled to the floor.

'It's a bit hot,' she protested.

'You won't notice when the show begins,' Susie assured her.

Because Susie had taken so long to get ready, they were only just in time. A skinny young man with a jack-in-the-box spring in his step bounced on to the stage, his hair a wild shock of blond and blue that matched his T-shirt. He dived straight in with a barbed attack on his arrival in Edinburgh, his West Midlands delivery so fast and so heavily accented that Cat could barely make out one line in three.

The audience seemed to fare better, following the performance well enough to cheer, laugh and heckle in equal measure. It was a novel experience for Cat, and in spite of her discomfort, she found herself caught up in the atmosphere, clapping and laughing regardless of whether she'd got a particular joke.

Eventually the show came to an end, with whoops and cheers signalling that it had been more of a success than not. The one good thing about being so far back was that they were able to make a relatively quick getaway. It was almost dizzying to emerge into the relative airiness of the foyer after the closeness of the event. 'The bar,' Susie said, immediately dragging her away from the direction of the street and deeper into the bowels of the building. 'I'm gagging for a drink.'

The bar was no less crowded. People stood three deep waiting to be served. Susie groaned and glanced at her watch. 'Andrew will be here any minute; he can do the donkey work for us. Come on, let's find a seat, my feet are killing me.' Cat wasn't surprised. Even a teenager would have had more sense than to go out for the evening in the ridiculous shoes Susie had bought that morning.

Finding a seat didn't seem a likely prospect to Cat, but Susie was undaunted by the crowds. She spied a table occupied by a group of young people who were clearly together, bunched around wine bottles and glasses. Susie marched straight up to the table and plonked herself on the end of the banquette. 'Squeeze up, darlings,' she said, waving her hands in a shooing motion.

Despite their anarchic appearance, this was evidently a group of nicely brought-up students. They obediently squashed closer together, creating just enough space for Susie and a sliver of seat for Cat. But politeness didn't extend to including the pair in their conversation. Cat felt invisible and unattractive. All at once it dawned on her that she had never been in a crowded place where she didn't know most of the other people present. It was simultaneously thrilling and unnerving. The potential for romance or danger was all around her; it was time to embrace the unfamiliar, not shrink from it.

She turned to share her insight with Susie, who was scouring the room with a pout on her face. 'Unbelievable. I emailed and Facebooked at least a dozen of my best friends to say we'd be here tonight and there's not a single one of them to be seen. I wanted you to meet the Elliots, they've got a son around your age. And the Wintersons, their twin girls must be off to university at the end of the summer. But no. Not a soul in sight.'

Cat felt the bubble of excitement burst within her, pricked by Susie's discontent. But before she could say anything, Mr Allen appeared, pushing his way through the press of bodies.

'This is impossible,' he said, breathing a cloud of whisky fumes over them both. 'There's no pleasure in this. Let's just walk home and have a drink there.'

'But we'll miss seeing everybody,' Susie complained.

'You can't see anybody in this mob, never mind have a conversation. We'll catch up with people soon enough. This is no introduction to Edinburgh life for poor Cat. Look at the girl, she's practically melting in here.'

Cat was sure it had not been his intention, but Mr Allen's words only served to make her feel more unappealing and unsophisticated. Flushed, she stood up and stepped aside to free Susie from the banquette. As she set off in the wake of the Allens, one of the young men at the table put a hand on her wrist. She startled away from him and he winked at her. 'Cool top,' he said.

She took off after Susie before she lost sight of her flam-boyant peasant dress, even more hot and bothered than before. But as they emerged into the chill of the evening, she realised that brief final contact had made the entire evening worthwhile. Edinburgh really was a city of infinite promise.

3

Cat was surprised by how quickly her Edinburgh days fell into a routine. In the morning after a late breakfast, she and Susie used the excuse of art to get out of the flat and explore. It was true that they saw many paintings, sculptures and obscure installations, but more than that, they saw the city, from the regimented grid of streets of the Georgian New Town to the multi-layered maze of vennels and closes that formed the old town where Burke and Hare had plied their trade. Cat had googled the dark side of Edinburgh history, and it was she rather than Susie who enlivened their prowls through the city with tales of body-snatchers and Janus-faced citizens who held their sinister secrets behind the mask of respectability. On more than one occasion, Susie put her hands over her ears and laughed nervously, 'Stop, Cat, you're scaring me.' And that was before she even touched on the vampire lore she'd picked up on the Internet. Cat was in her element, seeing potential for terror and adventure around every twist and turn of the narrow streets.

Of course, neither art nor sightseeing was sufficient to hold Susie's attention for long. Somehow, their routes around the city centre invariably washed them up against some fascinating shop window like flotsam on the shore at Cramond. Cat understood it was the price she had to pay for the delight of exploring so exotic a city. That and Susie's constant complaint that she couldn't understand why she wasn't bumping into anyone they knew from their London days.

On the fifth day, they returned footsore to the flat to find Mr Allen laying the table with a selection of cheeses, meats and vegetable delicacies, several of which Cat was depressingly unable to identify. 'I was passing Valvona and Crolla on my way back from a rather promising show based on the songs of Chris de Burgh, and I thought I would treat us to lunch,' was his greeting. He distributed plates and cutlery then opened a bottle of pale white wine with a corkscrew that had the look of something that had won a design award. 'Oh, and this came by hand while we were out.' He nodded at a thick piece of card tucked into the flap of the sort of heavy white envelope that signals senders with a good opinion of themselves.

Curious, Susie picked it up and flipped the card over. 'Oh, Andrew, the Highland Ball! I've always wanted to go. It's been one of my dreams for as long as I can remember.'

He looked mildly surprised. 'You never said. They invite me every year. But I'm generally here on my own so I've given it a miss.'

'We are going to go, though? Aren't we?' Susie reminded Cat of her younger sister Emily faced with the prospect of the latest Pixar animation. She'd been like that once, but she preferred to treat her enthusiasms in a more mature way these days. Even her mother would have struggled to spot just how excited she'd been by the latest Twilight movie, for example. 'Oh, Andrew, *please* say we're going.' She turned to Cat. 'The Highland Ball is *the* social event of the Edinburgh season. Absolutely A-list, Cat. The perfect place for you to find a real catch.'

Cat felt the tide of colour rising from her chest up her neck to her cheeks. Mr Allen shook his head and gave his wife an indulgent smile as he sat down at the table. 'Leave Cat alone. Not everyone goes to the Highland Ball to find a man, Susie. But if it matters to you that much, we'll go. And we can take Cat.' He chuckled. 'The Highland Ball. That'll be an experience for you. All those men in kilts. You do know how to do Scottish country dancing?'

Susie subsided into a chair. 'Don't be silly, Andrew, where would Cat have learned Scottish country dancing? We'll have to get her some lessons.'

'Robbie Alexander's wife runs a class specifically geared to the Highland Ball,' he said. 'She told me about it a couple of years ago. Why don't you give her a ring and see if she can fit Cat in?'

And so that afternoon, Cat found herself on a bus to Morningside, where Fiona Alexander had commandeered the last available church hall in Edinburgh to impress the basics of Scottish country dancing on the novitiate. 'Think of it as war conducted by other means,' Mr Allen had said on her way out the door. It hadn't exactly reassured Cat about what to expect.

She sidled in, hoping there would be enough people in the hall for her to pass unnoticed. Luck was not her friend, however. There were fewer than two dozen potential dancers in the hall, mostly gathered in clumps of four or five, the young men nudging each other and horsing around, the women rolling their eyes or texting or gossiping with heads close together. Two or three older couples had gravitated to the far end of the room, where a woman of indeterminate age in a tartan skirt and white blouse, hair tied back with a tartan ribbon, stood frowning at a portable CD player. Cat presumed she was Fiona Alexander. She leaned against the wall and waited for something to happen.

After a few minutes, Fiona clapped her hands for silence. The mutter of voices died away and she launched into her welcome speech, moving seamlessly on to a brief explanation of how the session would be run. 'And so, ladies and gentlemen, please take your partners. We're going to keep the same partners, and it's generally easier if you work with someone you know already.'

To Cat's dismay, almost everyone seemed to be already paired up. Two other girls, both of whom she considered much prettier, and two young men were the odd ones out. They gravitated towards each other, leaving her stranded and terrified that she was going to have to dance with Fiona.

She was saved by a young man thrusting open the double doors of the hall and skidding to a halt on the threshold, panting and dishevelled from running. He bowed low towards Fiona, his thick blond hair flopping forward over his forehead. 'I'm so sorry, Fiona. I missed the bus and ran all the way from Bruntsfield. I think a bunch of old ladies thought I was a performance artist – they applauded me as I passed the coffee shop.' He stood up crookedly, one hand pressed against his ribs.

Fiona gave him a look of mock disapproval. 'Come in, Henry. At least you're here now. Which is just as well because this

young lady here—' she gestured towards Cat '—is without a
partner.' She smiled at Cat. 'My dear, I presume you're
Catherine Morland? Susie Allen phoned earlier. This unpunctual reprobate is Henry Tilney, who helps me out with my
classes. Henry, meet Catherine.'

As he moved towards her, pushing his luxuriant honey-blond
hair back from his brow, Cat had the chance properly to take
stock of him. Henry was the right sort of tall – a shade under
six feet, broad-shouldered but slim without being skinny,
graceful rather than gawky. His eyebrows and lashes were much
darker than his hair, and had it not been for his dark hazel eyes
she might have suspected him of tinting them for effect. His
forehead was broad and his cheekbones well defined on either
side of a prominent nose that saved him from being too pretty
for a man. His skin was pale and clear, unblemished by freckles.
He didn't have the confected good looks of a boy-band member
but his face was compelling and memorable. Heroic, even, Cat
allowed herself to think.

He dipped his head in greeting. 'Nice to meet you, Catherine.
I promise you, it's not as hard as it looks. I'll be gentle with
you.'

When she looked back on that first meeting, Cat would
wonder whether she should have been more wary of a man
who began their acquaintance with such a blatant lie. For there
was nothing gentle about what followed.

After an hour of being whirled and birled, of Gay Gordons
and Dashing White Sergeants, of *pas de basques* and *dos-à-dos*,
they broke for refreshments. Cat was uncomfortably aware that
she was sweating like an ill-conditioned pony and that Henry
seemed positively cool by comparison. She expected him to

peel away from her at the first opportunity, to make a bee-line for one of the tall blondes with the far-back vowels and hair bands, but he told her to stay put while he fetched her a drink.

She collapsed gratefully on a bench till he returned with plastic tumblers of fizzy water. He sat down beside her, long legs in raspberry-coloured cords stretched in front of him and crossed at the ankle. 'Phew,' he sighed. 'Fiona really does believe in putting us through our paces.'

'Why are you here? You totally knew what you were doing, every step of the way.'

'The Alexanders are neighbours of my father. Fiona mentioned that she was always short of competent men in her classes, so my father volunteered me. He likes to play the good neighbour. It stands him in good stead when he does something monstrous,' he added, almost too softly for her to hear.

Mysterious bad behaviour was naturally meat and drink to Cat. Now she was even keener to find out more about her intriguing dance partner. 'Well, I'm glad he did,' she said. 'This would be a nightmare if I was partnered with someone as clueless as I am.'

Henry gave her a wolfish grin, revealing small, sharp teeth. His eyes looked almost tawny in the afternoon light, like a lion stalking prey. 'You're welcome. But I'm failing in my Edinburgh duties,' he said, straightening up and ticking off his questions on his fingers. 'How long have you been in Edinburgh? Is this your first time? Do you prefer the Pleasance to the Assembly Rooms? What's the best show you've seen so far? And have you eaten anywhere decent yet?' He had a delicious accent; almost BBC, but with a hint of Scots in the vowels and the roll of the r.

Cat giggled. 'Is that the checklist?'

'Absolutely. So, have you been in Edinburgh long?' He gave her a wicked look.

'Almost a week,' she replied, stifling another giggle.

'Really? Wow, that's amazing.'

'Why are you amazed?'

He shrugged. 'Somebody has to be. And are you an Edinburgh virgin? Is this your first time at the festival?'

'It's my first time north of the line between the Severn and the Trent,' she confessed.

Now he looked genuinely amazed. 'You've never been north before? How on earth have you managed that?'

Cat felt shame at her untravelled state. 'I live in Dorset. We've never travelled much. My dad always says we've got everything on our doorstep – beaches, cliffs, woodland, green rolling hills. So there's no need to go anywhere else.'

Henry's mouth twitched, whether in a smile or a sneer she couldn't tell. 'Dorset, eh? Well, I can see the temptation to stay put. But you must admit, Edinburgh's pretty good fun. Worth the trip, wouldn't you say?'

Now she was on safer ground. 'I love it,' she said. 'It's beautiful. And there's so much going on, it makes me dizzy just thinking about it.'

'And have you been to the Assembly Rooms?'

'Our first night we went to a comedy show. God, but it was packed.'

Henry nodded. 'Always is. Have you seen any theatre yet?'

'We saw a wonderful play last night about coal mining. *Dust*. You should catch it if you can, it was very moving.'

'I'll add it to my list. What about music?'

Cat shook her head. 'The friends I'm with don't really have the same taste in music as I have. But I've got a whole list of writers I want to see at the Book Festival. Honestly, Henry, this is the most exciting time I've ever had.'

'More exciting than Dorset?' He was teasing, she could tell.

She laughed. 'Almost.'

'I had better work a bit harder, then. Otherwise I'm going to end up on your Facebook page as, "almost as exciting as Budleigh Salterton".'

She gave him a gentle punch on the arm. 'Budleigh's in Devon, you ignorant boy. And what makes you think I'm going to mention you on Facebook?'

'Because it's what you girls say. "Went dancing in Morningside, partnered with weirdo in red trousers who doesn't even know where Budleigh Salterton is. Duh!"'

She giggled. 'No way.'

'Here's what you should say: "Mrs Alexander partnered me with the best dancer and conversationalist in the room. Ladies, check out the fabulous Henry Tilney."'

Cat shook her head in pretended sorrow. 'Anyway, what makes you think I confide everything to Facebook?'

He gave her an incredulous look. 'You're female and, I'm pretty sure, under twenty-one. If you don't do Facebook, how are your sisters and your cousins and your best mates going to be provoked to teeth-gnashing jealousy of your trip to Edinburgh? How else will they know you're having the time of your life while they're doing whatever it is they do in Dorset? All you girls do it all the time – Facebook, Twitter. I have this theory. It's why you've all suddenly got so good at writing novels. Chick lit and the serious stuff. It's because of all the practice you get spinning yarns on your phones and iPads.'

'You're telling me that guys don't do exactly the same thing?'

Henry nodded. 'We do different stuff. We talk about sport or politics or who got impossibly drunk on Friday night. We don't do the chit-chat about our lives the way you girls do. We talk about serious stuff. Plus we have better punctuation and grammar.'

Cat hooted with laughter. 'Now you really are kidding. Here's one thing that guys do much more than women – trolling. You are the evil that stalks the Internet, with your shouty capital letters and your sweary insults and your truly terrible mangling of the English language.'

Now he was laughing too, enjoying the effect of what she realised was a wind-up. 'To be honest, I think the honours are pretty much divided between the sexes,' he said. 'Men are just as gossipy as women, and you girls can give as good as you get in the abuse stakes.'

Whatever Cat might have said in response was lost, as Fiona was shepherding them all back on to the floor.

'On your feet, girl,' Henry said. 'There are willows to be stripped and eightsome reels to be beaten into submission.'

Cat threw herself into the dance with renewed energy, discovering that the basic steps had finally sunk in. By the end of the afternoon, she could go for several minutes without having to apologise for crushing Henry's toes. When the final measures of the Canadian Barn Dance concluded and they collapsed on the bench again, she realised she'd had more fun with Henry than she'd ever had on a dance floor before.

'That was such good fun,' she said.

'You're all set for the Highland Ball now. I take it that's what this is in aid of?'

Cat nodded. 'I suppose you've been going your whole life?'

'I've been a few times. But I'm not sure whether we'll still be in Edinburgh by then.'

'We?'

'My family. My father gets a little stir-crazy in the city if he's here too long.'

Before Cat could ask why a grown man's schedule should be dictated by the preferences of his father, Susie Allen swept through the double doors in an elaborate multi-layered confection of muslins. 'Cat, darling, over here,' she called, as if her entrance hadn't already earned the attention of the whole room. She continued towards them in a cloud of floral perfume. 'I thought I'd better come and get you. Andrew's got us an invitation to a preview of Jack Vettriano's latest show this evening, and it's over the bridge in some little town in Fife, can you believe it? So he's outside in the car.' All the while she was speaking, her eyes were raking Henry from crown to toe, making a mental catalogue of his attributes. She gave him a sultry look that Cat feared was meant to be seductive. 'And is this your dance partner, Cat? Aren't you going to introduce us?'

Although she knew she ought not to grudge sharing Henry with Susie, who was the only reason Cat was there in the first place, still she felt a twinge of resentment. 'Susie, this is Henry Tilney. Henry, this is my friend and neighbour Susie Allen, who has very kindly brought me to Edinburgh.'

Susie extended a hand as if to be kissed. Instead, Henry jumped to his feet and shook it delicately. 'Pleased to meet you,' he said, head cocked as if assessing her for the pot. 'That's a lovely frock, by the way. I love the way all the layers are cut on the bias so they cascade like a waterfall.'

Susie gave him a shrewd look. 'Thank you. Are you in textiles yourself? A designer perhaps?'

He laughed delightedly. 'God, no. I just have a sister, that's all. Ellie likes to lecture me on the finer points of women's fashions. She's got her eye on a design course at the College of Art.'

Satisfied that he wasn't a gay man in disguise, Susie tucked a hand under Cat's arm. 'Sounds like she'd be a perfect pal for you, Cat. I hate to drag you away when you two are just getting to know each other, but we're on a tight schedule.'

Henry inclined his head politely. 'It's festival time. Everyone's always running to catch up with themselves. No doubt I'll see you around at the Book Festival. I usually grab a coffee there in the morning.'

''Kay,' Cat said. She followed Susie to the car, completely oblivious to the ache in her feet and ankles.

Amazing. Awesome. Astonishing. Henry Tilney had seen her at her worst, red-faced, sweating and cursing. And still he seemed keen to see her again. That was some consolation for knowing she looked such a mess. Whatever their next encounter might be, she couldn't look any worse.

4

er complete failure to recall anything about Jack Vettriano's latest collection of paintings was not something Cat was proud of. She'd always admired his work when she'd encountered it on cards and prints. It was the sort of art she could imagine practising herself one day. On any other occasion, she'd have been riveted to see the originals and she'd have snatched at the chance to talk to the artist himself. But Henry Tilney had driven all other thoughts from her mind. She'd even have been hard pressed to remember which town they'd been in, principally because she'd spent the entire journey on her phone researching Henry.

Her first port of call had been Facebook. Disappointingly, Henry didn't share his information with people who weren't his friends. And since they had no friends in common, there was nothing she could glean by a more circuitous route. Next she tried Google. There, she did find a Henry Tilney, but since this one was a much-decorated general who had made his name in the Falklands war before Cat had even been born, this obviously wasn't her dance partner. Out of curiosity, she clicked on the 'image' button. Even allowing for the scale of the photo on the phone, the resemblance between General Tilney and her dance partner was so uncanny that the relationship between them was immediately obvious. Father and son, no question about it.

General Tilney had made his reputation on a night operation against the Argentinian ground forces. He'd been a lieutenant-colonel at the time, which Cat thought sounded pretty impressive. In spite of his rank, he'd led the sortie himself, single-handedly accounting for an improbable number of the enemy before finally effecting a single-handed rescue of one of his men who had been wounded and trapped behind enemy lines. 'Almost superhuman,' one newspaper cutting said. Clearly not a man you'd want to cross, which possibly explained Henry's deference to his father's wishes.

'What have you found out about him?' Susie asked from the front seat.

'What? Who?'

Susie chuckled. 'Your dance partner. No point in pretending, Cat. I know what you're up to, tapping away on your phone. What have you found out about Henry Tilney?'

'Nothing much. His dad's a general.'

'General Tilney?' Mr Allen interrupted. 'The Falklands hero?'

'That's what it says on Google.'

'He owns Northanger Abbey,' he said. 'One of those medieval Borders abbeys. It got turned into a fortified house at some point. I remember a film company trying to rent it for some Gothic horror movie, but Tilney wouldn't even take a meeting. I can't imagine him being much of a dancer.'

'Pay attention,' his wife scolded. 'It's the son we're interested in, not the General.'

Fortunately for Cat, who was mortified by Susie's fascination with Henry as all teenagers are by adult interest in the objects of their attraction, they arrived at their destination.

On the return journey, Susie talked incessantly about the guest list, while Mr Allen managed to squeeze in a few comments on the paintings themselves. Left to herself, Cat hit on the brilliant notion of checking out Henry's sister. What had he called her? Allie? No, Ellie, that was it. Back on Facebook, Cat searched for 'Ellie Tilney', but without success. She tried 'Ellen' but that didn't help. She waited for her companions to pause for breath then asked, 'Susie, what's Ellie short for?'

'I'm not sure. Eleanor?'

And so it was that Cat found herself face-to-face with Henry Tilney's sister. Eleanor had the same thick blonde hair and brown eyes set in pale skin and a finer-boned version of the same features. Like her brother, not exactly beautiful, but striking. There were the usual photos of parties and dimly lit bars, Ellie mugging at the camera with an assortment of young men and women. Cat scrolled through the photos until she eventually came across one of Ellie and Henry leaning into each other at a sepulchral café table with espresso cups in front of them. Definitely the right Eleanor Tilney, then.

She clicked on the 'about' button and discovered Henry was indeed her brother. He was also a lawyer, an occupation that would have struck dread into the heart of most seventeen-year-old girls. Lawyer equalled boring, lawyer equalled know-all, lawyer equalled run for the hills. Except that Cat's brother James had just been accepted as a trainee barrister in a set of chambers in Newcastle upon Tyne and she knew James equalled none of those things. So his profession did not quench her interest in Henry as it might have done with another girl.

Mining Eleanor's Facebook page offered the information that she had another brother, Freddie, a captain in the army. But there were no other titbits about Henry. Still, at least now Cat knew he was respectable. And in spite of her longings for romance and adventure, deep in her heart she knew respectable was not something to despise. She gazed out at the gathering dusk, remembering the coolness of his hand against hers, the dancing laughter in his unusual eyes and the promised prospect of meeting at the Book Festival. Not to mention a Borders abbey. That was more than enough romance and adventure to be going on with.

The next morning found Cat suspiciously early at the breakfast table. She could barely contain her impatience while she waited for Susie to complete her morning preparations. Cat sat by the window, unable to concentrate on *Pride and Prejudice and Zombies*. She frowned at the clouds hanging low over the distant hills of Fife, wondering if she should read in them a portent of gloom to come.

But by the time Susie finally pronounced herself ready to set off for Charlotte Square Gardens and the tented village of the Book Festival, the clouds had scattered, bathing them in warm sunshine as they climbed the steep hill of Charlotte Street. This time, Cat was determined to subscribe to the pathetic fallacy. The sun shone; therefore only good things could happen to her.

The event for which they had tickets was not due to begin till noon, but Susie minded the lengthy wait as little as Cat did, for it gave her the opportunity to see and be seen. It also provided her with plenty of time to bemoan the fact that she still hadn't run into any of the legion of friends and acquaintances she knew to be in the city. 'Honestly, Cat,' she complained, 'a more paranoid person than me would think they were deliberately avoiding me. I've been tweeting my movements on a daily basis, even texting some of the girls, but somehow we keep missing each other. I really must make more of an effort, if only for your sake, darling.'

But Cat was paying scant attention to Susie. She'd managed to secure them a table with a clear view of the entrance. And if Henry was already listening to Janice Galloway reading or to a pair of historians debating the Arab Spring, he would be unable to leave without her spotting him. She was like a pointer, casting about in every direction for the faintest spoor of Henry Tilney.

Yet it was Susie's desire that was the one to be satisfied. At the next table, a woman dressed in the Edinburgh cultural uniform of linen and cashmere had been constantly glancing across at them. She would peer for a moment, frown then look away, only to turn back a moment later, her expression uncertain. After a few minutes of this behaviour, she leaned across the table and spoke. 'Excuse me interrupting,' she said. 'But are you by any chance Susan Armitage?'

Susie reared back in her seat, flabbergasted. 'I was once,' she said, as if caught out in a misdemeanour. 'But I've been Susie Allen for years. I'm sorry, do I know you?'

The woman had lost her air of uncertainty. 'I used to be Martha Collins. We used to sit next to each other in Speccy Barton's French class.'

Susie's hand flew to her mouth. 'Little Martha Collins? Oh my God, I see it now. How amazing. What are you doing here? And what have you been up to all these years?'

The former Martha Collins picked up her coffee cup and moved to their table. 'The short version? Married, one son, three daughters, widowed. I'm Martha Thorpe now. I've got a little business in interior design. We help people refurbish their period properties, that sort of thing.'

'Gosh. You've had an eventful time of it. Not that I'm complaining. I've been very happily married to Andrew for a million years. He's made his money investing in musical theatre.' Susie allowed herself to preen for a moment.

'And is this your daughter?' Martha nodded at Cat.

Susie looked startled, then guilty. 'Cat? No, not at all, no.' A look of pain flickered in Susie's eyes, gone almost before it could be named. 'Andrew and I have no children. Cat's a neighbour from Dorset. We've got a house there, it's where we spend most of our time. London's so crowded and dirty these days. Even in Holland Park.'

Martha's eyebrows rose. 'Holland Park. How lovely. We're in Crouch End. Even though I have a lot of clients in Chelsea and Notting Hill, I wouldn't be anywhere but North London. So lively. My girls love it there. Though I wouldn't wish three teenage daughters on my worst enemy,' she added with a laugh that sounded suspiciously forced to Cat's ears. As Martha expanded upon the achievements of her own brood, it gradually dawned on Cat that a previously unsuspected disadvantage of being childless was the lack of weaponry one had against the tidal wave of a proud mother's conversation. For once, Susie was rendered speechless because she had nothing to chip in with. Really, if the Thorpe children were half as gifted as their mother claimed, the only question in their future would be which of them would be Prime Minister. If Cat had not had her own lively interest in her surroundings to preserve her, she might have lost the will to live entirely.

Then, 'Here come my dear girls,' cried Martha, pointing at three fashionably dressed females who, arm in arm, were moving towards them along the wooden duckboards, the swagger of their passage forcing everyone else to detour on to the still-damp grass. They looked as if they'd popped out of the same mould, each having slightly less clean-cut lines than the previous sister. So the eldest had features that could almost be described as sharp, while the youngest still had a puppy plumpness that lacked such clear definition. All three had identical tawny hair and eyes of a blue that is sometimes described as icy but which Cat preferred to think of as Scandinavian, having watched too many subtitled TV detective serials.

The trio, who were giggling at some private joke, made a scant acknowledgement of their mother and pulled up more chairs. 'Girls, this is my old school friend Susie Allen. Can you believe it's over twenty-five years since we've seen each other?' Martha's tone was apologetic.

The eldest raised her eyebrows. 'I bet you didn't recognise her,' she said to Susie.

'Of course I did,' Susie said.

Martha butted in. 'Susie, this is Isabella—'

'Bella,' the eldest interrupted, rolling her eyes in a 'pity me' expression.

'—and then Jessica, and last but not least, Claire. Girls, this is Cat – I'm sorry, I didn't catch your surname.'

'Morland,' Cat said.

'Girls, this is Cat Morland from Dorset. She's a neighbour of Susie's, come to Edinburgh with Susie and her husband.'

Bella, who had looked bored up to that point suddenly perked up. 'Morland? From Dorset? OMG, girls. Look at this.' And she pointed dramatically at Cat.

Cat flushed. Was she so much of a country bumpkin that it was obvious on sight to these London sophisticates?

'Oh God, you're right,' Jessica said. 'I just thought we must have seen her out and about, but of course, that's what it is.'

'What are you girls on about?' Martha asked.

'Can't you see it, Ma?' Bella demanded. 'She's, like, his spitting image.'

'Jamie Morland,' Claire said wearily. Clearly her role in the trio was to clarify her sisters' gnomic utterances. 'Johnny's friend from Oxford who came to stay at Easter. From Dorset.'

'The one that Bella's been losing sleep over,' Jessica chipped in.

'I so am not,' her sister protested. 'Can I help it if he totally likes me? I mean, if somebody keeps texting you, it's really rude to not text them back, right?'

'So, let me get this straight,' Martha said. 'Are you Jamie Morland's sister?'

'We call him James,' Cat said. 'He was at St John's College.'

'He's our brother Johnny's sidekick,' Claire said. 'And he's very keen on Bella.'

This was news to Cat, who had thought until then that she and her brother were close. Obviously, when he was separated from his family, James had a very different life from the one apparent to those who thought they knew him. He had never mentioned Johnny Thorpe or his sisters round the family dinner table. Cat wondered why, since they seemed so fond of him.

'Hey, Cat, let's take a wander round and see who we can spot,' Bella said, jumping up and pulling Cat to her feet. She linked arms with her as she'd done previously with her sisters, but shook her head briskly at Jessica and Claire when they made a move to join them. 'Not now, brats. I need to get to know Cat.'

'Get the inside track on Jamie, more like,' Jess grumbled.

Ignoring her, Bella swept Cat along. Before she knew it, they were gossiping about the things that entertain young women of a certain age and type. It was all new to Cat, but as they strolled in the sunshine, she managed to appear as if she were entirely familiar with a conversational world that encompassed intimate gossip about people neither of them had ever met, current fashions and where the cool people were hanging out in Edinburgh. In short, a range of subjects that had no useful application whatsoever.

Luckily, Bella required little input from her companion when it came to conversation. She knew enough of the world to entertain both and Cat was sufficiently well brought up to provide the appropriate prompts. But eventually, even Bella ran out of steam. 'What are you seeing today?' Cat asked when it was clear she was required to pick up the baton of dialogue.

'We've got the hot ticket of the day,' Bella said. 'The open-air adaptation of Ginny Blackstock's *Cupcakes to Die For* at the Botanic Gardens.'

Cat squeaked with delight. 'So have we.'

'Wow. With your brother being Jamie and all, it's like we're totally meant to be bgfs,' Bella whooped. 'Oh, Cat, this is so going to be the best Edinburgh ever.'

5

Cat had convinced herself that in spite of Henry Tilney's failure to appear at the Book Festival grounds, he would surely attend the dramatic adaptation of last year's bestselling novel about love, zombies and patisserie, *Cupcakes to Die For*. Had they not touched on the subject of the fluency of women's writing at Mrs Alexander's dance class? Was this not the most sought-after ticket of the Fringe? And was not the Botanic Gardens the coolest of venues?

But again, she was disappointed. There was no sign of Henry among the milling audience at the al fresco performance, nor even anyone Cat could momentarily mistake for him. However, that evening there was some slight mitigation of her disappointment for now she had a friend to giggle and gossip with.

Bella had summoned Cat with an enthusiastic wave as soon as she had clapped eyes on her, and Cat had been glad to see her. With Bella, she could indulge her daydreams of Henry to the full. The very idea of discussing him with Susie Allen made the back of her neck turn chill with horror.

But before they could delve into the very depth of their

respective affections for James Morland and Henry Tilney, the young women were obliged to watch the play, which, unusually, turned out to be as entertaining as its advance publicity had promised. Even the weather joined in the fun, bathing the audience in warm sunshine throughout. In a momentary lull, Cat looked around in vain for Henry and noticed Mr Allen muttering eagerly into his phone. She wondered whether this was to be his next venture in the West End. If so, it would surely add another zero to his bank balance, and on the advantageous side of the decimal point.

Once the final applause had died away, Bella and Cat escaped on their own to roam the gardens and strengthen those bonds of friendship they had started to weave earlier. 'So, are you still at school?' Bella asked.

'I've never been at school.'

Bella's eyes widened. 'Wow, how did you get away with that?'

'We were all home schooled. My mum thought it was better that way.'

'Amazing. And Jamie got into Oxford. Your mum must be a totally cool teacher.'

Cat shrugged. 'I suppose. But I don't know what I'm going to do with the rest of my life. I'm not academic like James.'

'Oh, something will turn up. You could always get a job as a chalet girl over the winter while you decide.'

'What about you?' Cat was eager to turn the talk away from her lack of prospects, a subject that had begun increasingly to dismay her.

'Camden School for Girls,' Bella intoned as if she were revealing she'd spent her youth in a penal institution. 'Ma spent all the money sending our brother Johnny to a classy boarding school so there was nothing left for us girls. I've left now, though.'

'And what are you going to do?'

'I help out in the business. I'm learning as I go. It can be fun sometimes, but mostly it's pretty boring and Ma can't afford to pay me much, so it's a bit of a dead end. I need to find me a man to pamper me.'

Before Cat could comment on this novel idea, they were over-taken by the weather. Although it had stayed fair for the outdoors performance, they felt a few drops of rain and took refuge inside the humid shelter of the glass and sandstone Palm House.

'It's like the tropics in here,' Cat exclaimed. 'I read this novel last year, it was, like, a prequel to *Jane Eyre*, you know? It was kind of the story of the madwoman in the attic?' In spite of Bella's blank look, she pressed on. 'Anyway, it's really atmos-pheric, you feel like you're in the Caribbean yourself. And this—' She spread her arms wide. 'This is what it felt like.'

'I wouldn't mind being in the Caribbean myself, if I could be with Jamie.'

Cat still couldn't get used to thinking of her brother as 'Jamie'. It didn't fit him at all. 'I imagine he'd be quite good at knocking coconuts out of trees,' she conceded.

'I bet he goes totes brown in the sun, he's got that kind of skin,' Bella mused.

'We all do,' Cat said. 'My mum says it's because we all ran around half-naked like savages when we were small.' She spun round on the balls of her feet, peering between dripping fronds and sheltering leaves, half-convinced that Henry Tilney must be somewhere nearby. 'I really thought Henry would be here,' she said wistfully.

45

'If he was a zombie like in the play, he'd be lurking in some graveyard eating the dead,' Bella said, dropping her voice to spooky depths.

Cat laughed. 'I think I'd have noticed if he was one of the undead. They're a bit obvious, Bella. But if he was a vampire . . .' Her voice tailed off.

'Oh yeah, if this was, like, a Twilight movie, he'd have to hide indoors on a sunny day like this.' She gave Cat a gentle poke in the arm. 'That's it, he's a vampire. That's why he's not around this evening. It's way too bright for him to be outside.'

Cat giggled. It was a preposterous notion, but nevertheless it was the kind of absurd fantasy that they could have fun with. 'And of course, yesterday was cloudy so he was able to be out in the daylight, just like in the Twilight books. And he had run all the way across town, he said. And everybody knows vampires can run really far and really fast.'

'Was he, like, amazingly strong? Could you tell from dancing with him?'

Cat cast her mind back. It was true that Henry had manoeuvred her through the complicated dance moves with little apparent effort. She'd felt safe in his hands in spite of her clumsiness and there was no doubt that he had prevented her from violent collisions with other dancers on more than one occasion. 'He never let me fall. I know it doesn't sound much, but when you're whirling round in an eightsome reel, believe me, it's a big deal. Have you been to the Highland Ball?'

Bella rolled her eyes. 'Only, like, every year.'

'Then you know what it's like. It must be quite terrifying to have a partner who doesn't know what he's doing. I bet people get hurt all the time.'

Bella shrugged. 'I only dance with men who know what they're doing. I wish Jamie was here, he's a dreamy dancer.'

Cat frowned. She'd never seen her brother dance willingly at parties, never mind master the intricacies of Scottish country dancing. She thought Bella's assertion a wild statement of faith in someone she knew rather less well than she supposed. 'I guess we'll never know,' she said. 'Since he's not here.' She sighed. 'Do you think Henry's gone back home? Without saying?'

'Even if he has gone home, I bet he'll be back soon as.' Bella turned and took Cat's face in her hands, gently moving it this way and that to catch the light. 'I mean, now he's seen how pretty you are, he won't be able to stay away. Didn't you say he's a lawyer too? Maybe he knows Jamie. Maybe he can persuade Jamie to take a weekend off and come to Edinburgh? How hard can that be?'

They emerged into the evening air, relieved to be out of the humidity of the palm house. They found Martha Thorpe and Susie Allen sitting on a tartan rug sipping white wine spritzers on a grassy bank. Mr Allen was nowhere to be seen, and the women were engaged in a form of parallel monologue. Martha talked about her children and Susie about her wardrobe. Neither seemed to notice that their twin tracks had no connection; they were content to be in conversation with someone who never tried to wrench the discussion away from their favoured subjects.

Cat and Bella sat on the top of the bank, arms round their knees, leaning companionably into one another, comparing notes about the events they were most looking forward to at the Book Festival and discovering with delicious pleasure that they were of one mind on most of their selected authors.

The only surprise for Cat was that she seemed to have read much more widely than her new friend. But she supposed when you grew as old as Bella, there were more calls on your time and fewer opportunities to spend the evening on a chaise longue with a book. Certainly the Thorpes seemed to watch a great deal more television than the Morlands, whose viewing was, of financial necessity, restricted to those channels that were available free of charge. Their options were further circumscribed by their parents' conviction that all soaps and most dramas were absurd and therefore not worth the time they demanded. Cat found little hardship in this edict, since there was always something else she would rather be doing.

But that evening in the Botanics, she luxuriated in sharing an intense conversation about the novels she inhabited in her imagination. This was entirely a novelty for Cat, since she was the only member of her family who set any store by fiction. Their views baffled her; fiction seemed to Cat to be the highest form of the writer's art, depending as it did on the resourceful application of creativity and the necessity of direct communication with the reader.

For historians and writers of narrative non-fiction, all the building blocks of their work were already in place. They had nothing more to do than gather them and construct a pretty edifice. Conversely, the writers of fiction began with nothing other than the contents of their heads and their understanding of the human condition. They must comprehend the deepest and strangest elements of emotion and behaviour and render them accessible to those who lacked their wit and skill.

Poets, it might be argued, also relied on their own emotional and intellectual resources. But Cat had serious doubts about poets. She firmly believed that while some could thrill and excite, too many failed the fundamental test of communicating with their readers. The more obscure their verses, the more praise they appeared to garner. Annie had attempted to convince her that T. S. Eliot was a writer of incomparable ability but Cat had rebelled on the second page of *The Waste Land*. 'Honestly, Mum, how can you say someone's a great writer if you've no hope of understanding their work unless you've got a stack of reference books next to you? It's just showing off. If I behaved like that in front of other people, you'd totally tell me off when we got home. So why is it all right for T. S. Eliot to swagger about like a complete know-all and make the rest of us feel stupid?'

Not for the first time, Annie had struggled to find an answer to her eldest daughter's candour. 'It's a challenge,' she'd finally said. 'It makes you think. It makes you look beyond your own narrow horizons.'

'But reading the Twilight novels makes me think,' Cat replied defiantly. 'Just because you're not interested in thinking about the same things doesn't mean it's worthless.'

It wasn't solely her mother who dismissed the power of fiction within the Morland household. Richard naturally read the Bible, though rather less than his parishioners might have hoped. He read a great deal, having the excuse of a weekly sermon to sprinkle with erudition. Most of his reading consisted of philosophy and natural history, with occasional forays into biography. The Internet had also afforded him access to a bewildering array of blogs, which he dipped into like a man sampling an all-you-can-eat buffet. He claimed he approached his reading with a measure of scepticism. Cat was less certain about that; she thought sometimes the blogs more closely resembled the condition of fiction than her father was willing to admit.

Her brother James wasn't much of a reader. He'd dutifully read the Harry Potter books, but that was the last fiction he'd embraced. In his early teens, he'd discovered the true crime genre. Since then, his reading for pleasure had consisted of exploring the warped lives of serial murderers and spree killers. It was a fascination that puzzled Cat. It couldn't even be explained as preparation for life at the bar, for James had no intention of pursuing criminal law. He was destined for family law, something of his father's social conscience having rubbed off on him. And yet, he remained fascinated by the perverted actions of a psychopathic few.

And so Cat was stranded on the shores of fiction alone, save for the occasional forays of her younger sisters, both of whom preferred to fiddle with Facebook or tattle-tale with Twitter than sit down with a book. Cat had briefly cherished hopes of Emma becoming a reader like her when her younger sister had picked up the first volume of the *Hunger Games* trilogy. But it soon became clear that her interest had only been pricked because she'd seen the film of the book at a friend's house, and that she had no sincere love for the written word *per se*.

And that was why Cat revelled so thoroughly in the company of Bella Thorpe, who might not have been the most assiduous reader in the city of Edinburgh, but who at least understood enough of the joys of novels to seek out the presence of their authors, if only to have her copies of their work signed. For once, Cat felt the fiction lovers were in the ascendancy. All they lacked was Henry Tilney who, she was sure, would only have enriched their conversation. But as her parents had been careful to teach her, Cat knew you couldn't have everything. At least, not all at the same time.

6

Two days later, Cat rushed into the Spiegeltent at the Book Festival grounds, hot and damp and five minutes late. Bella waved at her from a far booth and she excused her way across the busy café and subsided on to the bench opposite her friend.

'Where have you been?' Bella's voice was plaintive. 'I've been waiting, like, forever.'

'I'm hardly late at all,' Cat protested mildly, taking off her father's elderly Panama hat and shaking the rain from it. She had brought the hat to shelter her from the sun but so far it had done more service as protection from the squally East Coast showers.

'Love the hat – that is so cool. I need one just like it. But seriously, what kept you?' Bella pouted.

'Well, technically it's your fault.'

'My fault? Like, how can it be my fault that you're late? I even left early because it looked like rain and I didn't want to get caught in it, which by the way I managed better than you did.'

Cat smiled, not caring that the sudden shower had left her

a little bedraggled. It was a condition familiar to her at home, and Susie Allen was still at the flat and so had not been able to chide her for being less than perfectly turned out. 'It's your fault because you got me into Morag Fraser. I'd never even heard of the Hebridean Harpies series till you dragged me along to her event. And now I am totally hooked. I was reading *Vampires on Vatersay* till one in the morning. I just had to finish it. And then I started *Banshees of Berneray* at breakfast and I could hardly drag myself away from it to come and meet you.'

Bella squealed. 'Have you got to the bit with the long black veil?'

'How did you know? That's exactly where I stopped.'

'You stopped? How could you? Are you not wild to know what's behind the long black veil?'

'Of course I am. But I had to get out the door and up the hill or you'd be even more cross with me. I'm dying to know the dreadful secret behind the veil.'

'Well, I'm not going to tell you,' Bella said stoutly. 'I'm not going to spoil it for you. But I swear you'll have a heart attack, literally.' She fished her phone out of her pocket and brought up a website. 'I'm going to email you the link. It lists the whole series in order.'

'What are they? Go on, tease me, tempt me, tell me.'

'*Ghasts of Gigha, Werewolves on Wiay, Poltergeist Plague of Pabbay, Shapeshifters of Shuna, Killer Kelpies of Kerrera* and the latest, *Maenads on Mingulay*.'

'That sounds so cool.'

'You don't know the half of it, girlfriend. You are going to be screaming like a Berneray banshee before you're finished.

You're going to be looking over your shoulder every time you turn a corner.'

Cat gave a delicious little shiver. Already, she'd categorised the dimly lit narrow alleys that threaded between the streets of the New Town as ripe territory for supernatural creatures to lurk among. Now, thanks to the apparently ordinary Morag Fraser, she'd have terror on one shoulder and horror on the other as she walked the streets after sunset. It was probably as well that Susie took care to stay close when they made their way back from evening events. 'And they're all as good as *Vampires on Vatersay*?'

Bella bumped shoulders with her. 'They get even more scary, trust me. And it's not just me saying that. My friend back home, Madison Crowley, she's read them all too, and she says the same. She had to sleep with the light on for a week, she was so totally terrified after *Shapeshifters of Shuna*.' She pouted. 'I wish Maddy was here, you two would bond like sisters. Of course, she'd be left out a bit, she hasn't got a gorgeous man in her life like Jamie or Henry. I'm always giving guys a hard time for not fancying her the way they do me.'

Cat struggled to make sense of Bella's words. 'You give boys a hard time because they don't fancy your mate?'

Bella tossed her tawny hair back and tucked it behind her ear. 'Well, duh. She's my mate, so I have to put myself out for her. That's what friends do for friends. I totally put my friends first. Like, we were at this party, some guy my brother Johnny knows was all over me and poor Maddy was all on her own, so I said to him, "You don't even get to dance with me unless you dance with Maddy first. Because she is lovely inside." He wasn't happy, but he did try. She wasn't having it, though. I guess he wasn't her type. Anyway, that's just a for example of how I am for my buds. If anyone dissed you, I would be all over their faces.' She smiled. 'But that's not going to happen, you're not going to be a wallflower. You'll have to beat the guys off with a stick, you're so pretty.'

Cat blushed, not least because she knew Bella was only being kind. She was well aware of how nondescript her looks were. 'Now you're having a laugh.'

'No, but you are. See, you're bubbly. And that's what lets Maddy down. She can be really banal, you know? Now, when we were leaving here last night, there was this guy watching you, you could see he really fancied you. That would never happen to Maddy, she never does anything that would catch a man's eye. But you didn't even notice, did you? I bet he went home dreaming of you and you never even realised he cared. You're so caught up in the invisible Mr Henry Tilney that it's like all these other sweet guys don't exist.'

'I'm not that bothered about Henry,' Cat lied. 'He seems to have disappeared, anyway. So it would be pointless even if I was.'

'I don't believe you're not bothered.'

'Cross my heart. The Hebridean Harpies are much more interesting. I'm totally obsessing about what's behind the long black veil. There's no room in my head for Henry Tilney.'

'I can't believe you missed out on them, have you never seen the TV series?'

Cat shook her head. 'We're not big on TV in our house.'

'Weird.' Bella dismissed the subject. 'So, Henry, is he your type, then? Because if he is, we need to keep an eye out for guys that look like that, to take your mind off him.'

Confused, Cat frowned. 'I don't think I have a type. I either like people or I don't.'

Bella opened her eyes wide. 'Double weird. You're such a strange one, Cat. Now I know exactly the kind of man who makes my heart beat faster.' She looked dreamily around the bustling Spiegeltent. 'And I think you could probably guess what my type is without having to try very hard.'

'I don't—'

'No, no, don't embarrass me. I always give myself away.' She raked around in her bag and took out a tiny mirror and her lipstick. As she applied a fresh coat of scarlet to her lips, she carried on talking. 'There's two guys over by the coffee counter, they totally can't take their eyes off you.'

Startled, Cat followed her friend's gaze. One of the young men in question gave her a louche wink, then nudged his friend, who had turned away to pick up two cartons of coffee. A moment later, they were gone. 'You're mistaken, Bella. They've gone off.'

Bella tutted and flicked her hair out on both sides in a gesture of impatience. 'Oh, come on then, there's nothing happening here. I'm literally going to die of boredom if I have to sit here a minute longer.'

Without checking whether Cat was ready to leave, Bella strode off, apparently driven by some inner urgency to be away from the confines of the Spiegeltent. They emerged into the humid air trapped beneath the tented walkways of the festival. Bella paused, like a pointer sniffing the air, then hustled off towards the exit. Cat thought she saw the two young men from the coffee counter ahead of them, but she couldn't be certain.

'Do keep up,' Bella said impatiently.

And Cat obeyed, not quite sure why they were in such a hurry. But she had observed her friend with her sisters and understood that when Bella was in this mood, it was better to obey.

7

If the burghers of Edinburgh had conspired to transform the traffic flow of the capital into a circle of hell that Dante would have recognised, they could have done no better than their plan to bring trams back to the city. Road closures, diversions and temporary lights had made the centre almost impossible to navigate.

The junction of George Street and Charlotte Square had always been one of the most awkward street-crossings in the city, with a constant hurtling of vehicles back and forth and round the tight corners of roads built for carriages, not buses. But this year, the felony had been compounded by the closure to traffic of most of George Street. True, it had created a Continental feel the length of this major artery, with restaurant tables and temporary event venues in the middle of the road. But it had also funnelled the festival-fattened flow of traffic into ever fewer capillaries.

As they emerged on to the pavement, Cat was momentarily bewildered by the transition from the genteel crowds of the Book Festival. But Bella was as sharp-witted as ever. She pointed to her left, towards Bute House, the official residence of the

Scottish First Minister. 'Let's walk this way, Cat,' she urged, linking arms with her friend.

Cat couldn't help but notice that the two young men from the coffee stand were crossing the quieter side of the square towards the First Minister's grand grey Georgian pile. The realisation made her faintly uneasy, but before she could examine the feeling, the long bonnet of a bright scarlet sports car screeched to a halt beside them. Startled, she swung round to see two young men waving at her and Bella from their open-topped vehicle. As is often the way when we are confronted with those we know in unexpected situations, it took Cat some seconds to realise that the passenger was her brother James.

Any exclamation of surprise she may have uttered was lost in the screech of delight from Bella and the answering whoop from the driver.

'Johnny! And Jamie,' Bella screamed. 'I don't believe it. Totes amazeballs.'

The driver jumped out of the car without opening his door and bounded up the steps to the pavement level where the young women had stopped in their tracks. He threw his arms around Bella and the pair of them pogoed together in a tight circle that was clearly the product of much practice, all the while whooping like savages.

James Morland meanwhile made a more decorous exit from the passenger door and trotted up to his sister, giving her a quick hug. 'What are you doing here?' she demanded with a delighted laugh, pushing him away from her but holding firm to his upper arms.

'Spur of the moment, Sis. Johnny turned up at my flat last

night and persuaded me to join him. I think he's missing his mum – I swear he's got a boot full of dirty laundry for her.' James gave her his familiar quick and easy grin, but she was so excited to see him, Cat failed to notice how his eyes kept flicking across to her friend.

'Shouldn't you be working?'

James winked. 'My pupil master's extended his holiday in Tuscany, so I'd just be twiddling my thumbs in chambers. They told me not to bother coming in, then Johnny showed up and twisted my arm.' He was speaking to Cat, but his attention was all on Bella, whose ecstatic dance with her brother had just ended.

John Thorpe broke away from his sister and seized Cat's hand, swooping low over it in a mock-heroic gesture. 'And you must be the famous Cat Morland I've heard so much about from Bella and Jamie. I'm Johnny Thorpe, and you must be delighted to make my acquaintance.' He released her hand and beamed at her, his plain face revealing how pleased he was with himself and his attempt at humour.

Cat giggled uneasily, not quite sure how to handle so bombastic an introduction. 'Bella's told me all about you.' There was some truth in that, though his sister had not mentioned his paunch or his thinning hair.

He raised his eyebrows in an arch expression. 'God, I hope not,' he said in exaggerated style. 'So, Cat, I bet you can't guess how long it took us to drive up the bloody awful A1 from Newcastle.'

Cat, whose studies in British geography had left her with gaps the size of Wales in her knowledge, looked to James for help. 'I don't know how far it is.'

Her brother tore his attention away from Bella long enough to say, 'About a hundred and twenty miles.'

'More like a hundred and fifty,' John corrected him. 'Given the time it took. So, Cat, what do you think? How long?'

Cat frowned, trying to do the sums in her head. 'About two and a half hours?' she hazarded.

John slapped his thigh in a gesture of incredulity. 'Are you kidding me? Have you seen my flying machine? An hour and twenty minutes. I noticed the church clock on Shieldfield Green said ten o'clock as we passed it on our way up from the Quayside.'

James laughed. 'You've lost an hour, Johnny. We left at nine.'

John's chest puffed up under his pink and grey striped polo shirt. 'At nine?' He turned to Cat for support. 'Is he always like this? Picking a fight when he knows he's in the wrong? I tell you, just look at this car of mine and tell me you think it would take two and a half hours to travel a hundred and fifty miles.'

'A hundred and twenty,' James said weakly.

'It does look fast,' Cat said, trying to make peace between the pair before their mock argument turned, as they so often do between men intent on impressing women, into the real thing.

'Fast? She goes like the proverbial. Just touch the gas and she shoots forward like a bullet. She's hand built, engine tuned to within an inch of its life. Look at that cream leather interior, the black walnut dash, the perfection of that chrome. Spring-loaded drink holders, on-board wifi and subwoofers to blow your ears off. And don't get me started on the brake horsepower and the torque.'

Cat nodded politely, hiding the fervent hope that he would

not indeed get started on those perplexing matters. 'It looks very smart.'

'And you know what I paid? Three grand less than the list price. Three grand! Amazing, no? She's the perfect car for me. In the City, success is ninety per cent front and ten per cent balls. And this beauty makes a statement about me. She lets people know I'm a man to be reckoned with. She was built for a Christ Church man, to his spec. But I heard he'd been a bit too flash with his cash so he was looking to offload her for readies. I ran into him in that Slovakian cocktail bar up near Hilda's and he goes, "Johnny, Johnny, my man, do you know anybody who might be interested in the best car in Oxford? Only, I need to realise her capital value sharpish." Now, I'd just had a spot of luck at the casino, so I made him an offer he couldn't refuse. *Et voilà.*'

'I don't know much about cars, but it looks like you got a bargain.'

John gave a smug little smile and patted his hair in a self-satisfied gesture. 'A total bargain. But you know, I was helping the poor guy out. You need a favour, I'm your man. Always ready to do my bit.'

Before he could preen further, his sister exclaimed, 'Johnny, there's a traffic warden heading straight for us.'

'Buggering barnacles,' he swore, turning his back on them all and returning to the car, this time opening the door. 'Come on, girls, get in!'

Cat hung back, looking dubiously at the shallow parcel shelf behind the two seats. But Bella grabbed her hand and together they clambered inelegantly into the rear of the car. They'd barely squeezed in when John stamped on the gas and shot

63

down the hill in a throaty roar of exhaust. Cat and Bella clung to each other, shrieking.

At the first set of traffic lights, John resumed the conversation. 'I could have sold it for four grand more the day after I bought it. Jacko Jackson from Oriel offered me cash on the nail the next day in the King's Arms.'

'Yeah, but you're forgetting your parking permit was included,' James pointed out.

'Like I'd be dumb enough to sell my parking permit after the amount I had to bribe the college porter to get it in the first place. Duh.' The lights changed so once more communication was rendered impossible.

Before long, another set of traffic signals brought them to a halt. 'Do you like a rag top, Cat?' John asked.

'He means a convertible, Sis. With the top down.'

'Oh. Well, this is my first experience, unless you count a quad bike. But yes, I can see it might be fun if you were in a proper seat and not in fear of spilling out the back every time you accelerate.'

John roared with laughter. 'God, Jamie, you never told me she was so funny. Cat, I'm going to take you for a spin every day I'm here. With the top down.'

It wasn't that thrilling a prospect to Cat. 'There's a forecast of rain tomorrow.'

'We'll dodge the raindrops. I'll drive you up the coast for fish and chips.'

'Won't you want to take it easy after your long drive today?'

He laughed again. 'Call that a long drive? That was just a warm-up. No, it's a date. Fish and chips at North Berwick for lunch.'

'Oh, me too, me too!' Bella exclaimed.

'Are you kidding? I didn't come to Edinburgh to drive my sister around. Jamie, it's up to you to amuse Bella.'

And again, conversation was stilled by acceleration as they drove out across the Dean Bridge and down Queensferry Road a way towards the flat where Mrs Thorpe and her daughters were staying, some little distance from the Book Festival and most of the venues of the Festival Fringe. The one advantage their accommodation had over the Allens' apartment was that it lay just outside the city centre's restricted parking zone, so all that was required to find a parking space was for John Thorpe to drive round the block three or four times.

As they walked back up the hill to the Thorpes' flat, John fell into step beside Cat. Desperate to avoid another lecture on the subject of his splendid car, Cat cast about for something to say. Given that Bella was his sister, she reasoned that they might share some tastes in common. 'Bella has introduced me to the Hebridean Harpies series of novels,' she said.

'Oh my good lord,' he groaned. 'Spare me! Not another one. I've had Bella wittering on about those bloody books for ever. I don't have time to waste on novels, but if I did, it wouldn't be them I'd choose. Vampires and banshees – I ask you. Those books are dumber than a deaf mute with a mouthful of superglue.'

The image was so singularly unpleasant that Cat could think of no immediate riposte. 'So what do you read?' was all she could manage.

'Only what I have to for work,' he said. 'I don't have time to read. How can you bear to read when there's cars to race and dragons to slay?' He imitated the movement of his hands on a console controller, making the revving, screeching and gunshot sounds of a computer game.

'Surely it's just as dumb to slay imaginary dragons and drive imaginary cars as it is to read Morag Fraser's books?' Cat demanded.

He snorted. 'Obviously you're not a gamer, sweetheart. What I do sharpens my reflexes and keeps me on top of my game. Reading those stupid books just fills your head full of nonsense.'

It was true that there had never been a games console in the Morland household. But Cat had been in other homes where the children had had apparently unlimited access to a staggering range of virtual experiences. And from those encounters, she dredged up something she hadn't known till she'd looked up Hebridean Harpies on Wikipedia. 'Do you play *DragonSky*?' she asked.

He nodded with enthusiasm. 'I used to play it all the time. Not so much now that *Felony Driver IV* came out.'

'Did you know that Morag Fraser was one of the writers on *DragonSky*?'

Taken aback, he goggled at her. 'I don't see how,' he said. 'You sure she didn't just make the credits for being somebody's girlfriend or something?'

Before Cat could muster a response, Bella, who had been walking ahead with James, turned and pointed at the building where their flat occupied part of the second floor. 'This is us, Johnny.'

Although she had begun to feel quite cross with John Thorpe, the warmth with which he greeted his mother and sisters restored Cat's general spirit of goodwill. Even so, she was taken aback by the apparent rudeness of the banter the Thorpes exchanged with one another. 'Ma, dearest,' John said, hugging his mother so tight she squealed. 'Where in the name of God did you get that hat? It makes you look like the Wicked Witch of the West.'

Martha Thorpe smacked him affectionately on the shoulder. 'You are the worst boy in the world, turning up without warning.'

'And where are the two ugly sisters?' he called, bringing his siblings rushing from their bedroom to perform the same whooping dance he'd earlier conducted with Bella. However brutal it all seemed compared to Morland family life, it appeared to please the Thorpes.

'You've put on weight, fatso,' Jessica said.

'And you've got five more zits on your nose,' her brother riposted. 'Ma, have you got a washing machine here?'

Martha sighed. 'You've brought your washing, haven't you?'

'Clever girl,' John said. 'You guessed. I'll bring it up later. But look, Ma, see who I've brought with me.' And he hauled James, blushing, into the ring of Thorpe women. 'You can squeeze us in here, can't you?'

Martha looked doubtful. 'I don't know where.'

'Oh, Ma, you can sleep on the sofa, and Jamie and I will share your bed,' John said with the cavalier ease of a man who has never had to pay the piper. 'Now, Jamie, sit yourself down and Ma will get us a coffee to revive us after our drive.' And he was off again, regaling the company with a paean of praise to his new car.

By the time Cat and Jamie escaped from the crowded flat, Martha had accepted a collective invitation to a ceilidh that evening at the grand New Town home of one of her clients,

Bella had dragged her to one side to tell her that Johnny thought she was the cutest thing he'd ever clapped eyes on, and John himself had informed Cat that he was going to dance her legs to stumps at the ceilidh. To be the centre of such attention left Cat a little breathless. It was very far from what she was accustomed to, and it was hard to sift through the swirl of mixed feelings she was enduring.

'He's pretty full on, is Johnny,' James said as they set off to walk back to the Allens' flat.

Were it not for the friendship between the two men and the flattery of John Thorpe's interest in her, Cat might have answered with more acerbity. Instead, she simply said, 'The whole family are pretty full on.'

'But he's a good guy. He's always up for a laugh.'

'He's certainly never short of something to say.'

James laughed. 'There's no pleasing you girls, is there? You're usually complaining that guys have got nothing to say for ourselves, but when we do talk to you, apparently you don't like that either.'

'Whatever. You seem to be everybody's favourite in that family.' The comment was innocent enough, yet James flushed.

'They made me really welcome when I stayed with them in the Easter vac,' he said. 'You like them? Martha and the girls?'

'I do, very much. Bella especially. We totally hit it off.'

'That's great. But then, what's not to like? She's smart and funny—'

'And so beautiful and cleverly dressed and well read,' Cat butted in. 'Exactly the kind of girl I always wanted as a best friend.'

'And she's easy-going and relaxed,' James added. It wasn't

quite how Cat would have described her friend but she let it go because James continued, 'And she thinks you're great too. She texted me to say she'd met you and how cool she thinks you are. And when a girl like Bella thinks you're cool, then you know it's the truth.'

'Wow! She said that? Awesome. I didn't realise you were such good mates. You know, Bro, you hardly said anything about her when you texted me after you stayed with them.'

They were in the middle of the Dean Bridge as she spoke and James turned away to lean on the parapet, gazing down at the treetops below. 'I hoped you'd get to meet her yourself soon, and I didn't want to influence what you thought of her. I'd be as happy as you if the pair of you ended up best friends.' He swung round and smiled at her.

'That's very sweet of you, James. Oh, and by the way, what's with the whole "Jamie" thing?'

He shrugged and resumed walking. 'It was Bella's idea. She said they knew too many Jameses and she didn't want there to be any confusion who she was talking about. So she started calling me Jamie and they all followed her lead. Though, to be honest, I think Johnny's taking the piss a bit.' James spread his hands in a wry shrug. 'That's blokes for you.'

'Still, he obviously likes you. And it was really thoughtful of him to stop off in Newcastle to see if you wanted to come all this way to see me and the Allens. He must have thought I'd be missing you all.'

James gave her a quizzical look, which she took to mean that he was surprised at her effusiveness. 'Yeah,' he said. 'Right. Thoughtful. And how is everyone at home?'

Cat's exposition on the home life of the Morlands occupied

them all the way back to Queen Street, save for one brief digression on Bella's sense of humour. The Allens were delighted to see James, and to hear that they too had been invited to the ceilidh. Mr Allen begged off, on the grounds that he had to endure a one-man version of *A Farewell to Arms*, but Susie was ecstatic to have so early an opportunity to wear the dress she had bought only that afternoon from the sweetest little boutique in the Lawnmarket.

By mid-afternoon, Cat was exhausted with people and conversation and was quite delighted to sneak off up the hill to the Book Festival to listen to three Shetland poets reading from their work. Luckily they passed her comprehensibility test and they wove a web of words around her, its dreamlike quality the perfect preparation for an evening's dancing that would be at once systematic and spontaneous. The first time she'd done Scottish country dancing, she'd been whirled around emotionally as well as physically. Who knew what the second occasion might hold?

8

The Thorpes, the Morlands and Susie Allen arrived simultaneously on the doorstep of the grand mansion on Rothesay Terrace. Cat and Bella were so delighted to see each other after seven hours of abstinence that they immediately formed a two-person huddle, admiring each other's dresses, their hair and their make-up as they moved oblivious through the gleaming marble and glittering crystal of the entrance hall and into a ballroom transformed for the night with tartan silks and indifferent Victorian Highland landscapes.

The party settled round an oval table midway down one side of the room and they had barely secured drinks and a tray of hors d'oeuvres when the ceilidh band struck up. Two fiddlers, an accordion, a keyboard player, a drummer and a pair of guitarists occupied a small stage at the far end of the room and it was quickly apparent that they were a gifted ensemble. No sooner had the dance caller announced a Gay Gordons than James was on his feet, reminding Bella that she'd promised him the first dance. Bella half-rose, then looked around. 'Where's Johnny?'

'He's gone through to the card room,' James said. 'He's feeling lucky.'

Bella pouted. 'Well, I'm not going to abandon Cat just because Johnny has no manners. If we get split up now, it'll be the Dashing White Sergeant and Strip the Willow before you know it and we'll never see each other again all evening. Honestly. Men.'

James sat down, crestfallen. Cat had never seen him so eager to take to the dance floor. But at the end of the first section of the dance, he cast a beseeching glance at Bella, who rolled her eyes. 'Oh, all right, Jamie. If you insist.' She put a hand on Cat's arm. 'I'm sorry, but what can you do? He's gagging to get me on the dance floor, it would be cruelty to refuse him. You don't mind, do you? Johnny will be back any minute, win or lose, I promise.'

And she was gone, drawing James after her. He cast a quick look back at his sister with a worried frown, but she put a brave face on it and waved him off, even though that left her to the tender mercies of Martha and Susie and their seemingly endless conversations about fabrics and Pantone colours. Not only did she want to be on the floor, caught up in the excitement and movement of the dance, but she felt too the shame of being one of the wallflowers. In all her fiction-fuelled fantasies, she'd never been one of the dis-regarded ones, and it hurt to find herself overlooked. She'd read enough to know that it was the heroine's part to suffer the smug scorn of others, but that didn't make it any easier to keep a smile fixed on her face. But she was damned if she was going to pout or sulk over John Thorpe. She would suffer, but nobody would know.

And just then, as if to reward her silent stoicism in the face of torment, her gaze fell on a far more welcome sight than her friend's brother. There, less than three metres from their table, was Henry Tilney, unmistakable even though his back was to her. He was immaculately dressed in a perfectly tailored Argyle kilt jacket, nipped in at the waist, and fishtail-back tartan trews. He stood watching the dancers, then turned to face the entrance to the ballroom. His lively profile, handsome and dark-eyed, brought a blush to her cheek which faded as soon as she realised he had no notion that she was there. As she watched, a pretty young blonde in a white Empire-line dress with a tartan sash that matched his trousers sidled up to him, standing on tiptoe to kiss his cheek. For a moment, Cat's stomach lurched at the thought he might already be spoken for, but then her good sense kicked in and she recognised Ellie Tilney from the Facebook profile she'd studied on her phone. Relief flooded through Cat in a second scarlet tide and she told herself it spoke well of Henry that he had so affectionate a relationship with his sister.

The Tilneys moved closer to Cat's table, still oblivious to her presence. But a woman edging up the room ahead of them stopped abruptly with a little scream of delight. 'Martha Thorpe!' she exclaimed, lunging forward to air-kiss her friend.

It was enough to make both Tilneys stop and turn towards Cat. Henry gave a slow smile of recognition, his dark eyes appearing to grow even darker in his pale face as they drank her in. Cat felt a silly grin spread across her face as he moved towards her, Ellie in his wake.

He nodded to Susie. 'Mrs Allen. How lovely to see you again.'

Susie simpered and batted her thickly mascaraed eyelashes at him. 'Why, hello, Henry. When we didn't see you at the Book Festival, I was beginning to think you'd left town without saying goodbye.'

'You're spot on, Mrs Allen. I did have to go out of town unexpectedly for a couple of days. Urgent business, I'm afraid. But now I'm back again.'

'I dare say you're not sorry about that,' she said coquettishly. 'There's nowhere like Edinburgh at this time of year. Anywhere else would feel dull, don't you think?'

He caught Cat's eye momentarily. 'Since everyone worth spending time with is here, I'm bound to agree with you.' He gave Susie another courtly nod.

By now, Martha and her friend had introduced themselves to Ellie and invited her to join them. 'Plenty of wine to go round,' Martha said, pouring Ellie a glass in spite of her protestations that all she wanted was water.

Now, at last, having fulfilled the obligations of good manners, Henry turned his attention to Cat. Before he could say anything, however, the dance ended and the caller invited the gentlemen to take their partners for the Military Two-Step. Henry raised his eyebrows. 'Did we get that far with Fiona?'

Cat made the effort of recall. 'Heel and toe, and heel and toe and forward, two, three? Is that the one?'

'Splendid. Well done, Cat.' He extended a hand to her. 'Shall we?'

But before she could slip her fingers into his waiting grasp,

a familiar loud voice boomed in her ear and a hot, beefy hand
snatched hers. 'Not so fast, mate.'

It was John Thorpe, back from the card table at precisely
the wrong moment. He glowered at Henry, who gave Cat an
enquiring look. Before she could say anything, John continued
as he had begun. 'She's with me, buster.' He moved towards
the dance floor, presuming that Cat would follow. And she
did, to avoid the embarrassment of being dragged off her
chair.

Henry stepped to one side, a look of concern on his face.
'Are you OK with that?'

'I said I would dance with him, that's all,' Cat said over her
shoulder, uncertain whether he had heard her or not.

Once they were on the dance floor John acted as if nothing
untoward had happened. He made a perfunctory apology for
keeping her waiting, then launched into a rambling account
of the polo ponies, cars and dogs of the men he'd been
playing poker with. Whenever the configuration of the dance
made it possible, Cat couldn't help but gaze longingly
towards the part of the room where she'd left Henry. But
she could see not a sign of him. Nor could she see Bella and
her brother. She felt cut off from everyone she cared about,
abandoned into the custody of a man who seemed to disregard
everyone but himself.

As soon as the dance was over, she thanked him then
scuttled back to the table, where Martha and her friend were
still deep in conversation with Ellie Tilney. But Henry was
nowhere to be seen. There was some consolation to be had,
however, for Martha introduced her to Ellie then swapped
seats so the two young women could chat to each other. In

the absence of Ellie's brother, there was nobody Cat was happier to talk to.

Ellie, as Cat had previously noted from her Facebook profile, had striking good looks, sharing the same marble-white skin and unfathomable leonine eyes as her brother. Her dark blonde hair flowed back in waves from a widow's peak, framing her delicate features. She was more formal than Bella and her sisters, more restrained in her style and conversation, and had none of their flirtatiousness towards the young men who eyed them up as they promenaded past, looking for partners. But Cat sensed an interesting personality behind that reserve and desperately wanted to know her better, suspecting they might well become friends irrespective of Henry. However, since they knew almost nothing about each other and since Cat was too proud to enquire as to the whereabouts of her brother, they struggled to find enough in common to trigger a close conversation. Once they had worked their way through the charms of Edinburgh – its architecture, its museums and galleries, and its festivals – neither girl seemed to know what to talk about next.

Before their constraint became uncomfortable, they were swooped on by Bella, who threw herself on the chair next to Cat and exclaimed, 'There you are. At last. I've been scouring the dance floor for you for ages. You totally missed the Dashing White Sergeant, and I was buzzing for you to make up a three-some with me and Jamie.'

Cat's face fell under her friend's attack. 'I'm sorry. I looked, but I couldn't even see you.'

James arrived just in time to take a gentle punch in the arm from Bella. 'I told your hopeless brother to go and look for you but he wouldn't leave my side. Honestly, Cat, men are so lazy.'

'It wouldn't have done any good if I'd found Cat only to mislay you,' James said in his defence.

Bella rolled her eyes. 'Hopeless.'

Cat leaned back in her seat so she could include Ellie in the conversation. But her new friend was already on her feet. 'I have to go,' she said. 'I promised my father I'd meet him in the supper room. It was lovely to meet you.' And she bowed with curious formality before backing away and making for the exit.

'Who on earth was that?' Bella asked. 'She acts like she's in *Pride and Prejudice*.'

'That's Henry Tilney's sister, Ellie.' Cat stared after the disappearing figure. There was something about Ellie, something out of time and out of style. Like there would be if you were a two-hundred-year-old vampire, she thought with a mixture of dread and delight.

'Is he here?' Bella looked around eagerly. 'Is he half as good looking as she is? Where is the all-conquering brother? Point him out to me, I'm totally dying to see him.'

'What are you both on about?' James asked.

'Honestly, you men talk about women gossiping, but you're just as bad. Actually, no, you're worse. You're like little old women, you put your heads together and gossip, gossip, gossip about cars and women and sport. Well, Jamie, this is our little secret and we're not sharing.' Bella prodded him in the chest to drive home her point.

James laughed. 'You're just trying to hide the fact that you've got nothing important to say.'

'Cheeky boy,' Bella complained. 'Honestly, Cat, you've done an atrocious job of bringing up Jamie. He has no idea at all of how to treat a woman. You'd better stop eavesdropping, Master Jamie, or you might hear something you don't want to.'

The banter continued between Jamie and Bella, freeing Cat from any responsibility to contribute. She was grateful that the subject of Henry had been sidetracked, though there was a tiny part of her that was disappointed by Bella's swift loss of interest in a subject that was so dear to Cat's heart. She might not want to discuss him, but she wanted to have it confirmed that he was worthy of discussion.

When the band struck up again, James was immediately on his feet, picking up Bella's hand as he rose. 'Come on, Bella, it's a St Bernard's Waltz. You like to waltz.'

Cat wondered how he could make so confident an assertion, considering how little he knew Bella. And how brief she assumed his own acquaintance with Scottish country dancing to be. However, her friend responded, 'I don't like to waltz, I love it. So dreamy. But my evil sisters will tease us if we dance together all night, Jamie.'

'You're confusing me with someone who gives a toss. They're just jealous. I want to waltz with a beautiful woman, but I'll make do with you, Bella.' His smile was impish, his words free of sting.

'You are so bad, Jamie. Will you be OK, Cat? I don't know where my hopeless brother has got to . . .' She looked around, distracted. 'Oh, I'm sure he'll be back in a minute.' Without further pretence at reluctance, she followed James on to the dance floor and let him draw her close as the dance permitted.

Cat felt her shoulders slump in spite of her determination to remain straight-backed and cheerful in the face of her disappointment. Martha Thorpe leaned across and patted her arm. 'He'll be back soon, then you'll be happy again. He'll have you tripping the light fantastic again. What an adorable couple you make.'

It took her a moment to realise Martha was speaking of her son. 'I'm fine as I am, thank you,' she said.

'Of course you are,' Martha said condescendingly. 'But you must feel deflated after enjoying John's high spirits on the dance floor.'

Susie interrupted, saving Cat from having to find an anodyne response. 'Did you see Henry?'

'No, where is he?'

Susie looked around, puzzled. 'He was with us just now, when you were talking to Bella and James. He said he was tired of lounging about and he wanted to dance. I thought he was coming over to ask you.'

Dismayed, Cat cast an eye over the dancers as they turned and glided past her. And there she saw Henry, smiling down at a frankly dumpy little woman whose dress didn't suit her in the slightest.

Susie caught sight of him at the same moment. 'Oh. He's dancing with someone else.' After a short silence, she added, 'He really is a lovely young man.'

'You're so right,' Martha chipped in complacently. 'I shouldn't say it about my own son, but there is not a more charming young man in the city, never mind in this room.'

Cat and Susie exchanged a look, both bursting to giggle at Martha's misapprehension. But that was Cat's last moment of levity for the evening. Before the dance was over, John Thorpe returned and dropped like a stone into the chair next to her. 'Shocking hands I've just had to endure through there. I thought I might as well come back here and take you for another turn round the floor.'

'That's very kind of you. But I've danced enough for one evening. And my feet hurt from when you stood on them before.'

He looked dumbfounded. 'I stood on your feet? I think it's more like you misplaced your feet and put them where mine needed to be. Come on, let's have another crack at it and see if you can't manage it better this time.'

'Honestly, I'm too tired.'

He gave a heavy, put–upon sigh. 'OK, then let's go walk–about and see who we can rip the piss out of.'

'Really, I'm happy where I am. On you go, though. Don't let me spoil your fun.'

He looked as if he was about to make another attempt, but just then his sister Jess came by and he snagged her arm. 'Jess, let's go and see who we can wind up. Come on, we'll show them how to have a good time.'

For the rest of the evening, Cat skulked round the fringes of the fun. She moved between the ballroom and the supper room, trying to look purposeful. She even took a couple of selfies to post on her Facebook page so she could pretend to her sisters that she was having the time of her life.

Later, as the balmy night air filled her bedroom, she studied the photos more closely, the better to decide which to post. In the background of one, to her surprise and consternation, was the unmistakable figure of Henry Tilney, his dark inscrutable eyes fixed unswervingly on her.

9

Cat's reaction to the photograph was not, as might be supposed, unmitigated pleasure. Instead, she was filled with an overwhelming desire to eat chocolate. Mr Allen came home towards midnight to find her working her way through the remains of a chocolate fudge cake from the fridge. 'The raging munchies,' he said, eyebrows raised, a smile twitching the corners of his mouth. 'Tell me you've not been smoking dope, Cat.'

Shocked that he would even think such a thing, Cat exclaimed, 'Even if I did take drugs, I would never abuse your hospitality like that.'

Seeing that he had genuinely upset her, Mr Allen sat down at the table and helped himself to a broken chunk of fudge icing. 'Relax, Cat. I was only teasing. But if you ever did need a non-judgemental place to smoke a joint, you could do a lot worse than to come round to our house.'

'Are you saying you and Susie do *drugs*?' This was the final disappointment of what had been a profoundly anti-climactic evening. It was not that Cat was a prig; simply that home schooling meant she had never been offered illicit drugs nor was she aware of anyone in her immediate circle who indulged. What she knew of drug-taking she had learned from books and films and it had awakened no desire in her to partake.

Mr Allen chuckled. 'Not any more. But we did enjoy our misspent youths. It's OK, Cat, I didn't really think you'd been getting stoned, it's just that I've never seen you working your way through great slabs of cake at any time of day, never mind last thing at night. And one of the side effects of dope is that it makes you want to stuff yourself with sweet things.'

Unwilling to share the reason for her comfort eating, Cat wrapped up the last of the cake and replaced it in the fridge. 'I just didn't get much to eat at the dance,' she said. 'Good night.'

Cat went to bed determined to lie awake and wallow in her misery. Instead, she was asleep in minutes and when she woke nine hours later, her despair had evaporated, replaced by a buoyant optimism that spawned fresh hopes and fresh schemes.

Phase one of her plan was to develop her new acquaintance with Ellie Tilney. She told herself that it was for the girl's own sake, but in her secret heart she knew she sought to reach the brother through the sister. She had gleaned from their conversation that Ellie had tickets for three events at the Pleasance that day. Cat checked the Fringe programme and discovered that the first of these was due to take place at noon. She determined to make her way over there after eleven, so she could appear to be a fellow audience member when Ellie arrived.

To pass the time, she curled up in an armchair with the Hebridean Harpies. Being part of a large family had allowed Cat to develop the habit of selective deafness, so she was more or less immune to the random remarks and exclamations of

Susie, who, having so little to occupy her mind, was determined to share whatever trifle happened to cross it. Whether it was an intriguing item in her Twitter feed or a stain on her dress, a traffic jam in the street below or a particular pigeon on a ledge across the street, Susie had to pass comment, regardless of the reactions of Cat or Mr Allen.

But it was impossible to ignore the shriek of delighted astonishment that Susie let out at the sight of something in the street below. 'What is it?' Cat asked, dragging her attention away from *Ghosts of Gigha* to present company.

'Look,' Susie exclaimed. 'It's Johnny Thorpe in an amazing red sports car. And your brother and Bella in . . .' She tailed off.

Mr Allen, who had joined her at the window, completed her sentence. 'A rather clapped-out Triumph Spitfire, unless I'm mistaken.'

'Oooh! Johnny's jumped out, he's coming up!' Susie clapped her hands over her face. 'Look at me, I'm wearing rags, I'm hardly made up at all! What will he think?'

'I don't imagine it's you he's come to see,' Mr Allen said drily. And now there was a hammering at the door. 'Bloody boy doesn't know what a doorbell's for,' he grumbled as he went to answer it.

Johnny bounded in, a cheeky grin on his face, tight jeans and a striped shirt on his body. A throat-closing swirl of pungent aftershave hung in the air around him. 'Well, Cat, here I am. Have you been waiting long? It took your brother longer than he expected to sort out the loan of a set of wheels. Good morning, Mrs Allen, bloody good night last night, wasn't it? I went back to the tables after you left, made a few hundred at the blackjack table. Splendid night, all told. Come on then, Cat, we're on a double yellow and we're all waiting for you.' He rolled his hand from the wrist, imploring her to get on with it.

'What do you mean? Where are you all going to?'

He rolled his eyes, which brought home his resemblance to his sister Bella. 'Going to? What have you got instead of brains, Cat? Have you forgotten our date? A run out to North Berwick for fish and chips? We're all ready and waiting.'

'You mentioned it in passing, I don't remember a firm arrangement being made. You could have texted me or Facebooked me.'

He looked affronted. 'What, you think I'm the kind of man who just makes idle promises? Cat, I work in the City now, where a man's word is his bond.'

'Or not, as has apparently been the case with some of our bankers,' Mr Allen cut in darkly.

'Whatever. Text or no text, you'd have kicked off royally if I hadn't turned up, I bet.'

All Cat wanted from the day was to see Ellie Tilney. And she knew that her new friend had tickets for three events at the Pleasance. The run out to North Berwick couldn't take that long. She was bound to be back in time to catch Ellie later in the day. And if she dug her heels in and refused to go, it would only cause bad feeling that would spoil the day for her brother and her friend. The only thing that could override John's insistence and not reflect badly on her would be if Susie vetoed the outing because of pre-existing plans. She cast her a beseeching look and said, 'Is that OK with you, Susie? It's not interfering with your plans?'

Susie either failed to notice the entreaty or misread it alto-
gether for she said, 'Of course, you must go off with James
and your friends. You don't want to be stuck with fuddy duddy
me all day, do you?' And she shooed them out the door like
a mother hen, busily telling John how wonderful a young
woman Cat was and how he must spoil her as she deserved to
be spoiled.

Cat hurried down the stairs in John's wake, emerging to the
sound of Bella whooping with joy at the sight of her. 'Hey,
girlfriend! What kept you?' Cat ran across the pavement and
embraced Bella, who muttered in her ear, 'I totally need to talk
to you about last night, but it'll have to wait till these guys are
done with driving around like Formula One maniacs.'

'Come on, Cat.' John was already in the driving seat, drum-
ming his fingers on the steering wheel.

As she turned away, she heard Bella say to her brother,
'She's such a sweetie, Jamie.' It was a gratifying moment, given
how unloved she had felt the previous evening. She let herself
down into the low-slung passenger seat and John revved the
engine, filling the street with its low boom.

'I warn you, I'm one hell of a driver,' John said, slamming
the car into gear and shooting forward. The acceleration thrust
Cat back into her seat, but she was almost immediately thrown
against the seat belt when the next traffic light turned red and
they were forced to stop with a screech of brakes.

Hell was right, she thought, as they proceeded east out of
the city in a series of sudden leaps and abrupt halts. On a
couple of occasions, Cat managed to glance behind at her
brother and Bella, who seemed to be keeping up with them
despite travelling in a far less violent fashion. Through it all,

John maintained a steady monologue, requiring nothing more from Cat than the occasional grunt, which was just as well since she felt beyond speech.

'I love having the top down. The wind in your hair, the sun on your face, the feeling of freedom.'

The traffic fumes and the dust in your eyes, Cat thought.

'Wait till we hit the A1, then I'll show you what she can do. Your brother will never keep up in that old rustbucket he borrowed.' And so on, and so forth.

As they turned into London Road, John abruptly changed the subject. 'Old Allen – is he Jewish?'

Catherine had no idea what prompted the question and it made her slightly uneasy. 'Mr Allen? He's not that old. And I don't think he's Jewish. They come to church at Christmas. Why does it matter? Why are you bothered?'

'Just curious.' He gave a harsh bark of laughter. 'He's got all the financial acumen of a Jew. They're still top of the tree in the finance business, you know. And he's definitely made plenty of money over the years, no?'

'I suppose so. They have a lovely house in the village and a flat in Holland Park. And they're always taking exotic holidays.' There was no envy in Cat's words, merely a statement of fact.

'They've no kids of their own, right?'

'That's right. Susie says she never wanted kids, but some-times I wonder.'

'But they're your godparents, right?'

Cat frowned and grabbed the side of the car as they lurched round a milk float at speed. 'No, they're just family friends.'

'But you're special to them, right? Or else why would they bring you to Edinburgh with them for a whole month?'

'Mr Allen thought I would be company for Susie while he's working.'

'You sure it's her you're here to keep amused and not him?'

When Cat understood his meaning, she was so annoyed she would likely have jumped out of the car if they'd been stationary. 'That's a horrible thing to say,' she told him. 'You make him sound like some dirty old pervert. And he's nothing like that at all. That's a revolting idea. He doesn't even tell smutty jokes. He's a genuinely nice man, I don't know how you dare to suggest otherwise.'

John grunted, as if dissatisfied with her response. 'I heard he's got health problems.'

'He had a minor heart attack in the spring, he's supposed to take things a bit easier. That's why Susie's here for the whole month this time – she wanted to keep an eye on him.'

'But he's still knocking back the Scotch, right? I saw him the other night at a whisky tasting and he was giving it some welly for a man who's supposed to be looking after his heart.'

'I think that's his business, don't you?'

'I'm not saying it's a bad thing,' John said. 'Living in this country is so bloody depressing you need something to cheer you up.'

'Yes, I hear you students apparently needed a lot of cheering up. My dad says it's shocking how much you lot drink compared with what it was like in his day.' This was as close to waspish-ness as Cat was capable of.

John laughed loudly. 'This new lot are all lightweights when it comes to drinking, trust me. When I was a fresher, we'd think nothing of knocking back two or three bottles of wine each on a good night, with a few brandy chasers. But I hear this year's lot were falling over their feet after a single bottle.'

'Maybe they weren't as well off as your crowd,' Cat said. 'Maybe they'd been preloading on the cheap vodka. James told me that's what people do in Newcastle.'

He shook his head, pityingly. 'Then they need to find a way to earn enough money to drink properly.'

'You don't have to be a big drinker to get on, though. James hardly drinks at all.'

John snorted like a pig. But whatever he said was lost in the growl of a massive articulated lorry sitting next to them at the lights. Cat remained unenlightened as to the true extent of her brother's indulgence in the Oxford high life.

Once they could hear each other speak again, John launched into a detailed explanation of precisely how rubbish her brother's borrowed car was. 'I bet it hasn't even got an MOT,' he shouted as they turned on to the dual carriageway of the A1 and he stamped on the accelerator. Cat narrowed her eyes against the scourging wind and held her hair in a tight ponytail to prevent it whipping painfully against her face. She could barely make out the speedo, but she managed to discern that they had left the speed limit in the dust.

By the time they reached North Berwick, she was freezing and nauseous. She had never been happier to see a car park. 'It'll be ages before Jamie and Bella get here. We can get a head start on the drinks,' he announced, making for the entrance of the gastropub he claimed produced the best fish and chips in East Lothian, according to his boss in London.

Cat caught up with him by the door and grabbed his sleeve. 'I'm not going back with you if you have a drink,' she said mutinously.

His lip curled in a sneer. 'Then how will you get back?'

'I'll go with James. He doesn't drink and drive. And neither should you.'

He cocked his head, considering her. For once, the words of someone else had penetrated the thick shell of his self-esteem. 'For the sake of buggering barnacles,' he said, rolling his eyes. 'All right, Miss Goody Two Shoes. I'll stick to mineral water. Just for you. But remember that when I want a favour from you.'

He strode into the pub, oblivious to her saying, 'Obeying the law isn't a favour.' Wearily, she followed him inside and found him at the bar ordering two sparkling mineral waters. 'If I can't drink, neither can you,' he said dismissively.

'I'm still only seventeen so I can't drink legally in a pub anyway,' Cat said, taking her glass and crossing to a table in the window. She prayed her brother would not be much longer for she did not know how much more of this conversation she could endure.

Her companion was all brag and bluster, exaggeration and embellishment, hyperbole and histrionics. Nothing in Cat's life had prepared her for John Thorpe. Her own family were direct and matter-of-fact to the point of dullness. Even the Allens, who moved in relatively exalted circles, never boasted about their connections or inflated their own worth at the expense of others. But John was a man who never owned a mistake, whose every anecdote showed him in a glowing light, whose skills and abilities were second to none. Cat was certain she was supposed to marvel that he had deigned to honour her with his presence.

It was all very perplexing because it was so unexpected. Bella spoke of him with such warmth, praising his sense of fun and his generosity. And James, her sweet-natured, clever brother, had told her that women found him irresistible. Neither had so much as hinted at how wearyingly self-absorbed his conversation was. Briefly, Cat considered the problem might lie with her and her undoubted lack of social sophistication. But when James and Bella finally joined them, the atmosphere changed completely and Cat found herself having fun.

The drive had given them all an appetite for the fish and chips – excellent as billed – and they were soon back on the road, much to the relief of Cat, who was mindful of Ellie Tilney's schedule for the afternoon. She gritted her teeth and blotted out both the return journey and the blowhard bullshit of her companion with a full-blooded daydream of how the rest of the day would play out.

When they arrived back in Queen Street, Cat felt obliged to invite them in for tea and cakes. Bella was halfway out of the car when she looked at her watch and screamed. 'Look at the time. OMG, how did it get so late? It's past three o'clock and Ma has tickets for a play at Summerhall at four.'

'For us too?' her brother demanded, sounding disgruntled.

'Yes, she managed to get her hands on a pair of returns this morning.' Bella got out of the car and wrapped Cat in a tight hug. 'This is so stupid, when am I ever going to get to talk to you? This totally sucks. We're going on to dinner afterwards with some family friends, so boring. I'd much rather we were together.'

Cat was torn between missing their intimate chats and wanting to be rid of them all so she could track down Ellie Tilney. 'It's OK,' she said. 'Susie has tickets for the Book Festival this evening. A crime writer and a historical novelist.'

John rolled his eyes. 'Rather you than me.'

'Will we see you later?' Cat asked her brother.

Looking faintly embarrassed, he said, 'Like Bella said, her mum managed to get a pair of tickets. I don't want to let her down after she put herself out for me like that.'

'And he might as well come to dinner since he's staying with us,' Bella added. 'So we'll see you tomorrow, yeah?' She air-kissed Cat on both sides then jumped back into the car with a cheerful wave.

Cat ran upstairs, reckoning she just had time to brush her hair after its buffeting in the car. And maybe to change into a fresh T-shirt that didn't smell of petrol fumes. As she burst in, she almost crashed into Susie, who was hanging up her wrap. 'Oh, there you are,' she said, her capacity for stating the obvious undiminished by her exposure to Edinburgh intellectual life. 'Did you have a lovely time?'

Cat had been brought up always to have something positive to say about any experience. 'The fish and chips was excellent.'

'Martha said it would be. She was thrilled that the four of you were going off together.' She went through to the kitchen, Cat at her heels.

'You saw Mrs Thorpe this morning?'

'We met up for coffee in George Street. And who should we see but Ellie and Henry Tilney.'

Taken aback, Cat said, 'But Ellie told me she had tickets for the Pleasance today.'

Susie nodded sagely. 'That's right, so she did. But you know everybody's been raving about the South African production of *Macbeth* in the main festival, and it turns out that one of the family knows the company manager and he snagged them some tickets for this afternoon's matinee. So Ellie handed back her Fringe tickets and was all set for *Macbeth* with her father and Henry.'

'Oh.'

'We had a lovely chat. They're really charming, Henry and Ellie. They remind me of you and James, such good manners and such attractive personalities. Ellie was wearing a beautiful dress, cream with tiny sprigs of herbs all over it. Almost Regency looking. She's obviously got very individual taste, that girl.'

'Yes, apparently.'

'Martha's friend Helen was with us, and she told us all about the family after Henry and Ellie had gone.'

Now Cat was eager. 'What did she say?'

'Their family home is in the Borders, Northanger Abbey. Helen says they've lived there since before Flodden, whenever that was. And they're very well off.' Susie filled the kettle and turned it on.

'And are their parents both here in Edinburgh with them?'

Susie frowned. 'Now, what did she say . . . ? They can't both be dead otherwise who would have sorted the tickets out . . . I think their mother is dead. Yes, I'm sure she is, because Helen said Ellie inherited her mother's jewellery. Now what else was it she said . . . ? Oh yes. Apparently the mother was practically a recluse for years before she actually died.' Susie gave Cat a knowing look. 'And we all know what that means, don't we?'

'Do we?'

Susie raised her eyebrows. 'Well, there's no reason why you would know, my dear. You've so little experience of the world. But often it means . . .' she lowered her voice, '. . . mental health problems. Sometimes as a result of domestic abuse.

Physical or psychological. Not that Helen said that in so many words, but reading between the lines . . .'

Cat, lacking the experience to distinguish speculative gossip from truth, gathered the information as if it were gospel. 'That doesn't sound good. What about the other brother, Freddie? Did you pick up any info about him?'

Susie looked doubtful. 'She didn't say, I don't think. But it was lovely to run into them.'

'Did they ask after me?' She hardly dared ask the question, but she needed to know the answer.

Susie put a finger to her chin. 'Now I come to think of it . . . No, I don't think they did.'

Crestfallen, Cat enquired no further. She had heard enough, and she excused herself, rushing to her bedroom and throwing herself down on the coverlet. The knowledge of what she had missed festered in her heart, and the more she felt the anguish of missing out on the Tilneys, the more she disliked John Thorpe and his stupid red sports car. That, she vowed, would be the last moment of her time she would waste on that blowhard bore.

10

The following morning, Cat walked up to the Book Festival grounds with the Allens. Mr Allen was intent on listening to some economist talking about first world problems, so the two women were free to drink coffee and eat shortbread till their friends joined them. They'd barely settled themselves with lattes and biscuits when the entire female division of the Thorpe family arrived, along with James. Cat was thrilled by the absence of John Thorpe, but she said nothing in case it was construed as taking an interest in his whereabouts. And then someone might text him and summon him and her morning would be ruined.

While James queued to fulfil everyone's orders for hot and cold drinks, Bella slung an arm round Cat's shoulders, complaining about the length of their separation. 'At last!' she said, drawing her chair closer. 'How's tricks? I mean, not that I need to ask because you look stunning. You've done something different with your hair, haven't you? Man, you are trying to make yourself irresistible, nobody else in Edinburgh's going to get a look in, you evil witch. My bro totally fancies you, and obviously Henry Tilney feels the same way since he came back to Edinburgh and made a bee-line for you. Like, wow. My ma says he's practically edible. You have to introduce us, right? First chance? I'm buzzing to meet him. Is he around this morning?'

'I haven't seen him.'

'Oh, poo. Am I never going to meet this stallion? Oh, but, do you like my new top? Ma has this woman who makes stuff for her and I got her to do this to my own design. Cool, right? I thought Edinburgh would be more interesting fashion-wise, didn't you? But it's really quite dull. Considering they're all so creative, their clothes are like, totally similar. Jamie and I were just saying this morning how we're really tired of the city, and how we were gagging for the countryside. Honestly, you wouldn't believe how in tune we are. We think the same about everything. I'm really glad you weren't with us because you'd have been ripping the piss out of us.'

'Why would I do that?'

Bella poked her arm. 'Because you would have wanted to see us squirm. You'd have been teasing us about being made for each other or some other sick story like that. You'd have had me blushing as red as your T-shirt.'

'No way,' Cat protested. 'That's not who I am. And besides, it wouldn't have crossed my mind.'

'Hah! I know you better than you know yourself, missy. But here's Jamie, back with our lovely coffees.' She cooed at him while he distributed drinks and scones and shortbread and had him sit beside her at the cramped table.

As soon as they'd cleared their plates and emptied their cups, Bella linked arms with James and stood up. 'Time for us to go walkabout.' Almost as an afterthought, she said, 'Come on, Cat, let's see who we can see. I swear I saw Stephen Fry earlier, over by the Author's Yurt.'

Cat fell into step beside them but it soon became clear to her that she was only there as a sort of chaperone to stop the adult tongues wagging. James and Bella kept whispering in each other's ears so even if they'd wanted to include Cat, she wouldn't have been able to contribute to a subject whose identity was unknown to her. Besides, the duckboard walkways were too narrow for them to walk comfortably three abreast when there were other book lovers to be taken into consideration. Cat was on the point of making her excuses and heading into the bookshop when she caught sight of Ellie Tilney emerging from the Spiegeltent.

Cat cut across the corner of the grass and waved to Ellie, whose solemn face lit up in a smile. 'Hi, Ellie,' Cat said. 'How are you doing?'

'Good, thanks. And you?'

'I'm sorry I missed you yesterday, I got dragged off for a run out to North Berwick for fish and chips, thanks to my brother's friend who wanted to show off his new car.'

'Tedious,' Ellie said, falling into step beside Cat. 'Men and cars is a recipe for boredom.'

'Susie was telling me you managed to snag tickets for *Macbeth*, you lucky thing.'

Ellie nodded enthusiastically. 'It was brilliant. Really dark and sinister. They played it like the Macbeths believed they were invincible, like they had special powers.'

'What? Like vampires or something?'

'Exactly that. So it was all the more shocking when everything started coming apart the way it would for mere mortals. Henry hasn't stopped talking about it.'

Even the sound of his name made Cat tingle. 'Henry's such a good dancer.' The non sequitur was out of her mouth before she could check it with her brain. The line clearly surprised and amused her companion.

'I suppose,' Ellie said with a smile.

'I hope he didn't take it the wrong way the other evening. When that idiot Johnny Thorpe pushed in and stopped us dancing together. OK, I did say I would have a dance with him, but he made out that he was my partner for the evening, which was total crap. So rude.' She tried to stop herself babbling but without success. 'It was really nice to see Henry again, I thought he'd gone for good.'

'Oh no, when he met you at Fiona's, he'd just come up to make sure the house was all prepared for us. My dad's such a total perfectionist, Henry wanted to avoid any hassle with the rental company and the staff.'

That would never have occurred to Cat, it being so far from her own experience of the world. 'Right. So who was it I saw him dancing with after I got dragged off by Johnny?'

'Miranda Tait-Brown. Her mother and my mother were at school together. We've known the Tait-Browns all our lives.'

'She must have been well pleased to have such a good dancer for a partner.' And before she could stop herself – 'Do you think she's pretty?'

Ellie raised one eyebrow. 'Never have.'

'Is Henry coming to the Book Festival today, then?'

'No, he's gone on a ride-out with my father.'

'What's a ride-out? I've never heard of that.'

'Most of the Borders towns have a traditional ceremony where they sort of beat the bounds or mark something about the town's history. It's an excuse for a bunch of men to mount up their horses and ride over the fields then get horribly drunk. There might have been a good reason for it once but now it's just silly business.' Ellie glanced over at the book tent. 'Look, have you got a minute?'

Regardless of her commitments, Cat would have said yes. She followed Ellie into the temporary bookshop, where her new friend selected a large coffee-table book from one of the displays and beckoned Cat to one of the sofas arranged around the room. She checked the contents page and opened the book about halfway through, so it sat across both their thighs. 'This is the Langholm Common Riding,' she said, pointing to a striking photograph of a quartet of plump bowler-hatted men on horseback riding through a narrow street. 'These guys are called the cornets. You see, they're carrying the standard.'

She turned the page to reveal an imposing fortified house against a dawn sky. Cat had learned enough in Edinburgh to understand it was a hybrid of Gothic and Scots Baronial. In the foreground, a string of riders in scarlet coats and bowler hats cut a dramatic diagonal swathe across the photograph. 'That's Northanger Abbey and this is our ride-out.'

'OMG,' Cat breathed. The abbey was vampire heaven. It was the perfect setting for an adventure in the Hebridean Harpies series. She said as much, and Ellie raised her eyebrows, a wry smile quirking one corner of her mouth.

'You're not the first one to say that. It's not nearly as grand as it looks, though. Some parts of it are almost modern.' She pointed to the figure at the head of the ride-out. His face was unreadable in the limited light of the dawn, but his carriage was erect and his lean figure a sharp contrast to the Langholm cornets. 'That's my dad.' Neither her voice nor her face gave anything away about her feelings towards her father. She glanced at her watch. 'Oh God, is that the time? I'm supposed to meet my cousin for lunch out in Cramond. I have to run.' She dumped the book on Cat's lap and jumped to her feet. 'Lovely to see you again – are you going to the Highland Ball tomorrow night?'

'Yes, will I see you there?'

'For sure.' Ellie bent down and gave Cat a quick hug. Cat watched her leave, holding tight to the book, thinking that it would be hard to imagine how the day could have been improved upon.

Although Annie Morland had worked hard to convince her daughters that fretting over clothes was a waste of time and energy, she might as well have saved her energy. From the moment Ellie Tilney left her side until Cat arrived at the Highland Ball, nothing occupied her thoughts but how she could look good enough to captivate Henry Tilney. Had she paid more attention to her mother, she would have understood how little store men set by the cut of a woman's dress; at least, the sort of men it would be worth her while trying to attract. No man would notice her outfit except when it revealed too much; no woman would be happy unless they could find something to criticise. Cat had yet to learn that she would be best served by dressing to please herself rather than ceding control to another's taste, real or imagined. Instead, she was convinced that the wrong choice would destroy her chances of impressing Henry, so her entire day was spent in consideration of her wardrobe.

Having finally settled on a simple dark blue dress in a silky fabric that caught the light and made it dance, Cat walked into the Highland Ball in a ferment of expectation. Her eyes darted everywhere, eager to catch a glimpse of Henry Tilney, but equally eager to spot John Thorpe so she might more easily avoid him. She knew she'd be lucky if Henry Tilney came near her after the way John Thorpe had behaved, but she couldn't help hoping Ellie might have put in a good word for her. But that good word would be wasted if she was being monopolised by the man she devoutly wished not to see.

This sort of anxiety was entirely new to Cat. She'd only ever been pursued in a half-hearted way by village boys who were going through the motions of courtship, experimenting in a safe zone where it didn't really matter. Both sides understood these were flirtations with training wheels firmly attached; and besides, Cat had never found any of the local boys even momentarily worthy of her fantasies. This heart-quickening, breath-stopping feeling that hit her whenever she thought of Henry was some-thing she'd only read about, never mind the stomach-clenching dread of being pursued by someone she was growing heartily to dislike. She had no idea how to defend herself against his atten-tions and she was far too kind simply to tell him to get lost. And she did know enough to understand that being blunt with John could have awkward repercussions for her beloved brother and Bella, neither of whom she wanted to inconvenience.

Their party was barely inside the ballroom when they were waved over to join the Thorpes. Cat hung back, trying to keep at least one person between her and John. When he greeted her loudly, she pretended she couldn't hear him over the music. Luckily, she was soon drawn aside by Bella. 'I know what you're going to say, but honestly, I am so going to dance with Jamie tonight. I don't care what people say, he's such a sweetie. But you have to cover for us. You need to dance with Johnny, so it just looks like the four of us having fun.' She looked around for her brother. 'Damn, he's walking off. But he'll be back in a minute.'

There was nothing Cat wanted to say that wouldn't have hurt her friend's feelings, so she said nothing, staying put as Bella and James moved off towards the dance floor, resigning herself with heavy heart to being the focus of John Thorpe's bulldozer bluster. In a bid to avoid his eye, she fished out her phone and pretended to be absorbed in her Facebook page. When a shadow fell over her screen, she was almost too dismayed to look up. But if she had failed to do so, she'd have missed the welcome sight of Henry Tilney leaning towards her, a friendly smile lighting up his dark eyes. 'Can you drag yourself away from Facebook long enough to dance with me?' he asked mischievously.

Although the fantasy of this very moment had enlivened every waking moment of the day, it had not prepared Cat for the warm rush of delight that followed his request. 'I'd love to,' she said, thrusting her phone back in her evening bag and taking his proffered arm. She could scarcely credit her luck – not only had she avoided John Thorpe but she'd also won a fresh chance to charm Henry Tilney.

But no sooner had they made it to the fringe of the dance floor when a familiar voice boomed in her ear. There, right behind them, was her nemesis. 'Hey, Cat, what are you playing at? I thought we were supposed to be dancing together?'

'I don't know where you got that idea, since you never asked me.' Fifteen, love, she thought.

'I did,' he harrumphed. 'I asked you as soon as you came in.'

'You did no such thing,' she said. 'I haven't spoken to you all night.'

'Damn it, I only came tonight because you were supposed to be my partner. It's been fixed since the other night.'

Henry, smiling, said smoothly, 'Which is it? This evening or the other evening? You're really not very convincing.'

John glared at him. 'I remember now. It was when you were waiting by the cloakroom for Andy Allen to fetch your coat.'

'It's a wrap,' Cat said.

'And here I've been telling everybody I'm booked to dance with the prettiest girl in the room. And when they see you dancing with him, I'm going to look a complete twat.'

'Don't worry, they'll never think of me after a description like that,' Cat said, taking pity on him and patting his arm.

'Whereas that description of you . . .' Henry spoke so softly only Cat could hear and she had to stifle a giggle.

'So who is this tosser you prefer to me?' John demanded, glowering.

'My name is Henry Tilney,' Henry said. 'And I suggest you take some lessons in manners before you speak to Cat again.'

'Tilney? Don't tell me you're Freddie Tilney's baby brother?' John sneered.

'How do you know my brother? I can't imagine him having anything to do with someone so ill-mannered.'

'We're old friends, me and Freddie. I was his potboy at Fenners.'

'That was a long time ago. Now if you'll excuse us?' Henry stepped neatly between Cat and John. There was a moment when she thought John would take matters further, but when he turned away, pretending one of his sisters was calling him, she understood that he was the kind of bully who backed down whenever he was confronted. 'Thank you,' Cat said, turning back to Henry.

'Just as well he decided to retreat,' Henry said. 'Only an idiot takes on a lawyer in a matter of contract.'

'Contract?'

'You and I contracted to dance and he tried to pretend there was a pre-existing contract between you and him. But when his claim was tested, he had to withdraw, exposed as a liar and a cheat.' His response, which could have been dry and legalistic, was delivered with wit and a sardonic grin.

'I wasn't aware that agreeing to dance was a legally binding contract.' She matched his smile.

'Absolutely. Very similar to marriage, in fact.'

Cat laughed out loud. 'You're being silly now.'

'Not at all. Fidelity and mutual consideration are at the heart both of dancing and marriage.'

'And fancy footwork too, obviously. But people that marry are supposed to stay together forever. People that dance only whirl around the room for an hour or two then part.'

'Have you never heard of divorce, woman?'

'I've heard of it but we're not keen on it in my family. My father's a vicar, you see.'

'My father's a general, but we're not keen on it in my family either.' A momentary shadow fell across his face. 'Once you're a Tilney, there's no escape.'

'Does that go for dancing too, or just marriage?'

He laughed. 'Now you've got me. But please, can you allow me the luxury of fidelity on the dance floor at least? No more flirting and batting your eyelashes at other men?' His eyelids lowered as if he were not entirely joking.

Cat groaned. 'Johnny Thorpe is my brother's friend and my friend's brother. Ignoring him is too awkward. But apart from him, I don't think I know anyone else in the room who would even want to talk to me.'

'And that's the only reason? That you don't know anyone?'

Cat looked away. 'I don't actually want to talk to anybody else.'

'That makes me feel much happier.' He steered her towards the dance floor with an arm round her shoulder.

'What was all that about Johnny Thorpe knowing your brother? His potboy? What's that?' Cat asked.

'Freddie went to Fenwick House School. It's one of those places that has ideas above itself and has stupid invented names for everything. A potboy is like a fag. A first-year oik who has to run around after the senior men. Like a little servant. Freddie will have bullied the living daylights out of Thorpe, and he'll have loved every minute of it.' Henry's contempt was obvious. 'But let's not waste our breath on that idiot. Are you still enjoying Edinburgh? Not tired of it yet?'

'No way. This is the most exciting place I've ever been. There's so much going on, so much to do and see. I was afraid it would all be over my head, the theatre and the art and the comedy. But I've loved it all.'

'And yet all this lot will disappear like Scotch mist as soon as the festival is over. They'll flee back to London. Because London is where it's at, according to them. I've even heard them say there's no politics outside London.' He gave a bark of laughter. 'What in the name of God do they think is going on at Holyrood? A debating society? They're all so bloody smug and narrow. They come here to show how very adventurous they are, turn it into London-on-the-Forth for a month then bugger off again.' His disdain shone through his every word.

'If they think Edinburgh's a backwater, they should try a Dorset village. They'd die of boredom.'

'You don't like the country?'

'I love it. But you have to admit one day is pretty much like another. It's not like Edinburgh. Or London, I suppose. The only thing I wish is that I knew more people like the ones I've met here. Sitting in Susie's kitchen is mostly the closest I get to intellectual company.'

'Poor you! At least now you'll be able to entertain them with stories of your cultural adventures in Edinburgh.'

Cat groaned. 'Don't. I'm going to be the world's biggest bore on the subject. My sisters are already threatening to superglue my mouth shut.'

'Mmm. Lovely girls, by the sound of it.'

'They're good fun. I just wish they could both be with me to enjoy it here. They'd love it.'

And on that wistful note, the band struck up a Strip the Willow and all possibility of speech was postponed. At one point, when they were in the middle of the set and Cat was struggling to get her breath back, she noticed a tall, pale-faced man come forward and lean in to whisper something to Henry, who responded at once. The man wore a scarlet tunic with medal ribbons over tartan trews and he was strikingly hand- some in spite of his silver temples and somewhat gaunt features. His hair flowed back from the same widow's peak Cat had noticed on Ellie earlier. He nodded to Henry and melted back into the crowd lining the dance floor. Cat tried to catch his image in the long mirrors that lined one wall of the ballroom, but she was too late and could see no trace of him. Just as if he were a vampire, she thought with a frisson of amusement.

When next the couple came together, Henry said, 'That was my father. The man who spoke to me.'

But the dance separated them again before she could respond. They remained on the floor for a Canadian Barn Dance and an eightsome reel, but finally conceded temporary defeat when a Virginia Reel was announced. Cat and Henry found Ellie in the refreshment room and collapsed on the chairs next to her. 'I'm puggled,' Henry said. 'Cat has worn me out.'

'Wimp,' his sister said. 'I've just been up for the last three dances with Sandy Baird and I'm fresh as a daisy.'

'Really? I bet you'll feel it in the morning.'

Ellie laughed. 'Is that a challenge? Tell you what, let's all take a hike up Arthur's Seat tomorrow. That'll sort out the sheep from the goats. What do you say, Cat?'

Cat couldn't imagine how she would feel in the morning but she didn't want to miss any possibility of spending time with Henry. 'Sounds like a plan.'

'OK. We'll pick you up at noon. Deal?'

Henry agreed. 'Deal.'

Cat nodded, but before she could speak, Mr Allen appeared at her side. 'Cat, Susie's not feeling very well, so I'm going to take her home. Will you be OK coming back on your own?'

Cat jumped to her feet. 'I'll come with you.' She turned to her friends. 'I'd better go in case there's anything I can do for Susie. She's taken such good care of me while I've been here. And I'll see you tomorrow at noon?'

'Unless it's chucking it down,' Ellie said.

As she followed Mr Allen from the room, Cat cared not for her aching feet or her tired legs. Inside, her spirit was skipping. It was, she thought, only the start of the dance.

11

On the following morning, Cat was so absorbed by the state of the weather she could barely summon enough attention to eat her breakfast. A haar had crept up from the Forth, shrouding the city in thin mist, through which the sun appeared as a pale nimbus struggling to make an impact. Susie, who had spent much of the night in gastrointestinal discomfort, was curled in a chair by the window, gingerly sipping rooibos tea and wincing. 'If only this mist would clear, it would be a lovely day,' she said faintly.

'And if only the clouds would thicken up it would be a miserable day,' Mr Allen contributed from behind the paper. 'It is what it is.'

By eleven, flecks of rain started to appear on the windows. Despondent, Cat said, 'It's coming on rain.'

'I was afraid of that,' Susie said.

'It's just spitting, maybe it'll pass before noon.'

'You won't see a bloody thing up Arthur's Seat in this mist,' Mr Allen said. 'Not to mention how muddy it'll be.'

'I've never minded a bit of mud,' Cat said.

'How true,' Susie said with feeling.

'And at least I have the right clothes for being outside in bad weather. Oh, it's too bad, though. People are putting their umbrellas up. It's coming down harder, and I was so convinced it was going to be a lovely day.' Cat threw herself discontented into a chair and scowled at the rain.

'There'll be nobody up at the Book Festival this morning,' Susie said.

'Apart from the ones with tickets,' her husband commented.

'I meant, people to talk to, not listen to,' Susie said.

'Quite.'

The raindrops fattened and speeded up and the hands of the clock turned just as relentlessly. At noon, there was no respite. 'I doubt you'll be walking today,' Mr Allen said, shrugging into his waxed jacket and heading for the door. 'I'm off to the Stand for an afternoon of comedy. See you both later.'

Glum-faced, Cat stared at the rain coursing down the window pane. 'I'm going to give it another quarter of an hour,' she announced. 'I mean, it's not like one of those thunderstorms with monsoon rain that they had in *Banshees of Berneray*. The sky could be clear in no time.'

As if it was listening to her, the clouds began to thin and the rain to slacken. By half past twelve, a gleam of sunshine took Cat quite by surprise. The sky had begun to clear, and even as she watched, scraps of blue sky appeared between the clouds, gradually meeting to form large clear patches. Ten minutes more and there was no doubt that a bright afternoon was on the way. 'I always thought it would clear up,' Susie said smugly. 'But has it cleared up quickly enough for the Tilneys, that's the question.'

Or had it cleared up too much, Cat wondered, checking her

phone for a text or tweet that would explain her friends' lateness. She couldn't help recalling the conversation with Bella where they'd joked about Henry being a vampire. According to what she'd read, cloudy skies were OK, but full sunlight was out of the question. She shook her head, as if that would clear away such a crazy idea. After all, if that was really what was going on with Henry and Ellie, they'd have been knocking at the door with delight in the lashing rain.

Again Cat crossed to the window and looked down into the street, just in time to see the same two convertibles that had appeared there the day before. 'It's Bella and James. And Johnny Thorpe. They must be coming here. But I can't go off with them, can I? Ellie and Henry might still show up.'

John Thorpe's voice arrived before he did, echoing up the stairwell. 'Cat! Get a move on, girl, we're on double yellows, for God's sake,' he bellowed as he climbed. She opened the door and he sighed histrionically. 'At last. Get your coat on, we're going to Glasgow.' He stuck his head into the flat. 'Morning, Mrs A.'

'Glasgow? Isn't that miles away? Like, on the other side of the country?'

'You've seen how fast my wheels go, we'll be there in no time. Trust me. Come on, girl.'

'Plus, I've got some friends coming round. Any minute now.'

'They'll understand. It's not every day you get the chance of a stunning drive across to Glasgow. It'll be a cracking day out. Jamie and I had this brilliant idea at breakfast, only we thought it was going to be stymied by the weather. But no! Here's the sun—' He gestured expansively as if to take credit for the improvement in the weather.

'And I'm supposed to be going out with friends,' Cat said with finality.

A sly look crossed his face. 'What if I threw in a haunted palace?'

He could not have found a better way through Cat's defences. Her distaste for him dissolved at such a prospect. 'A haunted palace?'

He nodded triumphantly. 'Linlithgow Palace. The ruined pleasure-dome of the royal Stewarts. The birthplace of Mary, Queen of Scots.' He lowered his voice to a sepulchral hollowness. 'They say it's haunted by her mother, Mary of Guise.'

'And are there towers and long galleries and battlements?'

John nodded. 'All you could wish for in a royal ruin.'

Cat groaned. 'It sounds heavenly. But I can't go, I really can't.'

At that moment, Bella joined her brother on the stairs. 'Can't go? Are you crazy? It's haunted, for God's sake, Cat. Haunted.'

Cat looked over her shoulder towards Susie, both for support and to avoid meeting Bella's eye. 'I made arrangements with Ellie Tilney and her brother to go up Arthur's Seat. They were supposed to be here at noon, but it was raining, so they'll probably be here any minute now.'

Because she was looking away, she didn't see the look of guile that passed across John's face. 'Henry Tilney? Freddie Tilney's brother? The bloke you were dancing with last night?'

Cat turned back to face him. Her chin came up. 'That's right.'

John laughed. 'You'll be waiting a long time if you're expecting him to call today,' he said. 'I've just seen him going into Haymarket station with a very good-looking blonde. The pair of them had backpacks, like they were heading off somewhere for the day. I'd say you were the last thing on his mind.'

Seeing Cat's stricken expression, Bella said casually, 'Ellie probably thought it was too muddy to go hill-walking. She's a bit precious, Cat. I think so, anyway. The least she could have done was text you and not leave you high and dry. Come on, we'll have a brilliant time at Linlithgow and Glasgow. It'll be so cool, just like being in a Hebridean Harpies story.'

'What do you think, Susie? Should I go?'

Susie shrugged. 'It's up to you. But Bella's got a point: Ellie could have texted you.'

And so it was settled. Which was more than could be said of Cat's feelings, divided between the pleasure lost and the pleasure anticipated. In spite of her natural tendency to think well of people, she couldn't help a niggle of annoyance that Ellie had left her dangling without a word.

They bounced over the cobbles of Queen Street and Ainslie Place, juddering so hard that Cat feared for her teeth. As they screeched through the sharp right turn on to Queensferry Road, John shouted, 'Who's that girl?' before they lurched to a halt at a red light.

'What girl?'

He jerked a thumb over his shoulder. 'Blonde, back there at the lights. She was waving at us, and I'm bloody sure I don't know her.'

Cat swivelled round in her seat just in time to see Ellie Tilney and her brother crossing at the pedestrian light behind them, both dressed for walking in waxed jackets, thornproof trousers and hiking boots. 'Pull over, you—' She almost called him a moron, but stopped herself in time. 'It's the Tilneys. Henry and Ellie. I need to catch up with them. Pull over.'

But the lights turned to green and John accelerated wildly. 'You're seeing things,' he said, hammering across the Dean Bridge as if the hounds of hell were on his tail.

'That was the Tilneys, John. I bet they're on their way round to meet me right now. Please, please take me back.'

'Too late,' he said. 'Other plans.'

Angry now, and confused by his behaviour, Cat said, 'Why did you lie to me? Why did you say Henry was going into the station at Haymarket when he obviously wasn't? They must think I'm the rudest person on the planet, shooting past them in a car when I'm supposed to be meeting up with them. How could you do that to me?'

'Christ, Cat, it was an honest mistake,' he protested at the next traffic signal. 'Just chill, would you? If you're so bothered, text your girlfriend and tell her you got a better offer.'

If she could have thought of a message that would convey her combination of anger, humiliation and regret to Ellie, she would have done just that. But there was no nuance in a text and Cat knew better than to try and explain the complicated misunderstanding in that abbreviated form. All she could hope for was that an opportunity would present itself when she could explain the whole horrible saga to Ellie face-to-face. And sooner rather than later.

By the time she had worked all this out, they had left the city behind and were hurtling down the M9 towards Linlithgow and Stirling. But they had barely left the turning for the Forth Bridge behind them when John started swearing and gesticulating at his rear-view mirror.

'What is it?' Cat fought the slipstream and managed to turn around. Diminishing on the hard shoulder was a terrible sight. Smoke billowed from the chrome grille of her brother's borrowed car. Even as she watched, James and Bella climbed out of the car and up the grassy bank beside it. 'Oh my God. You'll have to go back, you can't just leave them.'

'How the hell can I go back? I'm on a bloody motorway.'

'Come off at the next junction and double back.'

'What about our trip?'

'Never mind that, we need to go back and help James and Bella. The car might explode, for heaven's sake.' She was close to punching him, so angry and frightened was she.

John grumbled extensively, but as the next junction approached, he pulled off and did as she had asked him. 'Bloody stupid bloody car,' he yelled as they set off back the way they'd come.

Within five minutes, they were pulling up behind the Spitfire, which seemed to have ceased its belching and spewing of smoke. They clambered up the bank to the others. Bella threw her arms around Cat and said, 'Thank God you came back for us.'

'I wouldn't leave you in distress,' John said, preening himself, apparently oblivious to Cat's incredulity. 'That's what friends are for. And brothers, obviously.'

'You're a mate,' James said. 'I don't know what I'd have done otherwise. I don't have roadside assistance.'

Neither, it transpired, did John. They might have been expensively stranded for hours had it not been for Cat. On their earlier trip to North Berwick, she had been so determined not to pay attention to the journey itself that she had memorised every detail of the car's interior, including the sticker with the emergency number for the car's dedicated rescue service. When John called them and explained the situation, they reluctantly agreed to help. Cat suspected it was easier to give in than to have John Thorpe hector everyone in the company hierarchy until he finally got the answer he required.

Nevertheless, it was late afternoon by the time their small convoy was mobile again. 'It's too bloody late for Linlithgow now,' John whined.

'And for Glasgow,' Bella said. 'We're supposed to be at Ma's charity poker evening tonight, don't forget.'

And so they set off to return to Edinburgh. 'If your brother had a decent set of wheels, we'd have had a great day out,' John complained bitterly. 'It's a false economy not to have a good motor.'

'It's not if you can't afford it.'

'And why can't he afford it?'

'Because he's not got enough money?' Cat knew she was being snippy and she didn't care. Besides, she'd come to realise that John Thorpe was so thick-skinned he didn't notice.

'And whose fault is that? If there's one fault I can't abide, it's being tight with money. It's a man's duty to spend his money and keep the economy turning, not hoard it like a miser. And money's never been cheaper.' He fulminated in this vein for a while, but Cat tuned him out. She was long past the point of being polite.

Back at Queen Street, the Thorpes and James invited them-selves up for a drink. Before Cat could even put the kettle on, Susie emerged from her bedroom wrapped in a silk kimono. 'You're back,' she said, ready to state the irrefutable as ever.

'Things didn't quite work out as planned,' James said, abashed. 'My fault, Susie.'

'That's a shame. You would have done better to stay here after all, Cat. Because you just missed Ellie and Henry. Not more than ten minutes after you'd left. They were terribly apologetic about being so late, but apparently the General had invited some people around for morning coffee and they had to hang around and make small talk. Too boring, Ellie said. But apparently when the General says jump, they all jump.'

'Couldn't she have texted me?' Cat said.

'She tried to, but when you swapped numbers last night, she got one digit wrong on your number. So she's been texting some complete stranger who finally lost her temper and sent back a really rude message. Poor Ellie. The girl was mortified.'

Bella made a sound that somehow conveyed both disbelief and contempt. 'So you see, Cat, you've got nothing to reproach yourself with. It was totally Ellie's fault after all. She's the one who cocked everything up. Me, I'd never put a friend through that, even if it meant falling out with my mother. John's the same, aren't you, sweetie? You can never bear to let a friend down.'

It was the final irony. And although Bella pressed hard for her to join them, Cat was not sorry to see the other three leave for their poker evening. She supposed she must have had a more disappointing day in her short life, but she was damned if she could bring it to mind.

12

Cat hated people to think badly of her; she was so distressed at the possibility of having unwittingly upset the Tilneys that she spent much of the night in restless wakefulness, rehearsing how she might explain the events that had overtaken her. At breakfast, she could barely eat, satisfying herself with nibbling toast and sipping tea. 'Is it too early to go round to the Tilneys?' she asked as the clock hands crept towards nine.

'I wouldn't thank you for turning up at this time,' Mr Allen said from behind his paper and his coffee.

'That's all very well, Andrew, but people have tickets for festival events from quite early in the day. There are Book Festival events that start well before ten, if you can believe it,' Susie said. 'Of course, if they're not early risers, they won't welcome an early visit.'

It was all very well lecturing young people about the value of listening to their elders, Cat thought mutinously. But what was she supposed to think when they gave completely opposing pieces of advice? She finished her tea and stood up. 'I'm going round to Ainslie Place right now,' she said.

'I'll walk past the house and see if there's any sign of life. And then I'll decide whether to knock or wait.'

Mr Allen grunted. 'Sensible girl.'

Although the sky was overcast with high thin cloud, Cat didn't think it looked like rain, so there was little risk in walking the short distance to the Tilneys' rented house without a coat. She set off briskly, but slowed as she turned into Ainslie Place, an oval of elegant Georgian buildings with private gardens in the middle. On one side, there were tall five-storey tenements, divided into flats. But the Tilneys had rented on the smarter side of the gardens. No mere flat for them; they had taken an entire house for the month of August. Cat had learned enough from the conversation in Edinburgh to understand that represented an eye-watering outlay of cash. The knowledge did not make her envious however; she was more than happy with her lodgings, more than delighted to be in Edinburgh at all.

Cat made her first pass of the Tilneys' house, surreptitiously eyeing the windows. All the curtains seemed to be open, and she could see dim electric light through the muslins that draped the ground-floor windows. There was definitely life inside the house. She walked to the corner and turned into the side street. She stopped, breathed deeply until her fluttering stomach had calmed itself, then walked back to the Tilneys' front door. She puzzled briefly then pulled a gleaming brass knob and heard the distant pealing of a bell.

A long moment passed then the door swung open soundlessly to reveal a gaunt, pale figure with perfectly barbered grey hair. His clothes were almost – but not quite – a military uniform. 'May I help you?' he said, his voice brusque, his brogue unmistakably Scottish.

Cat managed a faint smile. 'I'm looking for Ellie Tilney,' she said.

He looked her up and down. 'And who shall I say is calling?'

'Cat Morland. Her friend Cat. Catherine. Is she in?'

'I believe so. I'll go and see.' And the door was firmly shut in her face. Cat knew she was unaccustomed to the habits of the rich and powerful, but she couldn't help feeling there were better manners to be found in the villages of Dorset. She hung around on the doorstep, trying not to look like someone who might be intent on persuading the inhabitants to change their electricity provider. After what seemed like a very long time, the door opened again. 'I'm sorry,' the man said. 'I was mistaken. Miss Eleanor is not at home. I'll tell her you called.'

Before Cat could respond, the door was closed again. She couldn't remember the last time she'd felt so mortified. He'd treated her like she was completely insignificant. And as if that wasn't bad enough, she wasn't at all sure she believed what he'd told her. She climbed down the steps slowly, casting a sideways glance at the drawing-room curtains, as if she half-expected Ellie to appear at the window, making certain she'd really left.

Cat trudged down the street, head lowered and spirits lower still. When she turned the corner leading her towards Queen Street, she leaned on the railings and stared back down the curve of the street as if that would summon the Tilneys to her. In apparent answer to her yearning, the door swung open and General Tilney marched down the steps to the street. He looked back at the house and spoke sharply. To Cat's dismay, Ellie ran out of the house and caught up with her father as he walked on round the crescent away from Cat.

Disconsolate and dejected, Cat had no choice but to head back to the Allens' flat. She had been thoroughly humbled – no, humiliated – and she had completely lost her appetite for culture. In spite of Susie's attempts to get her to the Book Festival, Cat insisted on remaining at home, furious with herself but even more furious with John Thorpe and his forcefulness. She couldn't even bear to go on Facebook or Twitter because she didn't have the energy to lie or the chutzpah to tell the truth. It occurred to her that although she had initially seen Ellie Tilney purely as a conduit to her brother, she had quickly grown to like the young woman for herself. Losing the prospect of her friendship was almost as cruel a blow as losing the chance of becoming Henry's – dare she think it? – girlfriend.

When Susie returned late in the afternoon, laden with shopping and full of gossip that meant nothing to Cat in her mournful state, she was insistent that her young charge should get in the shower and prepare for that evening's excursion to the ballet. Cat was resistant at first, but it gradually dawned on her that she'd spent long enough being miserable without distraction, not to mention that she'd never seen a proper ballet even though she was quite certain dance was an art form whose language she understood. 'Besides,' Susie said, clinching it, 'you never know who you might see.'

Mr Allen's connections had provided them with a box, which Cat was excited about until she discovered Susie had invited Martha Thorpe along. Fortunately, only Jess and Claire had chosen to come; James and Bella had apparently managed to get tickets for the recording of a BBC radio comedy show, which they thought would be more to their taste than modern dance. 'Johnny's somewhere around,' Martha said vaguely. 'He doesn't like the ballet, but he enjoys socialising.'

Cat said nothing, simply grateful that John would not be joining them. She made the most of the box, leaning on the velvet-covered sill to scan the audience. She told herself she was people-watching but in her heart she knew she was Tilney-spotting. But no matter how keenly she studied the audience, she could see none of them. Perhaps they had no interest in ballet. It wasn't a likely pursuit for a general and his lawyer son, after all. Disappointed, she sat back and immersed herself in the performance, which she found almost as captivating as she'd hoped.

At the interval, the Allens and Mrs Thorpe went to the bar. But Cat stayed put, preferring to continue her scrutiny of the audience. Even without the Tilneys, it was still an interesting study. But when the curtain went up for the second act, her attention was drawn by a commotion in the box opposite them. There seemed to be some reorganisation of the seating going on. Cat kept half an eye on the disturbance, which was enough attention to spot the unmistakable profile of Henry Tilney, his attention fixed on the spectacle on the stage.

Cat saw nothing of the rest of the ballet. Her eyes were glued to Henry, willing him to turn his head. But he was clearly impervious to any power of telepathy she possessed for his gaze never wavered from the dancers.

Then there came a brief scene change, and he did look around. His eyebrows rose then lowered when he saw her and he gave her the briefest of nods before turning back to the stage. For Cat, it was almost worse than if he'd never looked across at all. She wished she had the nerve to leave the box and run around the gallery to confront him with her explanation of what had happened the day before. It never crossed her mind that most people would consider Henry's reaction to be an excessive response to an innocent error. Cat was determined to shoulder all the blame. Some might think that she was enjoying the opportunity to abase herself before him, but it should be remembered that she had been raised in a house where the notion of wifely obedience was honoured verbally at least.

When the applause died away and the house lights rose, there was no sign of Henry in the box opposite. Cat assumed he had left as soon as the curtain fell to avoid seeing her, in the same spirit exercised by his sister in the morning. But she was mistaken. Before they could leave their own box, there was a knock at the door and Mr Allen opened it to reveal Henry, who greeted Susie with calm politeness. 'I saw you across the theatre and thought I should come and say hello,' he said. He nodded at Cat, a look of dark reserve in his eyes.

'Henry! Thank goodness you came round, I've been dying to speak to you and Ellie. You must have thought I was the rudest person on the planet yesterday, but it wasn't my fault, was it, Susie. They told me you'd gone off with somebody else for the day, Johnny said he'd seen you walking into Haymarket station, and it was an hour after you said you'd be there, and he cornered me and I couldn't say no. And honestly, I would much rather have been with you and Ellie, you wouldn't believe the day I had—'

'Cat, you're crushing poor Henry against the wall,' Susie said.

'It's OK, Susie, it's very crowded in here,' Henry said, a more natural smile lighting up his face as they stood as close as partners in a tango rather than a reel. She could sense the heat of his body and the clean masculine smell that clung to his skin. But his eyes were unfathomably dark. 'At least you looked back and waved us on cheerfully when you passed us in Queensferry Street.'

Cat was dismayed at this further misunderstanding. 'Oh no, not at all. I mean, I did look back, but I was appalled, not cheerful. I begged Johnny to stop and let me out. As soon as I saw you, I told him. If he'd only done what I asked instead of taking off like a bat out of hell, I'd have run after you and we could have had our walk. I wouldn't have offended you and Ellie for the world.'

Her breathless entreaty would have charmed a harder heart than Henry Tilney's. He shook his head indulgently and said, 'Ellie was right. She insisted you'd never let us down deliberately. And we were horribly late, after all. Ellie blamed herself for putting the wrong number in her phone. She didn't realise at first that she'd done it. She'd sent three or four texts before the other woman finally lost patience with her.' He chuckled. 'It was quite funny, really.'

'Don't say Ellie wasn't angry, because I know she was. The man who answered your door—'

'That's Calman. He was my father's batman in the army, now he's our driver and man about the house.'

'Calman,' she said firmly, refusing to be diverted, 'said your sister wasn't in. And then, not five minutes later, she came out with your father. What's that if it's not being angry?'

'Ellie told me. She was mortified in case you saw her leaving. But she was going to a private view with my father and he hates to be unpunctual. If she'd asked you in, he'd have been furious. If she was here, she'd tell you herself how sorry she is. But my father does rather rule the roost.'

'So we've established that Ellie wasn't cross with me. But you were.'

He frowned. 'I don't know what you mean.'

'You gave me such a black look from your box.'

'If it was a black look, it was provoked by the dance, not you. Look, here I am. Would I have bothered to come round if I'd been angry with you?'

She had to own he had a point. 'So we're all happy again?'

He smiled. 'Bloody delirious. So. When are we going to take this famous walk?'

'Tomorrow?'

He made a face. 'The weather forecast says it's going to be hot and sunny. I hate climbing hills when it's hot, I get so uncomfortable and sweaty. Leave it with me, I'll work something out with Ellie.' They swapped phone numbers, both taking extreme care to enter the correct set of digits on their phones. 'I'll text you.' And he was gone, slipping away as suddenly as he had arrived.

Meanwhile, Martha Thorpe had opened the picnic basket she had brought with her and was handing round chilled canapés and individual cans of Pimm's. 'Just a little treat,' she said. 'We might as well make the most of the box while the crowds disperse.'

Cat gave Susie a questioning glance. Even though the younger Thorpe girls were tucking into their Pimm's, Cat knew she shouldn't be drinking under age in a public place. The occasional ginger beer shandy over Sunday lunch was permissible, but she didn't want to cause the Allens any difficulty.

'Get stuck in, Cat,' Mr Allen said. 'There's not enough alcohol in that to bother a toddler. I won't tell if you don't.' And he graced her with that charming smile of his, the one that made her understand exactly how he talked people into multi-million-pound projects. 'You sorted things out with young Henry, then?'

Cat nodded. 'I think so.' Dreamily, she drifted across to the edge of the box and looked around the almost empty theatre. To her surprise, at the rear of the auditorium, she spotted John Thorpe deep in conversation with General Tilney, of all people. From the way they kept glancing up at the Allens' box, she couldn't help wondering if she was the subject of their conversation, though she couldn't imagine why that might be. Cat did not consider herself to be that interesting.

She turned away and allowed herself to be drawn into conversation with Jess and Claire Thorpe, although she had little to add to their discussion of the relative merits of TV reality-show winners. As Martha cleared away their impromptu picnic, another male figure filled the doorway. This one was less welcome, however; John Thorpe stood tapping his watch. 'Come on, ladies, there's gin to be drunk at the Pleasance.'

In spite of her finest efforts, Cat couldn't avoid John's determined company as they made their way downstairs. 'I saw you talking to General Tilney,' she said, making the best of a bad job.

'Amazing bloke. Fit, active. Looks as young as his sons.'

'How do you know the General?'

'How do I know the General?' He gave her an incredulous look. 'I said the other night, I was Freddie Tilney's potboy at Fenners. He brought a bunch of us back to Northanger Abbey one Easter break. Three of his friends and us four potboys. I met the General then. And more recently, we've run into each other at the tables.' He preened momentarily. 'Playing poker, that was the last time. Down in London. I took him for a few quid and, fair play to him, he coughed up without a whimper. Rich as a Jew, so they say. And apparently he's a real foodie. Not that I've ever managed to fiddle an invitation to dinner. Only a matter of time, though. Especially since he thinks you're such a cracker.'

'Me? You were talking about me?'

'Absolutely. He thinks you're quite the prettiest girl in town. And what do you think I said?' He lowered his voice and murmured in her ear. 'I said, "Well spotted, General, that makes two of us." So I think that dinner invitation can only be a matter of time.'

Cat was too busy considering the General's opinion of her to notice the proprietary air of John Thorpe. He continued in the same vein of flattery, but she tuned him out as she had learned to do. All that mattered to Cat was that every-thing had been ironed out between her and the Tilneys. And, as it turned out, even the General liked her.

Going to bed, she congratulated herself on turning things around. No more gloom and misery. Now she was her happy optimistic self again.

Sorted.

13

s Henry had predicted, the following morning brought
the kind of day that shows Edinburgh at its brilliant
best. The sun brought warmth to grey stone that could
otherwise look forbidding and the greenery of the trees and
private gardens was a satisfyingly vivid contrast. Clearly it was
not the sort of day to attract Henry to clambering up the slopes
of Arthur's Seat.

Cat was not downhearted, however. She hugged the events of
the previous evening close to her heart, happy at the prospect
of seeing Henry again soon. Nothing could put a damper on
her good spirits and she set off with Susie for the Book Festival
full of cheerful anticipation. They had a sheaf of tickets for the
day's events, which included her mother's favourite food writer.
Cat had put enough money aside to buy his latest recipe book
and she queued contentedly for half an hour in the heat to
have it signed.

Towards the end of the afternoon, Ellie texted her.

Where r u?

@ bookfest. Where u?

Jst got bk 2 house. C u @ bookfest in 10?

OK. Outside spiegeltent.

When Ellie arrived, resplendent in a wide-brimmed hat, there was a brief moment of hesitation before they hugged and kissed each other on the cheek. 'Henry explained,' Ellie said.

Cat laughed. 'And Henry explained to me too. He should join the diplomatic service.'

'Ha! You wouldn't say that if you could hear him ranting about people who mess him about at work.'

'I'm so glad we got everything sorted out.'

'Me too. Let's go and get an ice cream, I'm roasting.' And so they linked arms and stood in line. After they'd been served, they sat down on the grass and savoured the sensual pleasure of cold vanilla on a hot afternoon. 'Henry says it's supposed to be cooler tomorrow,' Ellie said. 'He thought we could do the Arthur's Seat walk in the morning. What do you think? Are you still up for it?'

Cat nodded enthusiastically. 'Totally. Henry's right, it would have been a real slog doing it today in this heat. How early do you want to start?'

'We'll borrow the car and pick you up at nine, if that's OK?'

'Perfect.' She finished her ice cream and lay back on the grass. 'This is the best time I've had in my whole life.'

'Don't you miss your family?'

'A bit. But I don't miss being in the Piddle Valley, where nothing ever happens.'

Ellie snorted with laughter. 'Every time you say that it makes me giggle. The Piddle Valley, for heaven's sake.'

'Northanger Abbey does sound much grander,' Cat said wistfully.

'You'll come and visit, I know you will.'

Before they could make further plans, a familiar booming voice assaulted their ears. 'Here you are! Susie said you were kicking around somewhere. We've been all over the bloody Book Festival looking for you, Cat.' John Thorpe loomed over her, blocking out the sun.

Cat pushed herself up on one elbow. Her brother and Bella were by John's side, gazing down at her. 'It's not like I was hiding,' she muttered.

Ellie stood up. 'I'll see you in the bookshop,' she said, slipping away. Cat wished she could do the same.

'We've rearranged the run out to Linlithgow and Glasgow for tomorrow,' Bella said.

Cat's heart sank. 'But Jamie's car . . . Surely it's not up to the journey?' It was her last best hope.

'It's fine,' her brother said. 'It was just a busted radiator hose. It looked much more spectacularly worse than it was.'

'I can't go,' Cat said, taking the bull by the horns. 'The same reason I shouldn't have gone before — I've just made an arrangement with Ellie to go walking with her tomorrow.'

'Oh, for heaven's sake, Cat. You can go walking any old day,' Bella insisted. 'Surely Ellie won't mind if you swap days?'

'We can go to Glasgow any old day.'

'Possibly not,' John butted in. 'I might have to go back to London. Urgent business. And that would put the mockers on our little trip. I can definitely do tomorrow. But after that . . . ?' He made a wiggling gesture with his hand, indicating uncertainty.

'We need you to come, Cat, don't let me down,' Bella wheedled.

'No. I've already messed Ellie around once, I won't do it again.'

'Just tell her you forgot you had a previous engagement.'

'I'm not going to lie, Bella.'

Bella pouted. 'You're my best friend, Cat. I've hardly seen you for days. I know you, you're so sweet and kind, are you really going to make me suffer without you? I know you hate to let a friend down.'

'Ellie's my friend too, and I won't let her down.'

Bella tossed her head, her hair swinging about her shoulders. 'Oh, is that how it is? Ellie Tilney's your new best friend, is she? Even though you've only known her five minutes, I'm just chopped liver now. It's Ellie this and Ellie that and Bella can go hang.'

'You're weirding me out, Bella.' The extravagance of her friend's protestations made Cat quite ill at ease.

Bella's bottom lip quivered and she clung to Jamie's arm. 'I can't help it if I have such strong feelings for the people I love. I get jealous when I see myself pushed out because some stranger caught your eye. It's only because I care for you so much and I've missed you.'

Cat grew increasingly uncomfortable in the face of Bella's emotional incontinence. It was so far removed from her own family's behaviour. Of course they acknowledged each other's emotional states, but they would never have dreamed of spilling them out so publicly. She was about to point out that the main reason they had seen so little of each other was that the Thorpes had been monopolising her own brother when Bella took out a tissue and began dabbing at her eyes.

It was all too much for James, who burst out in indignation, 'Now look what you've done, Cat. Bella's crying, and all because you won't come for a day out with us. It was supposed to be a treat, now you've spoiled everything. I think hanging out with the Allens has ruined you.'

Cat scrambled to her feet, astonished. Her brother had never taken another's side over her, and it was a shock to realise how things had shifted between them. 'I'm exactly the same person I always was. The one who keeps her word.'

Bella put a hand to her chest and sighed. 'That's that, then. If Cat's not going, neither am I. I don't want to be the only girl among you men.'

'So take Claire or Jess,' Cat said, tired of attempting to be conciliatory.

'Oh, brilliant,' John exploded. 'Do you really think I came to Edinburgh to take my sisters out and look like a complete and utter twat? No thank you. If you're not going, neither am I. Your company's the only reason I wanted to go in the first place.'

'Like I care,' Cat muttered under her breath.

'I can't believe how obstinate you're being,' James said. 'And here I've been telling Bella how kind and sweet-natured you always are to me and our sisters.'

'It's nothing to do with being kind. It's to do with dealing fairly with people.' In her outrage, Cat failed to notice John sidling away in the direction of the bookshop. 'It's not always easy, but I do try to do the right thing.'

Bella sulked. 'It's not much of a struggle when what you decide is right happens to coincide with what you want to do.'

Cat's heart swelled at the unfairness of it, and they continued to argue the stalemate back and forth until the moment when John burst between them, rubbing his hands. 'That's it settled, then. We're off to Glasgow tomorrow with a clear conscience. I've been and made your excuses to Ellie.'

'You've done what?'

'I told her you'd sent me to say that you'd just remembered you'd already agreed to come out with us to Linlithgow tomorrow so you'd have to postpone your walk till the day after. And she had to admit that would suit her just as well. So we're sorted.'

Bella's misery dissolved instantly and James looked relieved. 'You are so smart, Johnny. And now, girlfriend, everything's turned out perfectly. You're off the hook and we are going to have a great day out.'

'No, that's not how it's going to be,' Cat said. 'How dare you, Johnny? Who died and made you my social secretary? You've got no right to lie to my friend like that. I'm going after Ellie right now.'

But Bella grabbed her arm. 'Don't be silly, Cat.'

And Jamie angrily blocked her way. 'Why are you being so difficult? Johnny just sorted everything out, you could be a bit grateful.'

'Grateful? When he's made me look like a complete – a complete – a complete *shit*?'

James stepped back in surprise. He'd never heard Cat swear in public before. A rebel and a tomboy she might be on the surface, but she had too much love and respect for their father to shame him with bad language where others might hear and judge. 'Nobody will think that,' he said uncertainly.

'They will too. I'm going to find Ellie and tell her the truth.'

'No point. She's gone home,' John said firmly.

'Then I will go after her. Wherever she's gone, I will go after her. There's no point in talking to you people. What kind of man are you? You think if I can't be persuaded into something, it's OK to trick me into it?' And with those words she pulled her arm from Bella's grasp and pushed past the others. John tried to go after her, but James grabbed him.

'Let her go. There's no talking to her when she's like this,' he said.

'She's as obstinate as—' But John could find no comparison that was fit for the consumption of the Book Festival crowd, who were already gawping at him.

Cat meanwhile was pushing through the press of bodies milling around in the sunshine. When she made it through to the street, there was no sign of Ellie. She ran to the corner and paused for a moment, torn between going straight down the hill and turning left or cutting along the bottom of the square and into Glenfinlas Street. She had no idea which her friend preferred, but she guessed at the latter because it was a quieter, more leafy route. She took to her heels in spite of the heat, convinced she would catch Ellie before she reached home.

But Ellie must have been walking briskly, for there was no sign of her until Cat skidded round the corner into Ainslie Place, when she caught sight of her quarry entering the front door. Putting on a turn of speed she didn't know she possessed, Cat sprinted down the street, taking the front steps at a leap and before she could pause to consider, diving past Calman as he began to close the door.

'Sorry,' she gasped, making for the open door on the left

that she guessed would take her into the drawing room. Ellie whirled round and stared at her in consternation, while her father and her brother looked up in wide-eyed surprise from the game of chess they were playing by the window. Short of breath and even more short of nerve, Cat made a nervous grimace that only someone who loved her could have called a smile. 'I hurried to catch you up – To explain the stupidity, the mistake – I never promised Johnny Thorpe any such thing – As soon as he brought it up, I said no, I was committed to you – I'm sorry, I didn't give Calman a chance—'

'Hello, Cat,' Henry said, getting to his feet. 'How lovely to see you.'

'Henry, hello. I tried to catch Ellie up because that high-handed idiot Johnny Thorpe took it into his head to tell her a pack of lies. He did, didn't he, Ellie?'

Ellie seemed uncertain how to respond. 'He said you'd made a mistake about tomorrow. That you'd promised to go on some trip with him and Jamie and Bella tomorrow so you wouldn't be able to come up Arthur's Seat with Henry and me.'

Cat made an impatient gesture with her hands. 'I knew it. Honestly, Ellie, that is a complete fantasy. A lie. I made no such plans. He just wants me to come on this stupid outing so he can show off his fancy car again. I am determined to go walking with you and Henry tomorrow, not go to Glasgow or Linlithgow with that idiot.'

'Well, that seems pretty clear,' Henry said.

'I'm sorry, I seem to leave a trail of confusion wherever I go,' Cat said.

General Tilney got to his feet and came towards them. 'That's what comes of being such an attractive young woman,' he said.

It was a line that from another might have seemed louche or inappropriate. But in the General's dry tone, it was impossible to take exception to it. 'Eleanor, are you going to introduce me to your friend?'

Ellie dipped her head. 'Father, this is Catherine Morland from Dorset who is here in Edinburgh for the festival with her friends the Allens.' It was curiously formal, but it seemed to be the style of the house, for the General acknowledged the introduction with a half-bow from the waist.

'A pleasure,' he said. He gave Ellie a sharp look. 'But you didn't come in together. Why did Calman not bring Miss Morland in? What was he thinking? We don't just barge into rooms in this house.'

'My fault,' Cat said, clapping a hand to her chest. 'I was incredibly rude. I ran straight past him. Poor man, he didn't stand a chance. And please, General, call me Cat. Everyone else does.'

He smiled. 'Come and sit with us. Calman will bring us tea and cakes, it's that sort of time.' He nodded at Ellie, who hurried out of the room, and waved Cat to a sofa near the massive marble fireplace. Now she saw him at closer range, she could see that although his features were very similar to his son's, his skin was covered in fine wrinkles as if he'd spent years out of doors in all weathers. But because his hair was the kind of light brown that disguised the strands of silver, he still looked amazingly young. *Like a two-hundred-year-old vampire*, Cat's wicked angel whispered in her ear. That same angel noticed there was a faint outline above the elaborate mantelpiece, as if the large mirror one might expect to find there had been temporarily removed.

Afternoon tea soon appeared, so lavish Cat was fascinated

by its generosity to the point where she failed to notice her companions ate hardly anything. Instead they all chattered as cosily as if they'd known each other for years. The General remained formal and somewhat aloof, but he was not averse to joining the conversation when he had something germane to contribute. Eventually, he stood up and apologised for having to leave them. 'I have some calls to make,' he said. 'But we would be very happy if you would stay for dinner.'

Cat was as dismayed as she was surprised. 'I'd love to,' she said. 'But I know Mrs Allen has tickets for a concert this evening and I mustn't let her down.' She also got to her feet. 'In fact, I really should get back. This has been a lovely afternoon. Thank you.'

'We'll see you tomorrow morning around nine,' Henry reminded her.

'I'll see you to the door,' the General said. He took her elbow as they left the drawing room. 'You have the spring in your step of a natural dancer,' he said as he opened the front door. 'I thought as much when I saw you dancing with Henry.'

It was the icing on the cake, to be complimented by a man as eminent as the General. Cat proceeded happily to Queen Street, taking note of that dancer's spring in her step that she'd never noticed before. What an afternoon of ups and downs it had been. She hated upsetting James and Bella but she had been determined to do the right thing. And it had been the right thing, in spite of Bella's snide suggestion that she was trying to justify what she intended to do anyway. If anyone was selfish, Cat told herself, it was Bella. She checked her phone and sure enough, there were half a dozen messages from Bella entreating her to change her mind, plus a couple complaining of her intransigence.

The Allens were both sitting in the window sipping white wine when she returned and she amused them over dinner with her adventures. 'For what it's worth, I think you made the right choice,' Mr Allen said. 'Gadding about in gaudy convertibles sends the wrong sort of message about the kind of girl you are, Cat.'

'You're so right,' Susie said. 'I don't think your father would approve. Much better to take a sedate walk with the Tilneys. Such a good family, by all accounts. Just the kind of young people your parents would like to think of you hanging out with, Cat.'

Generally, that would have been the opposite of a recommendation to a teenager. But Cat was so deeply mired in her admiration for the Tilneys that not even the potential approbation of her parents could divert her.

14

The following morning Cat was in a ferment of apprehension. The weather was fair; a thin layer of cloud kept the sun at bay, making it perfect for hill-walking. But that would also make it perfect for driving to Glasgow with the top down. Since Bella had not given up texting her till after midnight, Cat was by no means convinced that the others wouldn't turn up on the doorstep for a final attempt at persuading her away from the Tilneys.

But nine o'clock struck and Cat's vigil by the window was rewarded by the sight of a Mercedes drawing up outside and Ellie exiting the passenger door. Cat grabbed her daypack and raced down the stairs, meeting Ellie halfway. They hugged and filled the stairwell with gleeful teenage exclamations.

Henry was behind the wheel of the Mercedes and although she feared momentarily that she might have to endure another bout of extreme male driving, Cat's anxiety turned out to be groundless. Henry drove like a perfectly sane person, so it was possible for his passengers to exchange remarks that didn't include squeals of terror.

The car park on Queen's Drive was almost empty, which

boded well for their walk. 'I do hate crowds when I'm out walking,' Ellie said. 'It defeats the object of getting out of the city if the hill paths are as busy as Princes Street.'

'If you don't like crowds, you should avoid Dorset in the school holidays,' Cat said with feeling. 'Ever since they christened it the Jurassic Coast, it's mobbed with small boys hunting dinosaur fossils. And the rest of their families filling the beaches with all the paraphernalia of middle-class leisure. Windbreaks and portable barbeques. Bloody boules and beach cricket. You can't move for folding chairs and boogie boards and wetsuits drying on the shingle.'

'You make it sound quite lovely,' Henry teased as they set off up the main path leading to the gap between the crags.

'It is lovely. Just not when the tourist hordes descend. Come and visit, both of you, and see it for yourself. The coast is truly dramatic.'

'But what about the Piddle Valley? What's that like?' Ellie giggled. 'Is the River Piddle a gushing torrent or a feeble dribble?'

'Ha, ha,' Cat said sarcastically. 'It's an insignificant little river, but the countryside is exactly what English chocolate-box scenery is meant to be.'

'We shall have to come and see for ourselves,' Henry said. They were silent for a while, saving their breath for the steep uphill climb that brought them to the top of Salisbury Crags, with its panoramic view of the city, the Firth of Forth and the hills of Fife beyond. They paused for a breather and Henry took the opportunity to tell Cat something of the three-hundred-and-fifty-million-year history of the volcanic landscape.

'It's amazing, somewhere so wild and yet so close to the city centre. When I turn my back on the city and look up to the summit, I feel like I could be in the heart of the Highlands,' Cat said.

'I love it up here,' Ellie said. 'Whenever we're in Edinburgh I always try to sneak away and come up, even if I've only got time to come this far.'

'I've been reading the Hebridean Harpies books and somehow, being here in this landscape makes the books even more alive to me,' Cat said. She cast a sideways look at Henry. 'I don't suppose you read novels like that, do you?'

'Why would you think that?'

'Because they're not highbrow enough for someone like you?'

'I hate literary snobbery, Cat. Anyone who can't take pleasure in a good story well told is the worse off for it. I've read all of Morag Fraser's novels – Ellie turned me on to them a couple of years ago. They're real page-turners, and they're genuinely scary. I know some blokes think they're soppy girls' books, but that's because they've never actually sat down and read one.'

'He's not lying, Cat,' Ellie said. 'When the last one arrived in the post at Northanger, I was out with friends, and he opened the parcel. I got back that evening to find him curled up in his chair, totally gripped. I had to wait till he'd finished before I could read my own book.'

'I'm a vile thief,' Henry admitted. 'But I didn't think she'd be back so early. I thought I could finish it by morning and wrap it all up again like new and she'd be none the wiser. So now do you have a better opinion of my taste in books?'

Cat laughed in delight. 'I shall never again be ashamed of

reading the Harpies. But my brother despises the whole category of fiction, and I assumed he was a typical bloke.'

'I believe it's true that women read more novels than men. Certainly they buy more and they borrow more from libraries. But it may be that their brothers and boyfriends and husbands can't be bothered picking them out. It's like food,' Ellie said. 'They'd complain soon enough if the cupboard was bare and there was no dinner on the table. But they don't want to come to the supermarket with us. They just expect food to turn up. Maybe it's the same with novels.'

'You girls have such a low opinion of us men, I'm amazed any of you ever agree to go out with us,' Henry said, setting off up the escarpment.

'Well, I think it's cool that you like the Harpies books,' Cat said, walking alongside him.

'Cool?' Henry groaned. 'Meaning what? Delightful? Fashionable?'

'Henry, stop it. Cat's not your sister, don't be so sarcastic with her,' Ellie complained. 'He's so bloody pedantic, he's always on my case about the way I use language. Father's got an excuse, he's from a different generation, but Henry's just a fully paid-up member of the awkward squad.'

'What's wrong with "cool"? Surely what matters is that people understand you? And everybody understands "cool",' Cat said.

'Very true. And this is a very cool day and we're taking a very cool walk and you two are very cool young ladies. Man, it's such a cool word. It works hard for a living, that's for sure. Once, cool referred to the temperature, either literally or metaphorically. But now it's made half the language of description redundant. Nobody thinks twice before they open their mouth. Everything is "cool",' he said, using his fingers to approximate inverted commas in the air.

Cat laughed. 'That thing with the air commas? That's not cool, Henry.'

'Yes, Henry, you are definitely uncool. Whereas we are the very epitome of cool. So, Cat, what do you read apart from Morag Fraser?'

'I love novels that transport me into their world. When I was a kid, I adored Harry Potter and the Narnia books. But now I read all sorts. The last thing I read before I came away was *The Strange Case of Dr Jekyll and Mr Hyde*. And in the car on the way up, we listened to *Dracula*.'

'The original? Wow, I've never actually read that all the way through.'

'It's amazing. People are very sniffy about vampires, but I think they're incredible. They're brave and driven. They can be really heroic because they're always outnumbered. And they're so passionate,' Cat added enthusiastically.

'Oh, I know. They're so edgy. And you can't help falling for them.'

'Mmm,' Cat said dreamily. 'I love all that. But there's one kind of book I totally can't get on with, and that's those solemn history books. I think history could be much more interesting if it was about the unseen as well as the seen.'

Walking behind them, Henry shook his head in bemusement. 'I wish I knew what you meant by that,' he sighed. 'History is what tells us who we are.'

Cat turned to face him, walking backwards. 'Then why does it have to be so dull? I sometimes think the writers of history books sit down to write with the sole intention of torturing little boys and girls.'

'Isn't that the point of little boys and girls? To be tormented by their elders and betters? How else are we supposed to have fun?' Henry asked. 'But, Cat, really, you can't believe that's what serious historians are about? Surely you must admit that they're there to instruct us? Or do you think that instruction and torture are the same thing?'

'Here we go,' Ellie groaned.

By now they were at the base of the final steep climb that led to the summit. 'I've seen the look on my poor mother's face when she's trying to cram some knowledge into our thick heads. And I've been on the receiving end of that cramming enough to know that torture and instruction can be synonymous.'

'But if we didn't allow that torture to happen, you wouldn't have learned to read. Think how much pleasure you've had over the years from that little bit of torture. Consider – if you hadn't been forced to undergo those terrible hours, Morag Fraser would have toiled in vain.' He spread his hands as if there was no possible comeback. 'Game, set and match, I think.'

'I told you, once he starts there is no stopping him. He could argue black is white,' Ellie said.

'That's why I'm such a good lawyer.'

Again they fell silent as they scrambled onwards. Finally, out of breath and sweating, they reached the summit and stood with their hands on their knees getting their breath back and taking in the glorious views. Then Henry stood up and made a frame with his hands. 'This would make a great opening sequence for a movie. You start off up here, then you zoom slowly in, getting closer and closer to a segment of the city, then to a building then to a window then to a single room.'

Ellie joined in what was obviously a game they'd played before. 'And in that room . . . a vampire.'

Henry sighed. 'It's always a vampire with you. What about a zombie, for a change?'

'Or a murderer, planning his next evil crime,' Cat said, desperate to make a mark.

'Maybe. But look, check out this framing shot over here. If you set up the camera right here and went in tight on those rooftops, you could do something really dramatic.'

'And now you know Henry's deep dark secret,' Ellie said. 'He actually wants to be a film director, not a boring old lawyer. But Father wouldn't hear of it.'

'Do you have to do everything your father tells you?' Cat said. 'My dad hardly ever puts his foot down because he knows we generally don't pay the least attention.'

A muscle tightened in Henry's jaw. 'My father takes the view that anyone who lives under his roof plays by his rules. I wanted to go to film school but he refused point-blank to support me. So I went into the law. I haven't given up my dreams, though. I've still got plans.'

It was clear that he didn't want to discuss the subject further, so Cat sat down on a rock and took a packet of biscuits out of her daypack. She handed them round, casting about for something else to say. 'I heard there's something truly shocking brewing in London.'

Ellie looked startled. 'What kind of thing?'

'I'm not sure. Only that it's going to be more shocking and gruesome than anything we've ever encountered.'

Ellie's eyes widened and she clutched her brother's arm. 'Oh my God. How did you hear about it?'

'I got a text from somebody I know. There was a link to a video clip. It looked like it was made on a hand-held camera in a cellar. The guy was talking about murder and child abduction and monsters in the streets.'

Ellie squealed. 'In London? My God, how can you be so calm about it? Why is there nothing on the news? What are the police doing about it?'

Henry was struggling not to smile. 'Not a damn thing. There must be murder and abduction, or what justification would the police have for their existence?'

'I don't believe you. The police wouldn't just stand by while such terrible things happened.'

It dawned on Cat that Ellie had misunderstood her. 'No, Ellie—'

'Cat's not talking about reality, are you?'

'No, it's a new TV series. They made these viral marketing clips that look like they're real underground news reports, but they're just trails for a new Channel 4 series.'

Henry laughed at his sister's discomfiture, but not unkindly. 'Bless you, El. You've got such an imagination, you should be writing this stuff yourself. One word from you, Cat, and she's picturing a mob of thousands assembling in Hyde Park, the Bank of England attacked, the Treasury firebombed, the streets of London flowing with blood as the crazed zombies march on Parliament. But never fear, sister dear, before you know it, the gallant Captain Freddie Tilney will be driving his tank down Whitehall to save the Prime Minister and the Cabinet.'

Ellie punched him on the arm and Henry howled in

mock-pain, skipping away from her. 'She's not a complete simpleton, Cat. Truly. And I do actually have a very high opinion of the intelligence of women. I think you have a far better understanding of human behaviour than men do, and you apply it in the most subtle of ways. We are putty in your hands.'

'You see?' Ellie said. 'He can't even pay a compliment without being facetious.'

'Facetious? *Moi*? Never.'

'Oh, shut up, Henry. I want Cat to be my friend, so don't put her off. Any more of your silliness and I'll push you off Salisbury Crags on the way down.'

He poked his tongue out at her. 'And I will simply fly through the air on my vampire wings and wait for you at the bottom.'

Cat's heart gave a little jolt. Henry's manner was so playful that she had struggled all morning to know whether he was serious. And here he was, talking of being a vampire. Was he merely joking or was this some bravura double-bluff calculated to divert suspicion from his true nature? The more time she spent with the Tilneys, the more off-kilter she felt. Was that to do with her own emotions or their behaviour? And if it was them, was their conduct deliberately unsettling?

In a bid to change the subject, Cat picked up on Henry's mention of their brother. 'Tell me about the gallant Captain Tilney,' she said.

Ellie and Henry exchanged looks. 'He's half a dozen years older than me,' Henry said. 'He was sent off to boarding school before I even remember him. We went to different schools too, so we've never been close. We don't actually have much in common.'

'Father says he's a good soldier, according to his commanding officers. He's done two tours in Afghanistan and he's just come back on leave. We don't actually see very much of him at Northanger,' Ellie added. 'He finds us all a bit dull, I think.'

There was an awkward silence then Henry asked Cat what films she'd enjoyed recently. It was a more comfortable subject for all of them and their tongues were hardly still as they made their way down the extinct volcano, talking animatedly about films and TV shows they loved and loathed. Happily, it seemed that Cat shared the taste of both Tilneys, which only added to her conviction that there was already a special bond between them.

Her pleasure in the excursion was made complete when, instead of dropping her off in Queen Street, Henry left the car at their mews garage and all three of them returned to the Allens' flat, where Susie bustled round feeding them sushi and cheeses and fruit chutneys bought that morning from the finest little deli she'd discovered on Rose Street. The walk had given them an appetite and they fell on the generous spread as if they hadn't eaten for days. 'You are completely spoiling us, Susie,' Henry said. 'I think you're jealous because we cut such a fine figure on the dance floor and you're trying to slow us down. Either that or you're a secret cannibal, fattening us up for the pot.'

'Excuse my brother, Susie,' Ellie said wearily. 'He can be serious about nothing at all.'

Susie, who had looked puzzled at Henry's words, smiled uncertainly. 'I'm sure he means no harm.'

'Don't bank on it,' Ellie muttered to Cat. Then she spoke up again. 'Susie, we were wondering if you could spare Cat tomorrow evening? We'd like her to come round for supper.'

This was the best of news to Cat, who had a moment of delicious anticipation before Susie said it was no problem, because she knew someone who would be very happy to have Cat's ticket for an evening of traditional French folk songs. So even though the Tilneys left after lunch, Cat's disappointment at their departure did not run too deep since they were to meet again so soon.

She had more reason to suppose her luck had changed later that afternoon. She was standing in line with Susie to get into the afternoon show at the Stand comedy club when they ran into Jess Thorpe and a couple of her friends. 'Hey, Cat,' Jess said. 'Wassup?'

'Hey, Jess. So, did Bella and Johnny go off to Glasgow after all?'

Jess rolled her eyes in what appeared to be the Thorpe family's all-purpose gesture. 'They went really early, like, around eight. Woke the whole house up. Your bro and Bella, and Johnny took Claire. How pitiful is that, having to take your kid sister on a day out?'

'Yeah, but it's nice for Bella to have a bit of female company.'

'You think? When Jamie's around, it's like Bella's deaf and blind to the rest of us. But Claire wanted to go. Something about some haunted castle or whatever.'

'Didn't you fancy it?'

Jess pretended to stick two fingers down her throat. 'No thanks. Like I said to Em and Soph here, I'd rather stick needles in my eyes than hang out in some dreary ruined castle.'

Luckily Cat was absolved from further conversation because the door crew allowed them inside. But she was glad to know the trip to Glasgow had gone ahead. She sincerely hoped there had been no disasters with James's car and that they'd had as much fun on their day out as she had. That way, James and Bella might have forgiven her absence by the time they returned.

A girl could always hope.

15

Cat awoke to a text from Bella that seemed to indicate her hopes had been justified.

Soz we fell out, gf. Its coz I heart u so much. 4give, yeah? On my knees 2 u, come and hv brunch chez Thorpe. Need 2 talk to u, big news coming down. Bx0x

When she hadn't replied within five minutes, a second text followed.

Pse, pretty pse, we have PAIN AU CHOCOLAT, u kno u want it. Buzzing 2 c u. Bx0x

OK. C u soon. Cx

Cat didn't want to be standoffish nor did she want to gush as if she was indirectly admitting she was in the wrong. But she did want to return to the same friendly footing she and Bella had shared. And so she was willing to accept the olive branch Bella was so determined to extend. And after all, Cat realised her own reaction might have seemed a little harsh. Even though she had been right, she reminded herself.

When Cat arrived at the Thorpes' flat, there was no sign of Bella or brunch. Jess and Claire were in the living room, grooming each other's long hair like a pair of orang-utans. 'She's in the shower,' Jess said.

'Did you have a good time yesterday?' Cat asked Claire.

She did the trademark Thorpe eye roll. 'Not that you'd notice. We went to some shopping mall, which was totally a waste of time because me and Bella are, like, totes broke. Then Johnny insisted on going to some club for lunch that was full of suits and dino-saurs. Nothing to eat that wasn't half a dead animal. I mean, God. I haven't been so bored since school. Then on the way home, it started to rain. Only, the roof on Johnny's bloody fabulous car wouldn't go up, so I got totally soaked. It's a miracle I haven't got pneumonia. Just be grateful you got yourself off the hook.'

'What about Linlithgow? Did you not at least enjoy the haunted castle?'

Claire looked at her as if she was deranged. 'Haunted castle? What are you on about?'

'When Bella was trying to talk me into going, she promised we'd go to Linlithgow Palace on the way.'

Claire shrugged. 'Nobody said anything about a haunted castle to me. Why would you want to go and see a haunted castle, anyway? Gross.'

Before Cat had a chance to explain the romantic frisson of ghosts, Bella burst in with her hair wrapped in a towel. 'Oh, Cat, you came!' She embraced her friend. 'You've guessed, haven't you? One word from me and you worked it all out, didn't you, you clever clogs!'

Cat had not the faintest notion what Bella meant. 'Truly, Bella, I've no idea what you're on about.'

Bella gave her a friendly nudge. 'It's OK, you can admit it now. My secret was safe with you, but now it's not a secret any more.'

Her secret had indeed been safe with Cat, who was still at a loss to know what it was she was supposed to know already. 'I really don't—'

'I've seen the way you watch us. That knowing little smile of yours, Cat. I swear, you knew even before I knew myself. Obviously, you're so in tune with your lovely brother, you can sense his feelings.'

The introduction of her brother into the conversation allowed a little light to dawn on Cat. 'You mean, you and James? You're an item?'

Bella hooted with laughter. 'Don't pretend you didn't know. Honestly, he's so gorgeous, you must be used to women throwing themselves at him.'

Cat was aware of her brother's many good qualities, but considering him handsome was a novelty to her. In her eyes, his looks were serviceable, no more. Not like beautiful Henry Tilney. 'If you say so,' she said. 'It's hard for me to imagine anybody being in love with my brother, on account of I've known him all my life and seen him in so many situations that were the complete opposite of romantic.'

Bella giggled. 'You are soooo bad, Cat Morland. Because Jamie is an absolute sweetheart. I just wish I felt I deserved him. And your mum and dad, what will they think? They'll be, like, "She's not good enough for you, Jamie."'

For a start, Cat thought, they wouldn't be calling him Jamie.

Nor did she expect they would be silly enough to express anything other than a kind opinion of their son's girlfriend. 'It's not up to them who James chooses to go out with.'

Bella clapped a hand to her mouth. 'OMG,' she said. 'You're one beat behind the dance, sweetie. He's more than my boyfriend, Cat, he's my fiancé.'

The revelation completely altered Cat's reaction. Boyfriend/girlfriend was no big deal, not when you got down to it. People came together and split up all the time. But engaged to be married took things to a completely different level. This was a monumental event, a huge commitment, a totally grown-up thing to be doing. This, Cat felt sure, was a moment she would remember all her life, the moment when the first of her generation of Morlands truly stepped into the adult world. She threw her arms round Bella and squealed, 'You're going to be my sister-in-law!'

'I know, and you're going to be my chief bridesmaid. You're going to be far dearer and closer to me than Jess and Claire.'

'Well, thanks a bundle,' Jess muttered. 'Come on, Claire, we know when we're not wanted.'

They flounced out, and Bella said, 'Like, my point exactly. They're stupid little kids, not like you and me. I tell you, Cat, in no time at all you're going to feel like I've always been part of your lovely family.'

Not for the first time, Bella had gone too far for Cat to be comfortable. But still she continued. 'You and Jamie are so alike. The minute I saw you, I just knew we were going to be bgfs. That's totes how I am – I have an instinct. So I always know, right from first sight. That's how it was with Jamie. The minute he walked in the door with Johnny, my heart was lost. I knew he was the one for me. I can even tell you what I was wearing. My skinny black jeans from Harvey Nicks and my fuchsia scoop-necked top from H&M. I mean, if I'd have known I was going to meet the love of my life I'd have dressed up, but bless him, he saw past my scummy clothes to the real me. He's so sensitive.'

Now Cat truly understood the power of love. Not even her mother, who could be incomprehensibly blind to the faults of her children, would have accused James of sensitivity. Luckily, Bella required no encouragement from Cat to continue tripping down memory lane.

'I was on pins that night he first came to our house, because Tiggy Andrews was round and she was dressed up to the nines. I think she fancies Johnny. But she looked so cool, I was convinced that Jamie would be, like, "Wow, she's the one." Oh God, that was the first sleepless night your brother gave me.' She paused and gave a cat-like smile. 'But not the last.'

'So where is James?' Cat asked, desperate to shift the direction of the conversation away from what she feared might rapidly become embarrassing.

'He's having a shower. He's decided to go down to Dorset to tell your mum and dad face-to-face about us. God knows what they'll say.'

'They'll be cool. They'd never stand in the way of true love. They'll be so pleased that James is happy. But are you not going down with him?'

Bella shook her head. 'Better they get used to the idea first. I mean, it's not like I'm bringing anything to the party except my sweet self. Jamie could have his pick of any girl he wanted, he needs to convince them I'm the one so they can forgive him for bringing all these poor relations into the family.'

'Bella, you misjudge us. That sort of thing just doesn't cross my parents' minds.'

Bella patted her friend's arm and gave a pitying smile. 'Just because you would never think that way doesn't mean other people won't. I just wish the situation was reversed. If I was a millionaire, if I ruled the world, Cat, Jamie would still be my number one.'

It was, Cat thought, the sort of thing that the soppy sidekick of the heroine in one of her novels would say, a Gabrielle to her Xena. And like Xena, she would show her tolerance for friendship's sake. 'Don't worry about what my mum and dad will say. How can they not be delighted with you?'

'That's true,' Bella said. 'It's not like I'm one of those greedy, high-maintenance bitches. Really, a tiny income would make me happy as long as I'm with Jamie. Just a nice little house in Chelsea would suit us perfectly. Or even a flat, if it had a river view.'

Advising on interior décor must pay better than Bella had claimed if she was setting her sights on a house in Chelsea, Cat thought. 'Chelsea? But James is in Newcastle.'

Bella waved her hand dismissively. 'That's only for his pupil-lage. In six months, he'll be done with that and moving to chambers in London, I just know it. But we'll have to get somewhere big enough for you to come and visit, because I'll miss you too much otherwise. Oh, but this is pointless, I can't make plans until I know for sure what your parents have to say. Jamie says if he gets the train this morning, he'll be in Dorset tonight and he'll text as soon as he has an answer. I told him not to phone because we're going to the theatre tonight and I wouldn't be able to resist answering him. And that would be totally embarrassing.' She gave a heartfelt sigh, then brightened. 'And then we can go and look at wedding dresses and bridesmaids' dresses for you. And I suppose I'll have to have Jess and Claire as well or they'll whinge till the end of time.'

Just then James hustled in, hair tousled and wet, holdall in his hand. 'You heard the news, then, Sis?' He pulled Bella to him with his free arm and grinned.

Cat beamed at him, making no secret of her delight. 'I don't have to tell you how thrilled I am. Give my love to Mum and Dad and the girls.'

'Will do.' James released Bella and checked his watch. 'I need to get going or I'm going to miss the train.'

'I can't bear it,' Bella wailed. 'We're only just together and you're driving us apart.'

James looked pained. 'I can't help it, I have to tell Mum and Dad face-to-face, it's only right.'

'I know, I know, our happiness depends on their help. Off you go, away with you, Jamie, don't drag it out and make it worse.'

He finally managed to escape, leaving Cat vaguely puzzled as to the significance of her parents' help in the romance. But she had no chance to make sense of Bella's words for no sooner had Jamie left than Martha and Johnny bustled in laden with bags from Valvona & Crolla. 'Celebratory brunch,' Martha announced, laying out pastries and cheeses, breads and salamis, biscuits and fruit on the table. Drawn by some sixth sense for treats, Jess and Claire reappeared, falling on the food like underfed locusts.

'Dear Cat,' Martha said. 'It's such a delight to have you and Jamie as part of our family. You've felt like one of us since the day we met.'

'And your brother's a bloody good mate,' John said. 'Amazing that Bella's managed to snag such a good catch. Good times ahead for all of us, Cat, with your family joining mine.' He gave her a suggestive wink, which she missed because her attention at that moment was all on an olive ciabatta and a rectangle of Taleggio.

After they'd all eaten their fill, it was impossible for Cat to leave because Bella needed someone to share her fantasy future with Jamie. She would be the envy of everyone on Facebook, her Twitter feed would be green with envy and she'd have an engagement ring to dazzle everyone in North London. Cat tried to extricate herself after a couple of hours, suggesting that her brother could tell her about James's Oxford days. John, who had just returned to the living room after an hour's absence, snorted.

'I don't think he'd appreciate that,' he said. 'Nor would Bella, I suspect.'

'Wicked man,' Bella said. 'Are you ready to leave?'

Cat's ears pricked. Ready to leave? Could it be her nemesis was departing? 'Are you returning to London?'

He sighed. 'Some of us have to bring home the bacon, Cat. We can't all be gadding around Edinburgh for weeks at a time like Andy Allen.'

'Hang on, I need to get you those swatches for Camilla Osborne's curtains,' Martha said. 'Bella, come and give me a hand to sort them out.'

Left alone with John – her least favourite Edinburgh state – Cat cast about for something to say. She needn't have bothered, for John Thorpe, like nature, abhorred a vacuum. 'Well, so it's goodbye for now, Cat. But not for long, because this marriage thing is going to throw us into each other's path. What do you think of it, eh? Jamie and Bella? It's not bad, eh?'

'I think it's pretty good, actually.'

'So you're not one of these post-feminists who think that marriage is an evil exploitative tool of the patriarchy, then? I'm glad to hear it. And you're going to be Bella's chief brides-maid, right?'

'She asked me, yes.'

He crossed to the window, gazing down at the street below. 'And I'll be Jamie's best man, make no mistake about that.' He gave her a quick sideways glance. 'Maybe we'll end up like that old cliché from the movies, right?'

Not in this life, Cat thought. 'So how long will it take you to drive back to London?'

'Most people would take at least eight hours, but I'll do it in six or less with my wheels.'

'I'm sure you will.' Cat stood up. 'I have to go now, I'm having dinner with the Tilneys and I need to get ready.'

'Can't you wait till I'm gone? I mean, it's nice to talk to you, and I won't see you for a while. And it'll feel like a long while till I'm back in your company.' He looked expectant, like a puppy who hears the jangle of its leash.

'Then don't stay away so long,' she said, trying to sound as repressive as she could.

He smiled. 'That's kind of you. But then, you are kind. Amazingly kind. I don't know anybody kinder than you. Actually, I don't know anybody like you.'

'I can't believe you know so few people, Johnny. Anyway, I need to get off now.'

She took a step towards the door, but he rushed across the

room to move in front of her. 'Maybe I'll come and pay a visit to the Piddle Valley.'

'My mum and dad will make you very welcome,' she said, cool as the river on a spring day.

'And I hope you will too?'

She shrugged. 'We're a very hospitable family.'

He laughed. 'I had a feeling you would be. That's all I ask in life, to be around friends and family. And you'll be family soon enough. I'm glad to hear you think the same. But then, I suspect we think the same about a lot of things.'

'You think? I'm not sure I know enough about a lot of things to have an opinion.'

'Good point, I'm with you on that one. Why bother your brain with stuff that has no impact on you? I'm like that at work, too, I never waste my time on things unless they can bring me some return. Keep life simple, right? A lovely girl and a comfortable house and a good motor and what more can you ask, right? Who cares if she's rich or poor, so long as she makes me happy.'

'Well, I agree with that. As long as you've got enough to get by, that's all that matters. I hate the idea of money and love having anything to do with each other. I know some people who won't even consider going out with somebody whose family live in a rented house. That's just snobbery of the worst kind. And when it comes to marrying for money, that's just the pits. You should marry for love or not at all. Like Jamie and Bella.' She looked at her watch again. 'Oh God, look at the time. I really have to go, Johnny.' She side-stepped him and reached the door.

'And the Piddle Valley? I should come?'

'Sort it out with Jamie,' she said over her shoulder as she made her escape, not realising he was so obtuse that he had read into her discouragement its very opposite. And any desire she might have had to revisit the conversation was overwhelmed by the remarkable discovery that the Allens were not in the least surprised by her news. 'I thought there was something going on,' Susie said. 'I could tell from the way they looked at each other.'

Mr Allen chuckled. 'I could tell by the fact that he preferred to cram into the boxroom with Johnny Thorpe rather than bunk up with us here. Well, Martha must be bloody relieved that she's got Bella settled with such a good catch.'

'And lovely for Cat too, to find herself tied so closely to Bella. How marvellous for you all, to have such a wonderful new extended family,' Susie added.

She was right, Cat thought. To entertain any other view just because of Johnny Thorpe would be mean-spirited. And she had no time for the mean-spirited.

16

Anticipation is often the enemy of pleasure; our sights are set so high that disappointment is inevitable. So it was for Cat when she went to dinner with the Tilneys. There was nothing specific she could put her finger on. Although all three seemed to fall silent when Calman showed her into the drawing room, the General greeted her warmly and was impeccably polite. Both Ellie and Henry were more formal in their welcome than she'd expected, and the easy lightness that had grown between them on their walk seemed to have evaporated.

Thinking about it afterwards, Cat couldn't help feeling somehow let down. She'd gone determined to enjoy herself and left feeling disgruntled. She'd expected the closeness between her and Ellie to develop further but it had stalled. She'd hoped that the intimacy of a family party would allow her relationship with Henry to blossom further, but he had never been more silent and withdrawn in her company. In spite of General Tilney's constant kindness and compliments, in spite of the delicious dinner Calman served up to them, in spite of the fascination of seeing how the Tilneys lived, leaving their house had felt like a release.

She couldn't make sense of it at all. It couldn't be General Tilney's fault. He had been charming and entertaining, completely avoiding stories of his military successes. She could see where Henry got his looks and his easy manners. Obviously it wasn't the General who had put a damper on the evening. The best she could hope for was that Ellie and Henry's lack of animation was just one of those things. And maybe she had just been overawed by the splendour of her surroundings and the complications of a menu that had included ceviche of salmon and duck so rare she half-expected it to quack.

It was still early when she left Ainslie Place, so she texted Bella to see where she was and whether she'd heard from James.

In bar @ traverse, heard nothing, come @ once!

Came the reply. So Cat hustled across the West End to the theatre café bar, where she found Bella slumped in a corner with a glass of red wine in front of her. 'Not a bloody word from him,' she greeted Cat. 'He was due into Dorchester nearly three hours ago.'

'He'll be picking his moment,' Cat said. 'Don't fret. Ask me how my evening with the Tilneys went.'

Bella sighed. 'Don't tell me. Henry was even more gorgeous and cool than ever.'

'No, actually.' Cat gave Bella a quick run-down on the disappointments of the evening, and settled back in her seat ready for commiseration.

Unfortunately she was to be disappointed for the second time that evening. 'I knew it,' Bella said. 'Totes up themselves, the Tilneys. They think they're something special. Honestly, I don't know how you let them treat you like that. I always thought that Ellie was a supercilious snob.'

'I never said that, Bella,' Cat protested.

'Don't defend her, Cat. Not when she's treated you like a stranger in her own home. And Henry, who acted like he totally fancied you – he hardly says a word to you all through the meal?'

'Maybe he wasn't feeling great.'

'Stop kidding yourself, Cat. He's moody, you never know how he's going to be. He's so not like our brothers. He's just been playing with you, stringing you along. One minute he acts like the sun shines out of your arse, the next minute he's acting like you don't exist. I can't be doing with messing people around like that. You should make a decision and stick to it. I hate people being disloyal. Henry should take a leaf out of Johnny's book, he's totally loyal to the people he loves.'

'I don't think he means to mess me around,' Cat said. But before they could take the conversation any further, Bella's phone beeped with a text.

'It's Jamie,' she squealed. She closed her eyes and held her phone at arm's length. 'I can't look, tell me what he says, Cat.'

Cat squinted at the screen. '"Mum and Dad thrilled to bits,"' she read. '"Totally supportive. Will call tomorrow." See, I told you there was nothing to worry about.'

Bella screeched, turning heads all over the bar. 'Coooooool! It's all going to be perfect!' She hugged Cat so hard it hurt her ribs. 'Now we have to go out and celebrate. There's a party at the Roxburghe, some guy who works for Johnny's company. We're invited.' Bella began gathering scarves and bag together. 'But I warn you, I'm going to be shocking company because my

heart's in Dorset. And as for dancing, you'll have to find somebody else to hit the floor with because I am saving all my dances
for my husband-to-be.' She gave a long, shuddering sigh. 'How
amazing does that sound? Husband-to-be . . . Anyway, you
know how it is. When you're in love like I am, you glow and all
the guys see the glow and they want it to rub off on them. But
I am not sharing my glow with anybody except Jamie.'

The party was in a pair of large upstairs rooms. One held a
cash bar, a somewhat depleted buffet table and an array of
tables and chairs where people sat and chatted or chilled. In
the other, a DJ hunched behind his equipment, the dance music
thudding and the coloured lights flashing. The dance floor was
half-empty, but those who were dancing were throwing themselves into it wholeheartedly.

Bella grabbed a table and Cat bought them a couple of Red
Bulls; it was late and they were both in need of a kick of caffeine.
No sooner had she sat down than a trio of young men came
swaggering in. Cat blinked hard, for the first of the three looked
like a pumped-up version of Henry Tilney. Everything about
him was bigger, somehow – he was taller, his jaw stronger, his
shoulders wider, his chest deeper, his legs longer. And certainly,
his voice was louder. 'Get them in, Charlie,' he said to the third
of their group.

'Oh my God,' Bella said. 'Tell me that's not Henry in an
Iron Man suit.'

'It must be his brother Freddie. Ellie said he was due home
from Afghanistan on leave.' He was, she thought, more coarsely
attractive than his brother, and certainly more noisy. But he
had the same unreadable dark eyes and pale skin, though there

were two spots of high colour on his cheekbones. He had the trademark wavy blond hair swept back from that familiar widow's peak. Already, he was mocking his friend Charlie for even thinking about dancing.

'What? When there's drink to be drunk?' he said. 'We'll find ourselves some gorgeous girls soon enough, Charlie. All the nice girls love a soldier.' And he looked round the room, sizing them all up with a flirtatious grin and a wink.

Almost unnoticed, Henry had slipped into the room behind Freddie and his pals. Cat began to understand why Henry might have been off his food, knowing his loud, handsome, brave brother was in town. It would throw anyone off their stride.

Seeing Cat and Bella, Henry waved and came straight over. 'This is a nice surprise,' he said. 'I wasn't expecting to see you again tonight, Cat. And Bella, you look particularly radiant.'

'She's just got engaged to my brother, that's why.'

'Really? Congratulations. But where is he? If I was engaged to you, Bella, I wouldn't want to let you out of my sight.'

'Oh, Henry, you are such a schmoozer,' Bella said coyly, all her earlier criticisms of Henry apparently forgotten and forgiven. 'He's gone back to Dorset to give his parents the good news.'

Just then, Freddie planted himself in the fourth chair at their table. There was something dangerous in his expression, as if he was only moments away from losing the veneer of civilisation. Cat thought a lot of girls would find that darkness exciting, but it didn't set her pulse racing. She far preferred the more domesticated brother. 'Henry, you dog,' Freddie said. 'Are you going to keep all the gorgeous girls to yourself? Who are these visions of loveliness?'

With some apparent reluctance, Henry made the introductions. When he heard Bella was so recently engaged, Freddie opened his eyes wide in a look of mock innocence. 'Then you need a chaperone, Bella. Someone to protect you from all those predatory bastards gagging to steal you away from your fiancé. And to take you out of yourself. Come on, come and dance with me. I'll take good care of her for your brother,' he added, with a wink to Cat.

'Wow,' Cat said as they headed for the dance floor without a word of protest from Bella. 'He's a bit of a force of nature, your brother.'

'Mmm.'

'But that was kind of him, to think of Bella being alone and miserable without James while everybody else is having a good time.'

Henry made the kind of noise that purports to be a laugh but isn't. 'It must be lovely inside your head, always attributing your good-hearted motives to everybody else.'

'What do you mean?'

'There's no cynicism in you, Cat. You never think anything but the best of everyone. Not everyone has the best of motives, but you persist in thinking well of them.'

'I don't understand you.'

'Then I'm one up on you, because I understand you perfectly well.'

Cat gave a wry chuckle. 'Right. Because I can't speak well enough to be obscure and unintelligible.'

This time Henry's laugh was genuine. 'The perfect satire on modern pretentiousness. Well said.'

'But tell me what you're getting at.'

'I don't want us to fall out, so I think I'll just shut up now.'

'We won't fall out, I promise. Just tell me what you meant.'

He considered for a moment then shrugged. 'It's typical of you to take my brother at his word. To believe he meant it when he said he was asking her to dance to protect her and cheer her up. Me, I know him well enough to know that was the last thing on his mind. Which proves, if I needed proof, that you are probably the most good-natured person in Edinburgh.'

Cat flushed deep scarlet. 'You're making me blush,' she said. 'But here's the thing. Bella was so determined not to dance with anyone because she's so in love with James, that only kindness would make her break that determination. And she knows Freddie is your brother, so she trusts him.'

'That might be her first mistake,' he said grimly. 'Freddie's always found beautiful girls irresistible. And they seem to think the same about him. As soon as I walked in and saw you two, I knew he'd be across like a bullet from a gun. And no matter how firm Bella's intentions might have been beforehand, I knew they would melt under the heat of my brother's charms.'

'I think you're reading too much into a simple act of kindness, Henry. Bella is totally devoted to James. And she's a woman who knows her own mind.'

He threw up his hands in a gesture of submission. 'If you say so. But the other side of the coin of people who say they know their own mind is obstinacy. The secret is knowing when to give in. So maybe that's Bella's secret. She knows when to back down.'

'Which is a good thing. So, Henry, are you going to sit here gassing all night or are you going to cheer me up on the dance floor? Or do I have to get one of Freddie's buddies to shake his booty?' She jerked her head towards Freddie's companions at the bar.

Henry shuddered. 'I could never do that to you.' And so they followed the music next door and threw themselves into unstructured gyration with all the energy and passion they had previously devoted to the strict patterns of Scottish country dancing. Still, Cat had enough attention to spare to notice Bella and Freddie making the most of the music, dancing perhaps a little closer than Cat would have done in Bella's shoes.

It was past midnight when Cat and Bella extricated themselves from the party. Both Tilney men had offered to escort them home, but the girls had refused. 'We'll walk down to the Allens and call a cab for Bella from there,' Cat had insisted. Henry's words had made her a little more cautious where his brother was concerned, especially since he had had at least four beers and two whiskies that she had counted. Drink, she knew, could blur boundaries and make people behave in ways that would shame them afterwards. Better to avoid the possibility.

Arm in arm, the two girls tottered down the street on feet made sensitive by energetic dancing. 'I'm knackered,' Bella complained.

'It's your own fault. You said you weren't going to dance.'

'I took pity on him. Don't forget, Freddie's been out in Afghanistan risking his life, not swanning around courtrooms like his brother. He deserves a bit of cheering up. And it was so sweet of him to be concerned that I might be lonely without Jamie.'

'I don't know how thrilled James would have been about that.' Cat tried not to sound disapproving and dull.

Bella tutted. 'Jamie doesn't want me to be mis. Anyway, I feel like I did my bit for the troops tonight. My personal Help for Heroes. Poor boy, he's had such a tough tour of duty, he needed to let down his hair. And once he'd danced with me, nobody else would do. If I'd gone and sat down, he'd just have been pestering me non-stop.'

'That must have been flattering.'

'It was quite. Anyway, what are you complaining about? Me being occupied with Freddie meant you got to dance with Henry all night. He's a lovely mover, isn't he? Much more stylish than his brother. Positively hetero-flexible!' She giggled.

Cat wasn't in the least comfortable with pursuing that angle, not being entirely sure what it meant, but reasonably certain it was nothing that would bring her comfort. 'I suspect his conversation's a bit more interesting too.'

Bella groaned. 'You're not kidding. There's nothing modest about Freddie. He's a bit up himself, like all the Tilneys.'

'That didn't stop us having a good time, though.'

Bella squeezed her arm tightly. 'It passed the time. Because I'm on tenterhooks to talk to Jamie tomorrow, to hear what your parents said. I can't wait!'

17

As arranged, Cat and Susie met Bella and Martha at the Book Festival for coffee and croissants first thing the next morning. Both girls were in flat plimsolls, complaining of sore feet after their high-heeled adventures on the dance floor the night before. Bella was also whingeing about her lack of sleep. 'I'm so desperate to hear the full story from Jamie, I could hardly sleep a wink,' she said.

'Funny that,' Martha said. 'Because when I went to the loo in the middle of the night, someone was snoring their head off in your bedroom.'

'Ha, ha,' Bella sneered.

Cat was on her second croissant when Bella's phone rang. She jumped to her feet and ran across the grass to a more isolated spot. Cat watched as her friend paced back and forth, spare hand clutching her hair, head down, a frown of concentration on her face. Then she turned her back on them and walked behind the equestrian statue in the middle of the festival grounds, so she was entirely obscured from sight.

When she finally reappeared, Bella was pale, save for two spots of high colour on her cheekbones. It was not, Cat thought, a look that did her any favours. Bella sat down heavily and drained her cooling latte. 'Well,' she said. 'Now we know where we stand.'

'And where is that, exactly?' Martha asked.

'So, Jamie told his parents, and he says they were delighted. But they'd also just had a letter from a university friend of Mr Morland who's a barrister in York and he's offered Jamie a place in his chambers. So, I go, Jamie, you've got to be joking, right? York? I mean, it's in Yorkshire, right? The North, for God's sake. Then he admits he's been getting nowhere with all the London sets he's applied to and his dad says he'd be crazy to turn this down because it's really tough out there. Plus his dad says if he takes the York offer, they'll help him with the deposit on a house because they can afford that on account of house prices are lower up there because, duh, it's the North and nobody wants to live there.' Bella paused for breath. Her tone was dull and flat but even Cat registered that her words were not.

'I think that's very sensible of Jamie and very generous of your parents, Cat. I wish I could do as much, but of course I'm just a poor widow. I expect Mr Morland will do more for you once he sees you settled, for he sounds a lovely man, from everything Jamie has said,' Martha commented.

'I doubt it,' Cat said. 'He's only a vicar.'

Both Martha and Bella looked at her with some puzzlement, but Bella moved on regardless. 'But here's the worst bit. Jamie says he thinks we should wait for a couple of years at least before we get married because he just doesn't see how he can support both of us till he's got his feet under the table. Even with the little bit I bring in.'

'Now that does surprise me,' Martha said. 'It's not like you're a big spender. You're not one of those "want, want, want" girls.'

Bella sighed. 'I'm not thinking of myself, I'm thinking of poor Jamie having to work so hard just to earn enough for the basics. It's him I care about. I can manage with next to nothing.'

Martha patted her daughter's hand. 'That's just like you. So selfless. It's such a shame that the only reward it brings you is everybody's affection and respect. If all that love turned to money, you and Jamie would be millionaires. Frankly, I'm sure that when the Morlands meet you, Jamie's father will find a way to help you be together as soon as possible.'

Bella gave Cat a look freighted with an impenetrable meaning. 'Everybody has the right to do what they want with their own money.'

Cat didn't know what she could say to make the truth of her family's situation clearer. She looked to Susie for assistance, but she was staring deep into her coffee cup. 'I'm amazed my dad's offered this much,' she said. 'Honestly, he's always made it clear we'd have to make our own way in the world.'

'Dear, sweet Cat,' Bella sighed again. 'It's not the lack of money that's pissing me off – you know I despise people who are obsessed with money. It's the waiting. Two years? I'd run off with Jamie tomorrow and to hell with the money. But your father has obviously convinced him that he needs to be cautious and save up before we can get married. Save up for what? I'd live with Jamie in a bedsit.'

'Of course you would,' Martha said stoutly. 'You wear your heart on your sleeve, of course you'd be happy in a bedsit.'

'It wouldn't be easy for James, though, trying to prepare his cases in a bedsit,' Cat said dubiously. 'Couldn't you get a better-paid job in the meantime?' She wanted to believe Bella cared only about the delay, but there was a niggle at the back of her mind that the loss of the glamorous Chelsea life Bella had fantasised about was closer to her heart than she cared to admit.

Bella and Martha both looked blankly at her. 'But what would Ma do without me?'

'That's right,' Martha said. 'Bella's invaluable to me. And we love working together. It's so rare to find a job you truly love, and that's worth more than money.'

'I suppose,' Cat said dubiously, scolding herself for nurturing such thoughts about her friend. She took herself off to the bookshop so that Bella and Martha could thrash things out to their hearts' content while she distracted herself with the fresh display of that day's performing authors. It was there that Ellie Tilney found her with her nose in a book of poetry.

'Hi, Cat, what're you reading?'

'William Letford.' Cat showed her. 'His day job is a roofer, and he's really good looking. But the best bit is that his poems are really zingy, full of life.'

'That's wild. Listen, Cat, I've got some really boring news.'

Cat felt she'd had quite enough trial by news for one day, but she forced a smile. 'What's that?'

'We're leaving town tomorrow.' Ellie looked on the verge of tears. 'My father was supposed to meet up with a couple of his Falklands cronies, but they haven't been able to make it. And the weather forecast is for a few days of scorching weather and he hates being in the city when it's hot and stuffy, so he's decided we're all going back to Northanger in the morning.'

Cat had neither the skill nor the will to hide her dismay.

She couldn't bear the prospect of not seeing Henry again. 'Oh no, Ellie,' she wailed. 'I was so looking forward to spending more time with you and Henry.'

'And we feel exactly the same. So, I was wondering . . . I know it's totally out of order and totally short notice—'

'There you are, Eleanor.' General Tilney's unmistakable clipped accent interrupted his daughter's awkward attempt at making a request. 'I've been looking all over for you girls. So, what does she have to say, Eleanor? Shall I congratulate you on managing to bring us all some delight?'

'I hadn't actually got as far as asking her, Father, because you arrived.'

The General shook his head impatiently. 'If you want a job doing, do it yourself. Never rely on your children, Catherine. Bear that in mind for future reference. Now, here's the thing. Did Eleanor manage to convey the information that we are about to leave Edinburgh?' Cat nodded. 'She did? Good, that's something, at least. You know, Catherine, every year, I persuade myself it will be different – that I'll enjoy all the performances I've chosen to attend, that I'll engage in nothing but brilliant conversation and that my life will be a buffoon-free zone. And every year I am proved wrong.' He gave a rueful smile. 'I realise it's not like this for you young people, but Edinburgh grows tedious to me. And besides, I prefer to be at Northanger when the weather is hot. The only thing that would improve matters further would be if we could persuade you to drag yourself away from the endless pleasures of the festival—' here, he raised his eyebrows and turned his eyes heavenwards '—and give us all the pleasure of your company at Northanger?'

Ellie gripped her friend's hand. 'Please say you will.'

The General clapped a hand on his daughter's shoulder. 'I know our humble home will seem modest to you, but we will do our best to make you comfortable. There will be no galleries or theatres to amuse you, but equally there will be no opinionated idiots to annoy you or terrible performances to regret as soon as the house lights are dimmed.' He gave her his most charming smile. 'And we will do our best to make sure you enjoy your visit.'

Cat could hardly credit this fulsome invitation. Not in her most detailed fantasies had she imagined being swept off to Henry's home as an honoured guest. It was all she could do not to gibber and jabber her gratitude and delight. She wanted to caper and prance round the bookshop, prattling to passing strangers about this unexpected and flattering turn of events. Not just some casual suggestion that she might drop by, but a pressing request for her company. It held out such entrancing possibilities – thrilling, romantic, yet with a frisson of the dark and unknown. Somehow, Cat contained herself and managed simply to say, 'That's very kind and I'd love to come. But I have to check with my parents. And with Mr and Mrs Allen, of course.'

The General waved a dismissive hand. 'I spoke to Mrs Allen just now, when I was searching for you. And although obviously she's sorry to lose your excellent company, she is perfectly willing for you to join us down in the Borders. So I think it's pretty much a *fait accompli.*'

Such a divine French accent, Cat thought as she pulled her phone from her pocket. 'All the same,' she said, 'I still need to check with Mum and Dad.'

A momentary look of displeasure flickered across the General's face, but he gave a stiff smile. 'Eleanor and I will take a look at the history section while you . . .' he waggled his fingers to indicate the business of composing a text to her mother.

Ellie Tilney wants me 2 go & stay w her at Northanger Abbey for a few days. OK with Susie. OK with you? Please say yes! Cx

Easier to explain if she said Ellie had invited her, she thought. She didn't want Annie thinking there was anything weird going on. Especially if Northanger turned out to be the vampire heaven she believed it might be.

She perched on the arm of a sofa, hardly able to contain her impatience. Luckily for the state of her nails, her mother texted back almost immediately.

James says she's a lovely girl. If Susie thinks it's OK, I'm fine with it. Don't take advantage of their hospitality, don't outstay your welcome and email me pix! Just googled it and it looks amazing! Have fun. We miss you. XXX BTW, we can't wait to meet Bella, James says you two are best of friends, which is lovely for him.

Cat almost tripped over her own feet, so eager was she to pass on the good news to the General and Ellie. 'Splendid,' General Tilney said. 'I didn't see how they could object after Mrs Allen gave the plan her thumbs up. Good. Well, you girls can sort out the details. I have business to attend to before I leave town.' He patted both girls on the shoulder and marched out of the tent.

'I'm so excited,' Ellie said. 'I hardly ever have anyone to stay. Usually my father is irritated by my friends and he doesn't want them cluttering the place up, as he puts it. But he's really taken to you in a big way.'

'You can't be more excited than I am! I'm thrilled to bits that I'm actually going to be staying in a genuine old abbey. And with my new friends.' She pulled Ellie into a hug and spun round with her. 'This is the best thing that's happened to me since Susie invited me to come to Edinburgh with them. Ellie, you've no idea how electrifying this is compared to my usual life!'

They quickly sorted out the arrangements for the following morning, then Ellie had to rush off to meet Henry at a live poetry slam. Cat pulled a face. 'Rather you than me.'

Ellie grinned. 'We're only going because one of the poets is an old school friend of Henry's. See you tomorrow. But I'll tweet you when I get the chance.'

Cat collapsed into one of the armchairs strategically placed around the bookshop for ardent readers whose feet had had enough of Edinburgh pavements. She was the luckiest person in the world, she thought. All the constellations had lined up in her favour. First, she'd had the amazing fortune to be here in the first place, thanks to the Allens. She'd seen theatre that had literally stopped her breath, comedy that had made her laugh till she couldn't breathe at all, and listened to authors whose words had brought life into the dullest of her days. She'd learned to dance and put her new skills into helter-skelter practice. She'd made new friends and been present at her brother's ascension into the world of true adulthood. And she had – yes, she was going to admit it – she had fallen in love.

And now she was the General's chosen visitor, she would be cheek by jowl with the man of her dreams for as long as she was at Northanger Abbey.

And that was the icing on the cake. Cat's passion for atmospheric architecture was only just second to her passion for Henry. Her imagination had always been filled with images of pinnacles and buttresses, battlements and cloisters, priests' holes and secret passages. Long before she'd ever clapped eyes on Henry, they'd been the stuff of her fantasies. Her parents had family memberships of the National Trust and English Heritage, and those tours of castles, abbeys and noble houses had wakened her appetite for more thorough exploration behind the twisted scarlet rope. And now it was within reach. She could already see herself, trepidatious in long damp passages, thrilled in narrow cells with high window slits, terrified in the ruined chapel itself.

Cat was strangely touched by the General's description of this bounty as 'modest'. She was charmed by his lack of boastfulness about the quality of his home. It was a surprising humility she'd never have suspected, judging by his apparent self-confidence about everything else in his life. She wished Ellie was around so she could press her for more details about her home. When was it built? How did it come into the hands of the Tilneys? Were there legends and creepy tales from the crypt? The images she'd googled promised delicious excitement and more. But would it really be so unnerving in reality? Surely with Ellie and Henry in attendance, no matter how spooky it was, she would be safe.

For now, she could only speculate. But before long, she

would have the chance to savour every aspect of Northanger Abbey for herself. And she was determined to do just that. No matter how bloodcurdling it might be, it would be no match for Cat Morland.

18

In spite of her fixation on her own future, Bella was alive to the change in Cat's mood when she returned to their table outside the Spiegeltent. 'You look like the cat that's got the cream,' she said. 'So the General found you, did he? I suppose you said yes? I suppose you're off to Northanger Abbey in the morning?' It was hard to ignore her air of resentment.

'I had no idea they were going back so soon,' Cat said, determined not to let Bella deflate her good mood. 'Never mind that they'd ask me to go back with them. How lucky is that?'

'All right for some. I'm going to be stuck here in Edinburgh with nobody for company but Jess and Claire. I might as well just kill myself now.' She pouted.

'But James is coming back, isn't he? At least until he has to go back to work.'

'Sweet Jamie.' Bella dragged her eyes away from her study of the festival entrance and gazed heavenwards momentarily. 'I miss him so much.'

'Is that why you can't take your eyes off the people coming in? Do you think he's going to sneak up and surprise you?'

Bella sighed. 'Honestly, Cat. As if. You make it sound like I want to be hanging on his arm every minute of the day. It would be totally hideous to be together all the time. Everybody would laugh at us behind our backs. It's healthy for a relation-ship if you spend time apart, you know. Take it from me, a bloke like Henry Tilney would soon get pretty bored if you were the only company he ever had. So, no, I'm not looking out for Jamie. I'm just interested, that's all. There might be somebody I know from London, somebody to keep me company when you go gadding off to Northanger. You have to keep me posted, sweetie. Photos and texts and tweets and emails, the lot. I'm going to be glued to your Facebook page, you lucky dog. Is it haunted?'

Cat shook her head. 'I don't know. I haven't had the chance to talk to Ellie properly about it. As soon as I know anything, you will too, I promise. The first mystery I have to get the answer to is what happened to Mrs Tilney. All I know is that she was a recluse and now she's dead. I don't know when or how.' But her friend's attention had already wandered. 'Bella? Are you sure you're not expecting someone?'

With an effort, Bella dragged her eyes back to Cat. 'My eyes have to be pointing somewhere, Cat. If I stared at you all the time, people would think we were lesbians. You know how I always need to keep an eye on what's going on around me. Freddie says I've got an agile mind, that's why my eye is always wandering. Oh, and that reminds me. I nearly forgot. I had an email from Johnny. I bet you can guess what it was about?'

Cat would have struggled to care less, but she chose to humour her friend. 'His outfit for the wedding?'

'Hardly. Since the only thing he can talk about is you. The poor fool is head over heels in love with you.'

'With *me*?'

'Oh, stop it. Honestly, Cat, sometimes you take the whole "who, me?" thing too far. Just be straight with me and don't keep fishing for compliments. A drunken child of two and a half would have noticed him trailing around buzzing for you. And he told me you'd been encouraging him to think you cared for him too, just before he left for London. Which, I'll be honest, I was surprised about because I know how much you fancy Henry. But Johnny said in his email that he made it clear he wanted you to be an item and you went along with him. And I know you too well to think you would do that if you didn't mean it, so I reckoned you must be totally over Henry. And now Johnny wants me to put in a good word for him, to remind you what a good bargain he is. He doesn't want to be out of sight, out of mind. So don't come the innocent with me, lady.' Bella paused for breath and poked her none too gently in the ribs.

'It never crossed my mind,' Cat said indignantly. 'And since it never crossed my mind, how could I have encouraged him? I swear to God, Bella, I had no idea he fancied me. The only time I wondered was when he was so pushy about me dancing with him the day he arrived. But then I had other things on my mind—'

'Henry Tilney.'

'Yes, Henry. So I truly wasn't paying much attention to whatever Johnny was saying. I'm just totally bemused by what his email said. I mean, I think I'd have noticed him telling me we should be an item. Cross my heart, Bella. He must be bewitched. I don't even remember talking to him before he left for London.'

'You did, I remember. It was after Jamie left. Ma dragged me off to find some fabric samples and we left you and Johnny alone in the living room. I remember thinking it was now or never if he was going to make you his girlfriend.'

Cat blew out a deep breath. 'If you say so. But even if we were alone, I don't remember him saying anything that mattered. My head was full of thoughts of you and Jamie and the wedding, so I suppose I wasn't really listening. But honestly, Bella, I never encouraged him. I never wanted him to fall in love with me, never imagined he would. So you have to explain that, whatever he thought I said, that's not how it was. I don't want to put him down – he's your brother, just like Jamie and me, and soon we'll be related so I don't want any bad feelings. But you know how I feel about Henry. I could never even think about another man, never mind agree to be his girlfriend.' For once, Bella was silent. 'Don't be cross, Bella. He'll get over it. We can't let a silly misunderstanding come between us.'

'So you're dead set against getting involved with him?'

'I don't feel the way you say he feels about me. And God knows where he got that idea from.'

'You must have led him on a bit.'

'I so didn't. I mean, what is he on? I've never so much as kissed his cheek. I'm not in love, Bella, nothing like.'

Bella swept her hair back with a disdainful toss. 'You're just saying that because you think you've got a better offer. Because Johnny hasn't got loadsamoney and a place like Northanger Abbey.'

Indignant, Cat glared at her. 'That is so not me. The Tilneys are just my friends. And anyway, Northanger doesn't belong to Henry. Freddie's the oldest, he's bound to inherit.'

'If he lives long enough,' Bella said darkly. 'He's such a risk-taker – who knows if he'll make it back from Afghanistan. But as far as Johnny's concerned, you've clearly changed your mind. And that's OK. And let's face it, the Tilneys are pretty special.'

'It's not a competition, Bella. We're still friends, right?'

Bella half-turned away and sighed. 'Fine. Whatever. I've done what Johnny asked, and that's that. I'll be totes honest, Cat, I always thought it was a crazy idea. I mean, you and Johnny? What kind of a good time would you be able to have, since you never seem to have any fun money and he always spends it as soon as he gets his hands on any. You'd just sit around whingeing about being skint, there would be totally no future in it. God knows what he was thinking of. Obvs he didn't get my email about how tight things are going to be for me and Jamie . . .' Her voice tailed off and she glanced sideways at Cat.

'So you believe me? That I never led him on?'

Bella gave a little laugh. 'I don't pretend to know what goes on in your head, Cat. I mean, you were probably being a bit flirty when you danced with him, because that's just the way you are. I don't know if you even know you're doing it. But I'm not saying you did anything deliberately. I mean, who am I to judge you? We're young, right? And we're women. We're supposed to flirt and be changeable. A woman's prerogative, like Beyoncé says.'

'But I've not been changeable. I never flirted with him in the first place. You're describing something that never happened, Bella.'

But Bella was not listening, as was her wont when the words didn't suit her. 'Speak of the devil. Look, there's Freddie.' She waved enthusiastically at Captain Tilney, who cut across the grass and sinuously lowered himself down next to Bella. Cat thought he looked a little fragile, as if he'd eaten something that had disagreed with him. 'Hey, Freddie,' Bella said. 'Are you stalking me, or what?'

He gave a mock leer that nevertheless made the hair on Cat's arms rise. 'If I was stalking you, you'd have had it by now.'

Bella giggled. 'Promises, promises.'

'I saw what you put on my Facebook page,' Freddie said, a dark note in his voice. 'Ah, Bella, if you were mine, you wouldn't be saying things like that to another man. I don't think you have a heart at all.'

Cat could hardly believe her ears. Not only was Bella flirting shamelessly with Freddie, she was brazenly doing it in front of her fiancé's sister. She was afraid that if she stayed any longer she might overhear something she could not in all conscience keep from relaying to her brother. So she stood up and said, 'I'm going to see if Susie wants to walk down George Street for a coffee. You coming, Bella?'

Bella yawned. 'I'm knackered, Cat. Besides, if I move from here, I might miss Jess and Claire. They should be along any minute now. I'm just going to hang out here, if Freddie doesn't mind keeping me company . . . ?'

Freddie raised one eyebrow. 'It's not like that would be a hardship, babe.'

Her plan to separate them having backfired, Cat left with some uneasiness. She collected Susie and they set off for one of the many café bars along the pedestrianised street. But although Susie was full of the latest gossip, Cat heard nothing, so busy were her thoughts. It seemed to her that Freddie was falling for Bella, who, ironically enough, was doing exactly what she'd accused Cat of – unconsciously leading him on. It had to be unconscious, for there was no doubt about her attachment and commitment to James. Cat trusted her friend, but still, she had to admit that Bella's attitude had been very odd. She wished it had been one of their usual devil-may-care conversations without so much focus on money and practicalities.

And she wished that Bella had been less obviously thrilled to see Freddie. Maybe she needed to warn Bella to back off in case Freddie got the wrong impression and things kicked off when James came back to Edinburgh. After all, this business with Johnny showed how easy it was for people to get hold of the wrong end of the stick. Cat shivered as she thought of how appalling it would have been if Bella had launched into her Johnny conversation when Freddie – or even worse, Henry – had been in earshot. And Bella, she knew now, would certainly have been capable of speaking without thinking of her audience.

It had been quite a day of ups and downs. And it wasn't over yet.

19

Instead of staying in to pack for her trip to Northanger Abbey, Cat allowed Ellie to talk her into going to a comedy benefit night in aid of the blood transfusion service. The venue for the Bloody Comedy evening was arranged cabaret style, with the audience seated at tiny circular tables jammed together in a steamy basement. Ellie, Henry and Cat were squeezed between a sweating iron joist and the wall but their view of the stage was thankfully unimpeded. Henry produced several cans of Irn–Bru from his backpack. 'No chance of getting to the bar through this mob,' he said. 'Plus the bar profits don't support the charity anyway. Have some Irn Bru, it's Scotland's national soft drink. And it's good for the blood.'

For once, Cat wasn't on vampire alert, for she had caught sight of something that was far more upsetting than that possibility. At a table close to the stage she saw the unmistakable sight of Bella and Freddie Tilney, heads together, shoulders touching. As she looked on, Freddie's arm encircled Bella's shoulders and she leaned into him.

What was Bella thinking? All it needed was for someone innocently to snap a pic on their camera phone, post it on their

Facebook page and tag it 'Bella Thorpe and Freddie Tilney having fun at the Bloody Comedy night', and James would be wracked with jealousy and hurt.

Cat knew Bella loved a good time. Obviously she wasn't aware of how her behaviour could be misinterpreted, both by James but also by Freddie. Clearly he didn't know about her engagement to James, or he wouldn't be trying to seduce Bella. There was a great big disappointment coming his way, and Cat cared enough for the whole Tilney clan to mind on his behalf.

If the room hadn't been so tightly packed, she might have considered going over and having a quiet word with Bella, just to mark her card as to how she risked causing pain to both her fiancé and a heroic soldier who deserved a better reward for serving his country than to be led up the garden path by a woman who didn't even know what she was doing. But that wasn't an option. And besides, Cat was far from certain she could manage to make herself clear except in private, with nothing to distract Bella from her words.

Time was running out for that course of action, for in the morning she would be off to Northanger. But although Freddie was staying on in Edinburgh, Ellie or Henry would have the chance to take their brother to one side and explain the situation before they left in the morning. Now she had a plan, Cat leaned over and spoke in Henry's ear so he would hear her over the hubbub. Even in a room that smelled of drink and sweat, she could still discern his individual fragrance of cedar-wood and maple syrup. It made her feel hungry for him, but she pushed her own feelings to one side for the good of both their brothers. 'Freddie seems very fond of Bella,' she said.

'He's definitely got the hots for her.'

'But he's in for a big let-down. Obviously he doesn't know she's engaged to my brother.'

Henry gave her a pitying smile. 'He knows all right, Cat.'

'Does he? Then why does he keep hanging around her? Why doesn't he cut his losses and go after somebody single?'

Henry said nothing for a moment, then he picked up the flyer and said, 'This is a terrific line-up.'

But Cat persisted. 'Why don't you persuade him to leave her alone? The longer he wastes his time on her, the harder it will be for him in the end, when he's forced to accept that she's committed to somebody else. Even if he thinks he's in love with her, he'll get over it. There's plenty of available young women here in Edinburgh without him having to practically stalk my brother's fiancée. All he's doing is storing up more pain for himself.'

Henry smiled. 'I don't think Freddie would see it like that.'

'So talk to him. Make him understand. Persuade him to back off.'

'No point. When Freddie makes his mind up, he's as stubborn as my father. And that is stubborn, believe me. Look, I told him myself that Bella is getting married to your brother. He just laughed and said, "But she's not married yet, is she?"'

'How can he be so selfish? If my brother finds out that he's been chasing Bella, he'll be furious.'

'It takes two to tango, Cat. Freddie wouldn't be coming on to Bella if she wasn't encouraging him.'

'She doesn't even realise she's encouraging him. She's just being nice.'

Henry laughed. 'I've said this before, Cat, but it's still true. You have this absolutely charming belief that everybody is as well intentioned as you. And they're not. Trust me, Bella knows exactly what she's about.'

'How can you say that? You have no idea how much she loves James. She's been in love with him since the first time they met. She was in such a state before James spoke to my parents in case they wouldn't approve of her. And all she's been talking about for the past couple of days is where the wedding's going to be and what kind of frock she's going to have.'

Henry shrugged. 'It's not about James, though, is it? He's not here, is he? She's just one of those women who needs to have a man dancing attention on her. The fact that she's flirting with Freddie doesn't mean she's not in love with James.'

'I don't know how you can say that so calmly. A woman truly in love with someone shouldn't have any inclination to flirt with anybody else. How would you feel if your fiancée was letting another man come on to her in public?'

Henry's face froze. 'I would not become engaged to a woman who was capable of that sort of behaviour in the first place.'

'But how would you know? Because, as you said yourself, the whole point is that James is not here and Bella is just amusing herself.'

'You're like a terrier,' Henry said. 'You don't let go of a subject till you've shaken every last drop of significance from it.'

Cat bridled, not entirely convinced that she liked being compared to a small yappy dog. 'I just want to make sense of things. I don't speak for the sake of it. I only ask when I truly want an answer.'

'And that's a good thing. But I can't always be expected to answer what you want to hear.'

'But you must know what your brother's up to with Bella.'

Henry laughed, a bitter look on his face. 'I've no idea. All I could do would be to guess, and that's no good to either of us. Look, my brother is a hot-blooded man who loves adventure and risk. He's known Bella hardly any time at all and he's known all along she's engaged. He's also going back to his regiment in a week's time, so whatever he is up to will be done and dusted by then.'

It was clear to Cat that she had failed to enlist Henry in her attempts to protect her brother from public humiliation. 'Maybe I should speak to your father,' she said.

Henry's eyebrows shot up in alarm. 'That's really not a good idea, Cat. I think you're getting a bit carried away over a mean-ingless little flirtation. Not to mention you're putting things on James that might not be how he sees it. You seriously think he believes that his only security in love is that Bella never hangs out with another guy? I suspect that if he's anything like you, he trusts his lady and he prefers her to be out enjoying herself than sitting at home moping.'

'I suppose,' she said dubiously.

'I'm not going to say, "Don't you worry your pretty little head about it" because, apart from being condescending as hell, it's obviously not going to stop you fretting. But what you need to remind yourself is that you believe in James and Bella's love for each other. The kind of love that withstands jealousy and arguments. Plus nobody knows what goes on behind the closed doors of other people's relationships. Sometimes flirting with somebody else adds a little frisson to a relationship – lovers like to tease each other with how desirable they are to others, you know.'

'I couldn't bear that.'

'It wouldn't be my cup of tea either, but couples who play that sort of game know exactly how far they can go with it before either gets hurt. And they never tease each other beyond what turns them on.'

Cat shook her head. 'That is so not my idea of a good time. And it's not very considerate of the third person in the triangle who gets caught up in their selfish game. Poor Freddie.'

'He'll be OK. He'll have some fun in Edinburgh then he'll be back with the boys in the mess-room. He'll toast Bella Thorpe a few times at dinner, then she'll just be a fond memory. And meantime, Bella will be teasing James with how lucky he is to be marrying the woman all the other men desire. It'll be all right, Cat. Trust me.' He looked intently into her eyes, his dark hypnotic stare holding her pinned like a captive butterfly.

She wanted to believe him, so she told herself his argument was convincing. She was over-reacting, as he'd said, and every-thing would sort itself out. And indeed, Henry's words seemed to be borne out by the end of the evening. Bella spotted Cat across the room and followed her cheery wave with a text.

Hey gf. 2 packed 2 get 2 u here. Meet u bk @ Allens or ours afterwards? xox

The text gave Cat a happy glow. Even Bella wouldn't be so insensitive as to bring Freddie Tilney to her fiancé's sister's lodgings. Mr Allen might be a man of few words but Cat imag-ined he would expend several of them in that circumstance.

Two hours later, the friends were ensconced in the window seat with mugs of hot chocolate. Freddie, it transpired, had gone to meet his father at the casino to play poker. And that was all the mention Bella made of the gallant captain. Instead, she talked of missing James and how she was going to miss Cat. 'At least your brother should be back in a day or two. But what am I going to do without my bgf? Who am I going to gossip with and confide in? We'll just have to mainline Facebook. Because, honestly, Cat, until Jamie gets here I might as well shut myself up in a convent for all the fun I'm going to have.'

They said an emotional farewell and Cat finally managed to pack her bag for Northanger Abbey. Just as she was settling down in bed with the latest instalment of the Hebridean Harpies, she had a text that completed the job of allaying her concerns.

Hi sis. I'll b bk in Ed 2moro teatime. Will u be gone to N Abbey already? Hope not. Don't tell Bella, want it 2b surprise. James xxx

Smiling, Cat curled up with her book. Everything was going to be all right. And she was going on a vampire hunt.

20

Cat was touched by how sorry the Allens were to lose her company. 'You're always so cheerful,' Susie said. 'You've been a little ray of sunshine for us both. I'm going to miss your positive outlook, young lady. Hopefully it will have rubbed off on me.'

'And trying to pick events that would appeal to you has definitely broadened the range of what I've been to see,' Mr Allen added. 'I think you may inadvertently end up earning me quite a bit of money.'

Cat was taken aback at the prospect of having been so useful to her hosts. Much as her parents loved and fortified her, they had never encouraged her to see herself as a positive influence on anyone's life. 'It's lovely of you to say so, but I'm the one who should be saying thanks. If you hadn't brought me on this amazing trip, I'd never have met the Tilneys and there's no way I'd be going anywhere like Northanger Abbey. I'll never forget what you've done for me.'

There was a great deal of hugging and insistence on keeping in touch before Mr Allen finally managed to pick up Cat's bag and carry it down to the street. The Tilneys had invited her to breakfast, and Mr Allen was determined to deliver her to the door of Ainslie Place as if she were a package that might get lost in the post. Calman ushered them into the dining room, but in spite of the General's earnest invitation to stay, Mr Allen waited only long enough to see Cat settled at the table before he made his polite farewells.

Left alone with her new friends, Cat was surprised to be overtaken by shyness. She was acutely aware of how desperately she wanted to avoid doing the wrong thing. For a fleeting moment she was tempted to jump up and run down Ainslie Place after Mr Allen. Not even the welcoming smiles and conversation of Henry and Ellie could put her at ease, especially since the General's incessant attention to her needs and wishes was so insistent she began to feel like the fly invited into the spider's parlour. It was a tricky thought to contend with while confronted with a dizzying array of breakfast possibilities. Cereals, juices, fruits – some of which she didn't even recognise – breads, pastries, cheese, smoked fish, cold meats, kedgeree, miso, sashimi and all the components of a traditional Scottish breakfast – including haggis and tattie scones – occupied a sideboard which ran along one side of the room. 'I pride myself that there isn't a hotel in Edinburgh that can outdo a Tilney breakfast,' the General said. 'But if there's something – anything, some particular cereal or bread – that you would like that we don't have, just say the word and Calman will send out for it.' He could not have been more solicitous if she had been a member of the house of Windsor, and Cat, who hated fuss, couldn't help hoping it wasn't going to be like this at every meal in Northanger Abbey.

The experience was all the more disconcerting because the

General's unctuousness alternated violently with his expressions of rage about the non-appearance at the table of his elder son. It started with, 'Where in the name of God is Frederick?' then escalated into a rant about how much Captain Tilney had lost at cards the night before, how much drink he'd consumed at the tables, finishing with an outburst on how bloody lazy he was in general. When Freddie finally appeared, bleary-eyed and unshaven, he must have wished he'd stayed in bed until they'd left for the Borders, so sharp was his father's dressing-down. 'It's disgraceful,' he concluded. 'I'm ashamed of you, showing such disrespect when we have a guest. In my day, the army taught a man how to behave. These days, all you seem to learn is how to misbehave. Now sit down and eat your breakfast.'

Freddie gave Cat a rueful smile but he said nothing in response to his father's outburst other than a muttered apology. She wondered if the real reason for his late rising was that he'd been tossing and turning over Bella. She hoped she might glean a better idea of his personality, since this was the first time she'd had the chance to talk to him without Bella's presence. But like his brother and sister, Freddie didn't have much to say for himself while his father held forth at the breakfast table. He sat with his head bowed, stirring a raw egg into what Cat devoutly hoped was tomato juice.

The General swiftly despatched a plate of kidneys and black pudding, then stood up. 'Forgive me for leaving you so soon, Catherine, but I must check everything is in order before we leave. But please, eat your fill. There's no hurry.'

Once the door had closed behind him, Freddie gave a hollow laugh. 'No hurry, but God help you if you're not on the doorstep on the stroke of whatever hour he's decreed for your departure.'

'Shut up, Freddie, you'll make Cat wish she'd never agreed to come to Northanger,' Ellie said.

He sighed. 'Whatever. To be honest, Ellie, I'll be glad when you've all gone and I can enjoy what's left of my leave without him on my case all the time. I'll miss you and Henry, but not Genghis Khan. It's about time you two got out from under his thumb.'

'We're not under his thumb,' Henry said. 'We choose to stay close to him because we understand him.'

'It's his way of dealing with his pain,' Ellie said. 'The terrible things he saw in the Falklands, and then Mother's death. You should cut him more slack, Freddie.'

Cat couldn't help thinking she liked the younger Tilneys better for the compassion they showed their difficult parent. But Freddie was determined to put his side. 'He's not in pain, he's just a bully. You think I haven't seen my share of horror out there in Helmand? You think I don't hurt from losing our mother? But I don't come home throwing my weight around and making everybody else's life a bloody misery like he did with Mother. You two are too young to remember what it was like, but to a little kid, it was terrifying.'

'You seem to have got over it. The two of you are thick as thieves when you come home,' Ellie said tartly. 'It's not me or Henry he takes to the casino or to the races.'

Freddie spread his hands in resignation. 'What can I say? I know. And he's great company when he forgets he's my father. But as soon as we cross the threshold, it's like the monster inside is unleashed.'

'Enough,' Henry said, standing up and swallowing down his final cup of coffee. 'Cat, I promise nobody is going to shout at you at Northanger. Well, not unless you cheat at Monopoly or Scrabble. Father's just eager to make sure you enjoy your time with us. He gets over-anxious.'

As he spoke, the General's anxiety entered a new dimension. He threw open the dining-room door. 'Come along, come along. We need to be on the road by ten. I promised Lachie we'd be with him by ten forty-five.' The door closed behind him and Ellie shovelled the last forkful of corned-beef hash into her mouth.

'Who's Lachie?' Cat asked, trailing alongside Henry into the hall, where there seemed to be a great flurry of luggage and boxes of provisions.

'He was a gamekeeper at Northanger. Then he went to the Falklands with my father and lost a leg.' Henry threw open the front door and picked up Cat's case. 'Obviously, he couldn't go back to his old job. So Father lent him the money to buy a pub just outside Lauder. We always stop for a coffee and some of his wife's home baking when we're passing. It's a tradition.' He trotted down the steps and put the case in the boot of the smaller of the two Mercedes parked outside.

Henry leaned against the car and folded his arms. 'I suspect we're not at our charming best this morning. You must be wishing you were safe in the bosom of Susie Allen.'

Cat snorted with laughter. 'You always know the right thing to say to stop me winding myself up. I'm sure everything will be perfectly calm once we get under way.'

And so it proved to be. The chaos somehow metamorphosed into order and Cat soon found herself in the back seat of the larger Mercedes alongside Ellie. Henry was driving the General in the smaller car, while Calman drove the girls.

Coffee at Lachie's turned out to be a major production number. The pub itself was a cosy cottage, all dark wood and gleaming brasswork, but the coffee shop and bistro occupied a sprawling conservatory built on to the original building. The only other customers were a trio of elderly ladies twittering in the corner over coffee and scones.

Lachie's wife, a pleasantly plump woman in her mid-forties, saw them settled, then disappeared into the kitchen while the General and Lachie exchanged what to Cat were a series of meaningless sentences. Sandwiched between Ellie and Henry, she couldn't think of anything to say that might be of any interest. Luckily, Mrs Lachie bustled out of the kitchen, laden with cake stands. She set them proudly in front of her guests and Cat stared open-mouthed at the array of sweetness. She thought she'd never seen so much butter, flour, sugar and eggs in one place, not even at the Piddle Valley produce show.

'Amazing, isn't it,' Henry said, reaching to pass the scones, pancakes and assorted buns to Cat. 'And it tastes as good as it looks. When I'm driving back and forth between Northanger and work, I have to take the back roads or I'd be the size of a barrel.'

Mrs Lachie returned with pots of tea and coffee. 'Don't be daft, Henry, you've got the metabolism of a whippet. Eat up those meringues, now, I made them just for you.'

Cat found it impossible to stop once she'd started. Everything was delicious, but as soon as she'd finished one sweet delight, the General or Mrs Lachie would press another on her. Finally, she knew that if she ate another thing she would be sick. 'I can't,' she moaned, as Mrs Lachie proffered a plate of vanilla slices.

'I think you've done your duty, my dear,' the General said to Mrs Lachie. 'Wonderful spread, as ever. Best cakes in the Borders.'

Cat was impressed with the deference that Lachie and his wife showed the General. It was respectful without being servile and she thought it spoke well of her host. Even if he was brusque towards his family sometimes, he was clearly a man who was admired by the world. That couldn't be the case if he was a vampire, could it? Or if he'd been a brute to his vulnerable wife?

The party moved out to the car park more slowly than they had entered, weighed down by their overindulgence. General Tilney patted his stomach and groaned even though Cat had seen him eat very little. 'I need more space to stretch out after that,' he said. 'Ellie, why don't you ride with Henry and I'll take your place. It's roomier in there.'

Cat felt a pang of dismay. But her friend rode to her rescue. 'I'd rather ride with you, Father,' Ellie said quickly. 'I've had so much to eat I'll get car sick driving with Henry, the way he throws that car round the bends.'

The General harrumphed. 'You have a point. Very well, if Catherine doesn't mind Henry's deplorable driving?'

'I'll be fine,' Cat said cheerfully. 'My mother says I have an iron constitution.' Even if it had been a lie, she would have said something similar to secure her place in the car next to Henry. Her only regret was that it would be less than an hour before they arrived at Northanger Abbey.

'I'll open the sunroof, make sure there's plenty of fresh air.'

General Tilney frowned. 'I don't think so.' He looked up at the clouds. 'We don't want the noonday sun beating down and giving poor Catherine a headache.' And so the tinted glass sunroof remained firmly closed.

As soon as they set off, she was reminded of how much more pleasant it was to be Henry's passenger rather than Johnny's. He followed sedately in his father's wake, leaving enough distance between the two cars for her fully to enjoy the rolling hills and fields of sheep and cows they passed through. The landscape was more dramatic than the Piddle Valley, but it was similar enough for her not to feel any sense of unease.

'It's really kind of you to come and stay,' Henry said.

'Kind? It's a huge treat for me.'

'Well, I appreciate Ellie having some decent company for a change. I know you haven't known each other long, but she counts you as a real friend.'

'Doesn't she have other friends at Northanger?'

'It's a bit isolated. And because she's been mostly at boarding school, she never really made friends with the local kids. She's mostly stuck out there with Father, and when he goes off on one of his mysterious jaunts with the lads – which he does quite a lot – she's left to her own devices.'

'Are you not around, then?'

'Northanger isn't even half my home these days. I'm an advocate, most weeks I'm in Edinburgh between three and five days.'

Cat raised her eyebrows. 'You rattle about in that big house in Ainslie Place all by yourself?'

Henry laughed so hard she thought he would steer them into a ditch. 'God, no. My father takes a house just for the festival. I have a disreputable little flat off the Cowgate, which I rent out during the festival. And that pays my mortgage till Christmas.'

'It must be hard to go back to that after Ainslie Place and Northanger Abbey.'

'I'm always sorry to leave Ellie, it's true.'

'Not just Ellie, though. Swapping a Borders abbey for a flat, even in Edinburgh, must be hard.'

He grinned. 'You've got high hopes of the abbey, haven't you?'

'Of course. Ellie showed me a photo in one of those books of Scottish views. It looks gorgeous. The kind of historic building that ends up starring in a film adaptation of some heart-stopping book about vampires or Jane Austen heroines or ancestral ghosts.'

Henry shook his head. 'And are you ready for all the horrors that a house like that has to offer? As well as an iron constitution, are you fearless? Are your nerves up to it?' He dropped his voice to a ghoulish pitch. 'Can you handle sliding panels, priest holes, secret passageways hidden by ancient tapestries?'

Cat laughed. 'What, you think I'd be scared so easily? You don't know me, Henry Tilney. Besides, there'll be lots of people in the house. It's not like it's been standing empty for years and we're coming back to face down the old ghosts – which is what it would be if this was really a horror movie.'

'No. We do have electric light nowadays. No more feeling our way down the hall, lit only by the dying embers of a wood fire. And we've emerged from that period where we had to sleep on animal skins on the floor in rooms without windows or doors or furniture. But Mrs Danvers, our elderly crone of a housekeeper, does like to keep to the old ways. She insists on making our attractive young female guests sleep in the west wing all alone while the rest of us retire to the east wing with its flush toilets and hot water and wifi.'

'Mrs Danvers?' Cat squeaked.

'Mrs Danvers. She'll lead you up a different staircase from the rest of us. Down the gloomy passageways. Into an apartment never used since mad Cousin Onesiphorus hung himself from the hammer beams twenty years ago. An apartment lit with one forty-watt bulb barely strong enough to reveal the shadowy tapestries of mythical beasts and deformed grotesques. Will that be all right for you?'

'I think you're at the wind-up.'

'I've barely touched on what awaits you at Northanger,' he said, his tones sepulchral. 'A broken fiddle, a chest that can't be opened, a grime-streaked portrait whose eyes follow you round the room. And a dribble of unintelligible hints and malevolent stares from Mrs Danvers. And then she'll tell you about the vampires and the werewolves and the undead who wander the corridors around your room. She'll point out that there's no mobile phone signal anywhere in the abbey and then she'll leave you, straining to hear the echo of her receding footsteps, convinced you can hear a strange fluttering in the chimney. And then you'll discover the door has no lock.'

By now Cat was giggling. 'You've been reading too many Hebridean Harpies books. No wonder Ellie doesn't get many visitors. I don't believe your housekeeper is called Mrs Danvers either.'

Henry chuckled. 'You'll have to wait and see. But don't shriek when she introduces herself, that really annoys her.'

'Yeah, right, whatever. So what other delights can I look forward to, alone in the west wing?'

Henry's voice sank back to its tone of horripilating menace. 'Nothing more, on the first night. Once you overcome your terror enough to climb into bed, you'll fall into a restless sleep, broken by vile unsettling nightmares. Nothing more than that. The house will be lulling you into a false sense of security. But on the second, or maybe even the third night, there will be a violent storm.'

'Of course there will. Peals of thunder that will shake those thick stone walls will bounce off the surrounding hills. Gusts of wind will whistle in the chimney like the screeches of a banshee and ripple through that grotesque tapestry, making it seem to come alive.'

Now Henry was laughing. 'Are you sure you've never been to Northanger before? Never climbed out of bed in the middle of a storm to examine the peculiarities of a tapestry and discovered the secret door that lurks behind it? Never worked your way through a series of logic puzzles and sudokus to open it?'

Cat gave a little scream. 'Stop it!'

'And then, once the door falls open, you tiptoe down the wide stone stairs which are lit by an unearthly scarlet light. You hear a crunching underfoot and realise you are trampling dry bones underneath. But something drives you on and you emerge into a vast underground cave where a decadent troupe of vampires are feasting on the body of a white-skinned young woman. Who bears a terrifying resemblance to . . .'

'To who?' Cat was caught up in it now. Somehow, Henry had plugged into her own strange and secret fantasies.

'To whom, don't you mean?'

She gave his arm a gentle punch. 'To wit, to whom – it doesn't matter. Who does the victim look like?'

'Bella Thorpe,' he intoned, then burst into a cackle of laughter. 'I can't keep it up, Cat. You'll have to make up your own grand finale. But make it smart – as soon as we go round the next bend, we'll be within sight of Northanger Abbey.'

His words could not have thrilled her more. Any minute now, flesh would clothe her fantasies. She could hardly wait.

21

As is so often the case, reality fell short of Cat's expectations. When they rounded the curve, what caught her eye was not a stately pile but a pair of Victorian lodges built without architectural distinction in the local red sandstone. Each had a security camera mounted on it. A modern steel gate slid to one side to allow the General's car to pass and they followed down a well-maintained tarmac drive. All that could be seen of the abbey itself were the tops of two lines of ornamental chimney pots.

Parkland stretched to either side, dotted with dense copses of mature trees and shrubs, so that wherever one looked it was impossible to see an uninterrupted horizon. Then a sudden scud of heavy rain sprang out of nowhere, reducing visibility and making Cat grateful that the sun roof had not been opened.

Her first view of the abbey was obscured by the rain sluicing across the windscreen. Henry pulled up outside an ancient portico with crumbling pillars and ran round the car to open the door for her. 'Hurry,' he urged her. 'It's lashing down.'

Cat ran into the shelter and waited for him to unload the boot and join her. Now she had a moment to drink in her surroundings, she was reassured by a generic familiarity with church porches and vestibules she had known all her life. Although Northanger was built from a dark red sandstone that reminded her of blood oranges, in style and scale the portico was very similar to that of the parish church in Piddle Dummer, where her father held evening services every other Sunday. The only things missing were the parish noticeboard and the Oxfam posters.

She heard the boot slam, then Henry appeared through the pelting rain with a couple of suit bags and her own suitcase. 'There's a couple of boxes of food, but I'll leave that for Calman to sort out when he takes the car round the back,' he said. He dropped his burdens and turned to look back at the cascading rain.

'So much for the forecast of sunny weather,' Cat said.

Henry shrugged. 'It's probably tropical in Edinburgh now. We seem to get more than our fair share of rain here. Sometimes it's a lovely day just down the road in Kelso but it's cloudy and drizzly at Northanger. We're used to it, but it can be a bit of a shocker for guests.'

'Funnily enough, you didn't say anything about rubbish weather till you'd got me here.'

He gave her an evil leer. 'But you are my prisoner now.'

She laughed. 'Spare me, sir, I beg of you.'

Henry grabbed the bags again and gestured at the door. 'We should go in. Do you mind?'

Cat turned a large black iron ring set in the studded door and it swung open silently. They stepped into an ancient hall with a vast stone fireplace, dominated by the wide sweep of a stone staircase that split halfway up and led to either side of a gallery that surrounded the hall. Faded rugs were scattered on the stone flags and the walls were hung with gloomy landscapes dominated by dark crags and ominously tumbling water. Her heart soared. This was what she had dreamed of, this was what she had craved. This was no genteel converted church, it was a fortified house, a castle almost, steeped in history.

'I'll just run these bags upstairs,' Henry said. He nodded towards double doors on the left of the hallway. 'That's the drawing room. Father and Ellie will be in there. Just go on in.' He set off up the stairs at a brisk trot, leaving Cat feeling that she ought to knock. But this wasn't some Sunday-evening period drama, she reminded herself. This was the twenty-first century and this was her friends' home. So, cautiously, she opened the door and stuck her head round.

'Come in, come in,' the General called. Although he had arrived only moments before them, he looked as if he hadn't budged since breakfast, sitting in a stylish leather chair with the *Telegraph* open on his lap.

Cat slipped inside, letting her gaze move out from the General to encompass the room as a whole. After the grandeur of the hall, it was a massive disappointment. Not the scale; that was grand and well-proportioned, dominated by a circular turret that consisted of tall windows supported by a delicate tracery of sandstone beams. It was the décor that astonished and dismayed her. Instead of a massive carved fireplace, rough stone walls and a flagged floor, the room looked like an illustration from a Scandinavian lifestyle magazine. Blond wooden floors with bright modern rugs, plastered walls adorned not with stags' heads and salmon in display cases but with tapestries and hangings in contemporary style. The furniture flew in the face of tradition also; everything had been designed to within an inch of its life with comfort, beauty and function carrying equal weight. Treacherously, Cat remembered James talking about the family home of an Oxford friend – 'So cool it wanted to snog itself.' Given that she'd been expecting atmosphere and cobwebs, Cat felt almost distraught. It reminded her of nothing so much as the ultra-modern home of the vampires in the first Twilight film.

Seeing her look but perceiving nothing of what lay behind it, the General gave an expansive wave. 'As you see, Cat, we live simply. Nothing for show, everything for daily use. This used to be like a museum, but we took it in hand, didn't we, Eleanor? No more draughts, no more gloomy corners. Now it's all about comfort. We've not quite finished the project, as you'll see in your own room, but we're getting there.'

'It's lovely,' Cat said, thinking a little wistfully of the kitchen in the vicarage with all its draughts and unmatched chairs with their surprise cargoes of cats. Nobody had ever given it a design makeover; it would have reduced a TV presenter to tears. But it was welcoming and warm, not sterile with all the elegance money could buy.

The General glanced at his watch. 'I don't imagine anyone wants lunch after our visit to Lachie's? An early dinner it is, then. I'll tell Mrs Calman, service at six. Eleanor, why don't you show Catherine to her room? I'm sure you girls have plenty to occupy yourselves till then.'

No dismissal short of grasping the scruff of her neck could have been clearer. Cat followed Ellie out of the room and they made for the stairs. 'The drawing room's amazing,' Cat said.

'After my mother died, Father went through the ground floor

like a whirlwind. He didn't want anything that reminded him of her taste, of how she liked things. The entrance hall was the only bit that escaped – Historic Scotland dug their heels in and he couldn't get listed building consent to strip it out.' Ellie gave Cat a conspiratorial look. 'Even Father thought twice about defying Historic Scotland.'

'I'm glad,' said Cat as they began to climb the wide, shallow steps with their indentations made by hundreds of years of ascending and descending feet. 'There's so much atmosphere here.'

'I think you'll find your bedroom's pretty atmospheric,' Ellie said. 'Once he'd sorted out all the rooms he goes into routinely, Father more or less ran out of steam. It's not quite medieval in the guest wing, but it's not that modern either, apart from the plumbing. When Father came back from the Falklands, he had a real bee in his bonnet about efficient plumbing, so you will at least have a bathroom that works!'

Once they reached the gallery, Ellie pointed to a corridor on the right. 'That's the family corridor. Where Henry and Freddie and I have our bedrooms, and our sitting room. The middle corridor is Father's domain. And here—' she led the way into a long corridor that snaked away from the staircase '—is the guest wing. I had Mrs Calman put you right at the end because that's got the best views.' The stone flags echoed as the two girls continued through a dog-leg that cut off the view back to the main stairs. They reached the end of the passage and Ellie turned to a door on the right. 'Here we are.' Ellie lingered on the threshold, as if she was reluctant to enter. 'The door opposite leads to the back stairs, which brings you out opposite the dining room. I brought you this way so you'd know how to find our sitting room. It's at the end of the corridor I showed you at the top of the stairs. Why don't you join us there when you've got yourself settled in?' And she was off, walking briskly back in the direction she'd come from.

Feeling a little mystified, Cat let herself into the room. It was a generous, unremarkable cube. The walls were plastered and painted the pale lemon of weak sunlight. A large painting of a seascape hung on one wall. It reminded Cat of the McTaggarts she had seen at the Kirkcaldy gallery where she'd gone with the Allens to the Vettriano exhibition. It felt like light years ago now. The floor was covered in sisal matting, and the king-sized pine bed was set against a wall so that from it the occupant had a view through two windows across treetops to distant hills. A heavily ornate Victorian wardrobe and matching chest of drawers stood in the far corner, and in the shallow bay of one window there was a black japanned chest about four feet in height.

It was the only object in the room that excited Cat's interest, but this wasn't the time to explore it. A look wouldn't hurt, though. 'Oh, but you are so tempting,' she said, running a hand over its smoothly lacquered top. She took a moment to examine it, seeing that the front was split in two, as if it were two doors. But they were doors without a lock and without handles. Puzzled, she looked more closely and realised the lid over-lapped the doors and acted as a means of closure. Satisfied that she'd be able to return to it in her own time, she turned away and took out her phone, snapping several shots of her bedroom and the marble-lined bathroom beyond, with its roll-top bath and smoked-glass shower cubicle.

But when she went to send the photos to Bella and her

sisters, she was dismayed to see there was no phone signal. Nor was there any indication that there was an available wifi connection. Surely that couldn't be right? The Tilneys couldn't exist in this isolated place without digital connections, could they? She knew there were a handful of people in the village who didn't have email or mobile phones, but they were either old or weird. The General might be eccentric but she didn't think he was weird. There had to be a reason for this lack of connection, and the creepy little voice she didn't want to listen to had one or two ideas what that might be.

Giving herself a mental shake, Cat realised Ellie and Henry might be wondering what was taking her so long. She opened her bag and thrust her clothes randomly into the chest of drawers, then ran back down to the junction at the top of the stairs. She gave a curious glance down General Tilney's corridor, but she could see nothing but blank walls and closed doors. She scuttled on down past more closed doors until she arrived at one that was ajar. Through the door floated the sound of a guitar played with no little skill.

Cat pushed the door open and Henry looked up from a somewhat battered old guitar. He gave her a welcoming smile. 'You found us. Ellie was afraid she hadn't given you clear enough directions. Come in and join us. We like to think of this as the Slytherin common room.'

'Hardly,' Ellie said, rising from the comfy chintz sofa where she was sprawled. 'When you're around, it's more like Hufflepuff. Typical lawyer, all hot air and bluster.'

There was certainly a feel of boarding school common room about the place. Shelves groaned with books that ranged from children's classics to current bestsellers. Towers of board games and jigsaws leaned drunkenly in one corner. An electric keyboard, a drum machine and an expensive-looking sound system filled another. A TV, DVD and games console completed the possibilities. The furniture was battered and scruffy but everything looked comfortable. It was, Cat thought, almost like home.

She lowered herself into an armchair piled with cushions and luxuriated in the comfort. 'What a great room,' she said.

'It's always been the place we could escape from order and orders,' Henry said. 'Your room OK?'

Cat nodded. 'Better than OK. It's lovely. Great views.'

'Mother always said it had the best light in the house. When she was piecing a quilt she used to take her fabrics down there to see how the colours truly looked together,' Ellie said.

'There's no phone signal, though,' Cat said, taking out her phone and checking. Still nothing.

'Father refuses point-blank to have a tower on our land, so we're in a black hole here,' Henry said. 'Sometimes you can pick up one or two bars up by the lodge, but if you want anything decent, you have to go a couple of miles down the Kelso road. Sorry about that. If you need to phone home, there's not a problem, we've got a perfectly functional landline.'

'What about wifi? I've got nothing coming up in my phone menu.'

Ellie groaned. 'I know. I'm sorry. We do have wireless, but Father is completely paranoid about it. He's convinced that if he leaves the router switched on, all sorts of hackers and spies will crawl inside our computers to spy on us and empty our bank accounts.'

'They're welcome to mine,' Henry muttered. 'If they can find anything in it.'

'So he only switches it on when he wants to use it, which is almost never.'

'You mean, you don't get to use your own wifi?'

'I'm sorry,' Ellie said.

'But how do you do Facebook and Twitter and stuff?'

Ellie and Henry exchanged a look. 'When I'm here, we go into Kelso. There's a coffee shop with free wifi,' Henry said.

'And when he's not here . . .' Ellie looked embarrassed, 'the Calmans have their own wifi and I know the password. When they're both busy, I sneak up to the lodge and sit on their windowsill.'

What was it she'd read in that Scott Fitzgerald short story, that the rich were different, that getting things early made them soft? It looked like there was some truth in that. Cat couldn't imagine herself or any of her siblings giving in so meekly to such a ridiculous interdiction.

Unless of course the Tilneys had other reasons, deeper reasons for wanting to keep their privacy intact.

22

C at had hoped for an afternoon in the company of both Tilneys; as much as she enjoyed Ellie's company, it was Henry who brought out the sparkle in her. But he barely stayed with them a quarter of an hour, dragging himself away with apparent reluctance to prepare a briefing paper. 'Do you have to do it today?' Ellie asked. 'When Cat's just got here?'

Henry spread his hands. 'What can I do? It's for my devilmaster.'

His response startled and alarmed Cat, and both Tilneys burst out laughing at her expression. 'If you could see your face,' Ellie giggled.

'It's a Scottish legal term,' Henry said. 'Technically, I'm a devil. That's what they call a trainee advocate. In a couple of months, hopefully my devilmaster will decide I'm fit for purpose and he'll recommend to the principal devilmaster that I should be admitted to the Faculty of Advocates. But till then, I spend my days devilling.'

'What a bizarre name for it. My brother is a pupil barrister in Newcastle, he's never claimed to be a devil!'

'That's because he's not.' Henry put the guitar down and

stood up. 'It's one of those things that marks the difference between Scottish and English law. But perhaps your father would have put the blocks on you coming to visit a house with a resident devil?'

'I don't know if he believes in that kind of devil,' Cat said uneasily.

'What? He doesn't do exorcisms?'

'No, he's just an ordinary vicar.'

'Perhaps it's about time he started, if you're going to be hanging out with the devilish Tilneys.' It was Henry's parting shot as he left the room.

Left to their own devices, Cat and Ellie had no problem entertaining themselves. They put on a music DVD then talked their way through it, slumped on the sofa together. Who knows what they discussed; only that it was of no consequence to anyone but themselves. But at last, Ellie told an anecdote about a family holiday that featured her mother. And Cat found the courage to ask her about matters of more weight. 'How old were you when your mother died?'

Ellie shifted away from her. 'Thirteen,' she said.

'That sucks,' Cat said. 'I don't know how I'd have got through the last four years without my mum. I mean, sometimes she drives me completely tonto, but mostly she's like a great big security blanket.'

'That's a great way of describing it,' Ellie said. 'And when you lose that, it's like falling through space with no bottom.'

'Was it sudden, when she died? Or did you have time to get used to the idea? Not that I suppose you can ever get used to an idea like that.'

Ellie shook her head. 'She kept saying she felt tired, so

eventually Father took her off to some specialist in Edinburgh for tests. It was in the Christmas holidays.' She gave a sad little noise that might have been an attempt at a laugh. 'He wasn't very sympathetic. He thought the doctor would just tell her to pull herself together. When they came home, they both looked shell-shocked. They just said there was something wrong with her blood then shut themselves away in Father's study. Henry and I were terrified.'

'Anyone would have been. But, something wrong with her blood? What was it? Did you find out?'

Ellie gave a heartfelt sigh. 'Mother told us later that night. She had a rare form of leukaemia. It's got a long complicated name so they just call it T-PLL. It's very aggressive. She told us the chances were that she only had a few months to live.'

'Was there no treatment?' Cat couldn't imagine what it must be like to hear such news. She didn't think she could bear it if it happened to her mother.

'She didn't want to do the chemo. She said it wasn't going to save her from dying and she wanted to make the most of the time she had with us.' Ellie's mouth twisted in a bitter grimace. 'It turned out there wasn't much of that. She was dead inside two months.'

Impulsively, Cat put her arm round Ellie's shoulders and pulled her friend close. 'I'm so, so sorry,' she said. But she couldn't help a tiny niggling voice in the back of her head muttering about bad blood and vampires.

'It all happened so fast,' Ellie said. 'And Father just cut himself off from all of us. Freddie's useless when it comes to emotions, so that left me and Henry to cope on our own. I suppose that's why we're so close now.'

They said nothing for a time while the music DVD continued, irrelevantly upbeat about love and heartbreak. The mood was broken by a knock at the door and a short red-faced woman bustled in without pausing for an invitation. 'I thought I'd better remind you dinner's early tonight,' she said. 'You know how your father hates to be kept waiting.' Her accent was so broad Cat felt herself translating into English in her head.

Ellie sprang up like a guilty thing surprised. 'Mrs C! This is my friend Catherine Morland.' She turned to Cat. 'This is Mrs Calman. Calman's wife. Obviously. She runs the house for us. We'd be lost without her.'

'Everybody calls me Cat.' She wasn't sure of the etiquette. Should she shake hands or not?

Mrs Calman surveyed her from head to toe with small dark eyes like currants in a scarlet bun. 'Welcome to Northanger Abbey, Miss Morland. I hope you enjoy your stay with us. If you need anything at all, just see me.' It sounded more like a threat than an offer.

'Thank you.' Cat gave an uncertain smile. 'This is an amazing house.'

'Aye,' Mrs Calman said. 'If these walls could talk . . .' She turned to Ellie. 'Don't forget now, Eleanor. I'll be putting the soup on the table in half an hour. Whether you're there or not.' She nodded at them both and left, closing the door firmly behind her.

'Wow. She's a bit of a dragon,' Cat said.

'She used to be in the army. That's how she met Calman. I think they both think that working for Father is as close as it gets to still being in uniform.'

'If it was a novel, she'd have been the one who clasped you

to her bosom after your mother died and revealed her previously unsuspected heart of gold.'

Ellie snorted. 'Trust me, my life is definitely not a novel. We'd better get ready for dinner. I'll meet you at the top of the stairs in twenty minutes.'

Cat looked at her jeans and T-shirt. 'Should I get changed?'

Ellie gave her a critical once-over. 'Jeans are OK, but I'd lose the T-shirt. Father likes to pretend the last hundred years never happened.'

They parted in the hallway and Cat hurried back to her room. She decided to ditch both the jeans and the T-shirt in favour of a long floaty skirt layered in different shades of green and blue, topped with a plain white cambric blouse. If the General wanted to live in the past, she'd do her best to be a demure young woman. She looked longingly at the japanned chest, but told herself to be patient, to wait till the house had settled down for the night. Just as well she had, for only moments later, Ellie knocked on her door, impatient for her company.

Although Cat and Ellie arrived in the drawing room a full five minutes ahead of the deadline, pink and panting from running down the corridor and stairs, the General was staring ostentatiously at the elegant grandmother clock in the corner. Henry was already there, done with devilling, sipping at what Cat fervently hoped was a Bloody Mary. 'Just in time,' the General said. Cat thought she heard a tinge of disappointment in his voice and scolded herself for the unworthy thought.

As Mrs Calman served the soup, Cat drank in the details of the grand room. Everything gleamed and glittered with polished wood, silver and crystal. The table was easily big enough to seat a dozen or more, but it came nowhere near filling the space.

Seeing her scrutiny, the General said, 'You must be used to far grander dinners than this with your benefactors, the Allens?'

Surprised, Cat shook her head. 'No, not at all. The Allens don't do much formal entertaining down in Dorset. We generally go round for kitchen suppers.'

He nodded sagely. 'I suppose there's not much of a choice of guests down in that part of the country. Not like here in the Borders. It will be different with the Allens in London, I'd lay money on that. I'm sure that Mr Allen knows exactly what he's doing when it comes to impressing people with his success.'

Perplexed, Cat wasn't entirely sure how to respond to that. She knew Mr Allen had to impress people with his instinct for theatrical successes, but she didn't think he did it with ostentatious displays of wealth.

'He's certainly very successful,' Henry said, seeing her uncertainty. 'But not everyone feels the need to display their achievements materially.'

The General raised his eyebrows in disbelief, his face growing pale with annoyance. 'Then how are people to know where you have reached in the hierarchy of things? Sometimes, Henry, you sound almost like a socialist.' He said the word as if it were the worst insult he could hurl across a dining table with ladies present.

'I think people should live in the style that suits them best, so long as they can afford it,' Cat said. 'Not everyone has the good fortune to be able to live somewhere as wonderful as Northanger Abbey.'

Mollified, the General grunted and finished his soup. When he was so brusque, Cat couldn't help but think wistfully of the kindness and conviviality of the Allens. But when he left the young people to their own devices, Cat was as happy as she'd ever been. Thinking of the Allens reminded her that she had been unable to communicate with any of her nearest and dearest for almost a whole day.

'General Tilney?' She spoke with some diffidence as Mrs Calman cleared away the soup dishes and placed a selection of curries and side dishes in the middle of the table. 'I wonder whether it might be possible for me to use your wifi?' She caught the look of alarm shared by Henry and Ellie.

'The wifi?' The General frowned. 'Is that entirely necessary?'

'I wanted to check my email.'

'My dear girl, why? Your parents and the Allens know precisely where you are and have the telephone number, so if there were any urgent need to contact you, there would be no difficulty.' He spooned rice on to his plate and added some lamb methi. 'You don't have any kind of job yet, so there can be no urgent business communication awaiting you. In short, Catherine, there's no conceivable reason other than the purely frivolous for you to "check your email". Isn't that so?'

Cat was taken aback. Never before had an adult lectured her thus nor attempted to keep her from the constant to and fro of social media. 'I suppose,' she said.

'So there is no need for me to make myself vulnerable to the phreaks and hackers out there who are just waiting for the chance to read my secure emails and plunder our bank accounts. There is no reason why you should be aware of this, but I receive communications that could conceivably be useful to the enemies of our country. We use the wifi sparingly here. I choose not to take risks with my security or the security of the nation.' It was a virtuoso display of pomposity and self-importance thinly disguised by the General's tone of regret.

Chastened, Cat devoted herself to Mrs Calman's curries, which were spicy enough to take her mind off any grievance against the General. Before dessert was served, he left the table, saying, 'I have an MOD briefing to take a look at. Enjoy the rest of your meal. I'll see you in the morning.'

When he left the room, Henry said, 'He still does consultancy work for the army. He's very cautious about security.'

'Paranoid, more like,' Ellie muttered.

After dinner, the trio retired upstairs to their sitting room and played a supremely silly game on one of the consoles, laughing and mocking each other's efforts. The evening slipped by in an entertaining blur, and Cat couldn't help thinking how well Henry and Ellie would fit in with the Morlands. Provided, of course, that she was mistaken about the whole vampire thing. Perhaps she'd discover more clues to help her make her mind up when she explored the mysterious japanned chest in her room.

By the time they separated and went to bed, the night was stormy. The wind had been rising at intervals the entire afternoon, though Cat had failed to notice it. Now it howled in dramatic gusts, bringing noisy scatters of rain with it. It was awesome, Cat thought as she made her way down the long corridor to her room. She nearly jumped out of her skin when a particularly loud gust was followed by the distant slam of a door. It was impossible to escape the sensation of having been dropped into an episode of the Hebridean Harpies' adventures. *Northanger Nixies*, perhaps, given how much water was pouring down her windows when she finally reached her room.

Cat pulled the curtains closed but they didn't stop moving when she stepped away from them. 'It's the wind,' she said firmly. 'Just the wind.' To make doubly sure, she pulled each curtain swiftly back and checked the window seat. Then she put her hand up to the window and felt the damp draught where the ancient frames had warped enough to let the night in. 'It's the wind, you moron,' she said to herself, letting the curtains fall.

She eyed the chest, but, recognising the deliciousness of deferred pleasure, she decided to get ready for bed first. Then, with clean teeth and freshly laundered pyjamas, she approached the lustrous black chest. Cat gripped the edge of the lid and attempted to lift it. She was surprised by how cold and heavy it was until she realised it was made not from wood but from metal. She changed her grip and put more effort into it and this time she was rewarded with success. The lid rose and she rested it against the wall, careful not to make a sound. Not that it would have made any difference if she had, for by now the night's peace was regularly broken by rumbles and claps of thunder as the storm took hold.

To Cat's disappointment, what was revealed was nothing more exotic than a hand-pieced quilt. It was true that the fabrics were of rich, jewelled colours, the pattern mathematically precise and intriguing and the stitches tiny and neat. But still, it was only a quilt. Cat drew it out of the chest and shook it out. It was big enough to act as a spread for a single bed. A hand-written label in one corner caught her eye and she pulled it close. 'Margaret Tilney fecit 2001,' she read. Cat, who had learned a little Latin from the memorial tablets in her father's churches, thought 'fecit' meant 'did', which made a sort of sense. Margaret Tilney did it in 2001. She remembered Ellie that afternoon referring to her mother's quilting. This must be one of her quilts. She was holding in her hands the very fabrics that the General's dead wife had held. Her DNA was mingling with Henry's mother's even as she had the thought. Cat didn't know whether to be spooked or gratified.

She spread the quilt out on her bed then returned to her chest. She was surprised to see that the quilt was not the top item in a pile of bedding. Instead, it had sat in its own shallow drawer. She studied the chest again and realised it should now be possible to open the double doors at the front. She tugged at them, but they remained puzzlingly closed. She ran her hand along the inside of the drawer and her finger snagged on a metal hook almost flush with the wood.

Trepidatiously, Cat pushed the hook free of its fastening and at once the doors swung back, emitting the sort of creak that presages something blood-curdling in every vampire DVD she'd ever seen. Cat let out a little scream, but all that was revealed was a stack of six narrow drawers similar to the ones she'd seen in drapers' shops in TV period dramas. She drew in her breath and pulled open the drawer below the quilt shelf.

Eight white cotton pillowcases and a lavender bag. Cat breathed again.

The drawers below held, variously, a pair of sheets, four cross-stitched cushion covers, three embroidered dressing-table runners, half a dozen silk scarves and a rusty red-brown stain that sent Cat's heart into her throat.

The stain was on the bottom of the last drawer, about the size and shape of a blade. The sort of stain you'd expect if someone had laid a bloody knife there. She made a small mewing sound in the back of her throat and recoiled from the chest.

And yet, the streak of curiosity that ran through Cat as strongly as her blood itself could not keep from examining the piece of furniture. As her eye calibrated the dimension, she realised there was a gap beneath the bottom drawer of perhaps five or six centimetres. Could the answer to the bloodstain – for so she had already classified it without a waver of doubt – lie in the space beneath?

Cat clenched her fists as if this would strengthen her resolve, then started to jiggle the drawer out of its runners. It was stiff and unwieldy towards the end, but she persisted, and almost fell backwards on to the floor when the drawer was finally released.

The cavity that was revealed was difficult to examine because, unlike a drawer that could be pulled out, it was not easily accessible. By angling her head to one side, Cat could see there was a dark oblong at the back of the space, about the size of a book or a DVD box set. She tried to squeeze her hand into the gap, but she couldn't insinuate her arm far enough to reach whatever it was.

She stood up and fetched a hanger from the wardrobe then got down on the floor by the bottom of the chest. Using the hanger as a hook, she dragged the object towards her. When she realised it was indeed a book, her first sensation was one of disappointment. Still, she wasn't about to give up her quest until her curiosity was satisfied. She reached for the volume. Her fingers told her it was flexible, bound in soft leather, with thin pages.

Cat drew the book from its hiding place and stared at it,

open-mouthed with astonishment. That it was a copy of the Bible was not in itself remarkable. What was remarkable, however, was what appeared to be a bullet hole in the top right-hand quadrant, a bullet hole that went right through to the back cover.

Before she could open the book, there was a clap of thunder so loud and so close that Cat cried out in terror. The room was abruptly plunged into darkness and a second deafening thunderclap vibrated through the air. Cat curled into a ball and moaned softly. What terrible powers had her discovery unleashed?

23

Cat was surprised to wake up. If pressed, she'd have claimed she hadn't slept a wink since she'd felt her way across the pitch-black room and clambered into her bed. She'd lain terrified in the darkness, reading all kinds of fresh terror into the strange sounds of house and storm interacting. At one point, she'd have sworn her door knob rattled fiercely, as if someone was determined to enter. But eventually, exhaustion had overcome anxiety and she had drifted off into the level of sleep only attainable by teenagers.

'The Bible,' she exclaimed as soon as she had swum far enough into consciousness to recall her adventures of the night before. She jumped out of bed and pulled the curtains open to reveal a bright morning had succeeded the tempest of the night before. In the sparkling sunlight, the Bible lying on the rug looked innocuous enough. Until she picked it up, half-convinced her imagination had run away with her. But in the light of day, it still looked like a bullet hole. It wasn't a clean shot all the way through – it had barely torn a hole in the back cover – but Cat could think of nothing else that could have caused such an injury to the book. The density of the fine India paper must have been enough to stop the bullet.

But who would shoot a Bible? And why? She couldn't think of anything from her reading that would fit such a notion, unless it was a werewolf hunter with a silver bullet. But why would a werewolf be carrying a Bible for protection? It made no sense. And besides, Cat was pretty sure that if the Tilneys were anything, they were vampires. The clues and coincidences seemed to grow with every passing day. And the bloodstain on the drawer would seem to confirm that notion.

She clasped the book to her chest and headed back to bed. She remembered a conversation she'd had with her father about vampires. He'd been adamant that there were no such creatures, that they were not part of God's creation and she should stop reading about them. But she'd found a website that cited Bible verses to contradict her father's position. She quickly flipped to her favourite. Revelation 16:6: 'For they have shed the blood of saints and prophets, and thou hast given them blood to drink; for they are worthy.' When she'd run that one past him, he'd done that totally annoying thing of telling her she didn't understand what she was reading. Why couldn't he just admit he'd lost the argument?

Cat closed the Bible again, then, on impulse, opened the cover. Her heart jumped in her chest as she realised what she was looking at. There, in ink faded more than a dozen shades, was a list of births, marriages and deaths. The first date was 1713 and the last was 1878. The family name that ran through the records was Tilney. The Christian name of the oldest son of every generation was Henry. And unusually, those first-born

Tilneys seemed always to have made it to adulthood and families of their own. How likely was that, Cat wondered.

Unless of course there was only one and he was a vampire.

What also made no sense was that, in this generation, Henry was the younger son. Unless, because of the reckless choices made by Freddie over the years, Henry just looked younger. Who knew how much attrition two hundred years of hard living might produce?

She shivered at the thought. 'You're losing it, Catherine Morland,' she said. She climbed out of bed again and tucked the book away at the bottom of her bag. She knew she should ask Ellie or Henry about it, but she wasn't willing to go there yet. Just in case her crazy idea was right. And then they would have to kill her, she supposed.

She was about to get ready to go downstairs when she realised she'd been so excited by her discovery the night before that she hadn't bothered to replace the drawer she'd had to jiggle out of the cabinet in order to reach the cavity beneath. With sinking heart, it dawned on her that she had to put it back or risk the most embarrassing kind of discovery.

Cat knelt on the floor and picked up the drawer, shivering at the sight of the elongated triangle of rusty brown stain. She wrestled it into place, as she thought, but after a few inches, it jammed. She pulled it back and this time she tried to ease it in more gently. But again it seemed to stick on the runners.

'Soap,' she exclaimed, jumping up and retrieving the soap from the bathroom basin. She rubbed the runners with it, then for good measure, ran it up the sides of the drawer. This time, it went in almost all the way. Almost, but not quite. What was worse was that it wouldn't come out again either. It was rock solid, not budging a fraction.

Cat, who had been brought up with propriety, allowed herself to swear as volubly as she'd heard the Thorpe girls curse. It made no difference, however. Finally, she tried to force it home by closing the front doors of the cabinet. But it was hopeless. They wouldn't quite meet.

She glanced at the clock and realised she couldn't afford to waste any more time. She'd have to leave it for now and hope that neither Ellie nor Mrs Calman came in before she could fix it. Quickly she showered and dressed and hurried down to breakfast, head still buzzing with strange fancies and increasingly unlikely explanations for the Bible with the bullet hole. She found Henry alone at the table, eating toast and drinking tea.

'Morning, Cat,' he said, looking up from the bundle of papers beside his plate. 'I hope the storm didn't keep you awake? This place is so old, it creaks and rattles like a galleon under sail when we get a bad storm. We're used to it, but I imagine it must have been pretty unsettling for you?'

'Not really,' she said airily. 'I soon got used to it.' Desperate to move the conversation away from the events of the night in case she gave herself away, Cat cast about for another subject. 'What a beautiful flower arrangement,' she said, waving a hand at a tall vase of extravagantly coloured gladioli.

'Ellie brought them in from the garden this morning. She's good with flowers.'

'What kind are they?'

'Gladioli.'

Cat grinned. 'My first accomplishment of the day. I have learned to love a gladioli.'

'Gladiolus, if you want to be precise,' Henry said, mocking his own pedantry with a raised eyebrow. 'Gladioli is the plural. I'm surprised you don't know the names of all our British flora. I thought that's what young ladies were supposed to have at their fingertips?'

'Ha, ha.' Cat poured herself a cup of tea and sat at right angles to Henry.

'It's good for you to have a hobby. Gets you out in the fresh air.'

'Trust me, Henry, I don't need excuses to get out of doors. I love walking. I don't even need the dog for an excuse.'

'So . . . wouldn't it be an even richer experience if you knew what you were looking at?'

'I know the trees and the wildflowers, clever clogs. Just not all the cultivated ones.'

He made a shallow bow. 'I sit corrected. But it's good that today you learned to love a gladiolus. The habit of loving is definitely one to be cultivated.'

Before she could respond, the General marched in. 'Are you still here?' he said. Happily for Cat, it was clear he was addressing his son.

Henry glanced at his watch. 'I'm fine for time, thank you. My con isn't till noon and I've gone through all the papers.'

'Are you leaving?' Cat asked, dismayed.

'Afraid so. I have to go into chambers in Edinburgh for a meeting with a client. Then for the rest of the week I've got a case in Glasgow that's been moved up the docket.'

'Will you be using Woodston when you're on your feet in Glasgow?' the General asked.

'I thought so. It makes for a long day if I commute from here or from Edinburgh.'

The General looked across at Cat. 'We have a cottage on the banks of Loch Lomond, just outside Glasgow. Just a modest little place with four or five bedrooms, but we like it. And Henry finds it convenient to stay there when he has a case before the courts in Glasgow.'

'It's more appealing than my flat in Edinburgh.'

The General shuddered. 'Indeed. Your arrival at the bar cannot come soon enough so you can find somewhere more appropriate for a Tilney to lodge than that hovel on the Lawnmarket. The last time I visited, you didn't even have proper china.'

'Father, everybody has mugs these days. It's not a sign of debauchery and disrepute to drink tea from a mug.' Henry's smile had the uncertainty of a man who is not sure whether he's tweaking the tail of a cat or a tiger.

The General harrumphed. 'I'm sure Catherine has higher standards. Observe,' he said, raising an empty porcelain cup to the light. 'You see, Catherine, how the light makes this fine china seem to glow? You pour tea into a cup like this and the very liquid itself brightens. I freely admit, I'm something of a perfectionist when it comes to the vessel I choose to drink my tea from. It must be as fine as possible, yet strong and heat-retaining. It's an endless quest, to find the perfect cup.' He lowered the cup and gazed reverently at it.

Deciding this was quite the maddest conversation she'd ever had, Cat thought it wisest to humour him. 'That must have made life hard for you when you were in the army.'

He stiffened. 'I suppose it must seem trivial, when all around me men were sacrificing their lives.'

'No, that's not what I meant,' Cat said desperately.

'But you're right. I suppose that, having endured those hardships, I decided that in future I would have only the best in the areas that matter to me. And so I seek out the finest porcelain money can buy. I imagine you are accustomed to beautiful things when you dine with the Allens?'

'They don't go in for porcelain; they have hand-painted Italian earthenware. It's very pretty but it's quite heavy. Not delicate like your beautiful china.'

He gave her an indulgent smile. 'Alas, not everyone is blessed with an aesthetic instinct.' He turned abruptly to Henry and said, 'I really think it's time you were away.'

Henry dipped his head in resignation and stood up. 'I'll be gone three days at the very most. See you soon, Cat.'

And he was gone, leaving her to the conversational delights of the General. 'It's a lovely little cottage, Woodston,' he said. 'When I bought it, the grounds were a wilderness, but I found a local chap who's good with vegetables and now we have a delightful little walled kitchen garden. Whenever we're going over there, I call him and he stocks the larder with game and fish, so we are virtually self-sufficient. In fact it would be a perfectly charming home for Henry if he chose not to work at the bar, and I can assure you there's no need for him to have a job in order to live. Now, you might think it odd that in a family with as much profitable land as ours, I should send my sons out to work. But I think it is important for a young man to have some employment. It's not about the money, it's about gaining experience of the world. Money only matters insofar as it allows me to promote the happiness of my children. But there is more than one way to do that. And so even Freddie, who will inherit substantial property, is out in the world earning a living among ordinary men.'

It was an unanswerable argument. But Cat saw in it an opportunity. 'And Ellie too? Girls need careers as well. I'm thinking of training as a nanny. Not least because it's the only way to have money of my own that I can be proud of earning. Surely Ellie should go out into the world like her brothers? I know she'd love to go to art college.'

A flash of annoyance lit the General's face. 'I'm not sure I see the point of that. She has some money of her own, I give her an allowance. She will settle down in due course with a suitable young man. You don't need training for that.'

Cat flourished what she thought was a convincing argument. 'But she should gain experience of the world, surely? So that she doesn't settle for the wrong bloke because she doesn't know any better?'

'Surely that is the job of a father? To make sure the man his daughter marries is up to the mark?'

Cat giggled. 'That's all very well, General. But you might not have the same taste in men as your daughter.'

His eyebrows rose alarmingly and for a moment she thought she had gone too far. But he gave a strained laugh and poured himself a fresh cup of tea. 'I think you said yesterday that you wanted to see over the house and the grounds?'

'Yes, I'd love that. Ellie said we could do that this morning.'

'I shall take charge of the expedition myself,' he said grandly. Her heart sank but she smiled bravely. He glanced out of the window, where thin streaks of cloud were spreading across the sky, erasing the earlier brightness. 'The forecast is for it to be hot and sunny this afternoon, so I propose we take advantage of the cooler air and go outside now, this morning, before the sun beats down and makes walking uncomfortable.'

This seemed to Cat, who loved to be outside in sunny weather, to be the opposite of good sense. Unless of course one was a vampire. But vampire or not, there would be no changing the General's mind once he was set upon something. 'Lovely,' she said.

'Excellent,' he said, rising from the table and marching to the door. 'I'll have Mrs Calman tell Eleanor to present herself at once.'

Cat sighed and helped herself to more toast. She'd been looking forward to a long, gossipy morning with Ellie, perhaps ending with a trip up the hill to the Calmans' house, where they could sit on the windowsill and catch up with Facebook and Twitter. Or a walk with Henry where he could instruct her in the finer points of what she was looking at. Instead, there would doubtless be another one of the General's bizarre lectures.

Just then, Ellie burst into the room, still tucking her blouse into her jeans. 'Sorry, sorry,' she said. 'That bloody storm kept me awake half the night, then when I finally got off, I slept like the dead.' She caught sight of the used cup and dirty crockery in her brother's place. 'Have I missed Henry?'

'He's gone to Edinburgh. Then he's got a case in Glasgow,' Cat said. 'He's going to stay at Woodston.'

'Drat. Oh well, I'll just have to phone him and get him to invite us over for dinner. You'll love it, it has the most fabulous views over Loch Lomond. By yon bonnie banks, and all that.'

She grabbed a banana and gobbled it quickly. 'Ten minutes, he wants us in the hall in ten minutes. If you need a jacket or anything, best run now and get it.'

Cat swallowed the final piece of toast and headed upstairs to clean her teeth and put on some more substantial shoes. She had no great expectations of the morning, but it would surely be far less pleasant if it started with a scolding for being late.

The three of them met in the hall and the General marched them off at a brisk pace from the front door. Cat formed an impression of paths intelligently laid out, weaving between well-tended shrubberies and surprising secret gardens tucked round corners. After about ten minutes of gentle climbing on a path of fine pink gravel, the General stopped and ordered them to turn round.

Cat gasped. From their vantage point, the abbey was visible in all its grandeur. She didn't need any guide, not even Henry, to explain its splendour to her. The whole building enclosed a large central courtyard she hadn't realised existed. Two sides of the quadrangle were clearly visible, their flying buttresses, lancet windows and circular towers with pointed roofs plugging directly into her fantasies of the sort of place the Hebridean Harpies would happily haunt. A stand of Scotch pines and rhododendrons obscured the other two sides, though the gentle breeze revealed occasional glimpses of red sandstone that hinted at what lay beyond. A couple of matching turrets could just be discerned. From one, the blue-and-white Scottish Saltire waved limp in the faint air. Nothing she had ever seen spoke to her deepest imaginings like this. The Morlands had visited all the local stately homes their National Trust membership granted them access to, but none had stirred her like Northanger Abbey.

'It's gorgeous,' she exclaimed. 'How lucky you are to live here. Oh, it's just the most glorious house I've ever clapped eyes on.'

The General's expression was smug. 'We think so. Like all the Borders abbeys, it was built to the glory of God, but I do believe we've managed to improve on that.'

'The monks didn't have plumbing,' Ellie said. 'Come on, I want to show you the kitchen garden. I love it because every time you walk in, something has changed. Something has budded or ripened or been picked.' She led the way over the lip of the rise to reveal a vast walled garden.

'There's enough stone in that wall to build half a dozen houses,' the General said, opening a door and ushering them inside.

The area under cultivation stretched so far Cat could barely discern the far wall. It was bigger than the vicarage garden, the churchyard and the Silver Jubilee field all rolled into one. There were vegetable beds, soft fruit canes, and fruit trees espaliered to the walls. A long line of glass houses stretched down the middle of the garden, triffid-like leaves visible wherever she looked. There must be enough produce here to feed an entire village, Cat thought.

'I love a garden,' the General said.

'This is a plantation, not a garden,' Cat said. 'Wow.'

'It's not been the best of summers,' the General said. 'We've scarcely had fifty pineapples. You don't have gardens like this down in Dorset? You surprise me. I'd have thought the Allens would have led the way in this sort of thing.'

'They've only got one greenhouse, and Susie mostly uses that to overwinter her plants. I don't think they're very interested in gardening. My dad's got an allotment, though. He keeps us going in potatoes and onions all through the winter.'

'How lovely,' he said with a look of happy contempt.

The first blush of amazement soon wore off, as the General conducted them through every nook and cranny of the garden. When he paused for breath, Ellie added her occasional comments, which had the benefit of brevity. At length, another door in the wall came into sight. The General was droning on about wanting to check the gazebo but Cat edged towards the door. Ellie caught her eye and said, 'Let's go back down the lime-tree walk.'

The General flinched as if she'd flicked grit in his eye. 'Why do you want to go that way? The ground's sticky with the gum that drips from the leaves, and it'll be damp after the storm.'

'It's fine, Father. You go and check on the gazebo and I'll take Cat back to the house.'

He glowered. 'I don't know why anyone would want to go down that miserable avenue. I should have the lot of them chopped down and replaced with something more suitable. Cypress or plane trees.'

Ellie looked suddenly furious. 'Don't say that. Don't ever say that.'

It was the first time Cat had ever heard her friend stand up to the General and for a moment she was rooted to the spot as Ellie flung the door open and practically ran out of the garden. Then she gave him an uncertain smile and chased after her friend.

She caught up with her a few yards ahead. Ellie had stopped

and was breathing in deep gulps out of all proportion to the distance she'd run. Cat put her arm round her friend's heaving shoulders, looking back in time to catch the General watching them before he closed the door. 'What's the matter?' she asked.

'He's so harsh sometimes,' Ellie managed to get out. She took one final gulp and somehow recovered herself. 'This was my mother's favourite walk.' She waved an arm that encompassed the avenue of limes, so mature they almost met in the middle. 'I used to wonder why she chose so gloomy a part of the garden, but she said it always made her feel like a character in a Jane Austen novel. There's a bench down there where we'd sit and she'd recite that Coleridge poem. Do you know it? "Well, they are gone, and here must I remain, this lime-tree bower my prison!" It was our little private joke when my father went off to do something adventurous with the boys.'

It struck Cat as peculiar that the General was so hostile towards a place his late wife had loved so much. So hostile that he wanted to destroy it. 'Anywhere that was so dear to her must bring you closer to her,' she said.

Ellie sighed as they set off down the avenue. 'It does. I sometimes think I miss her more now than I did when she died. It's like I don't have anybody to show me how to be a woman, if that makes sense? I've got friends my own age—' She gave Cat's arm a squeeze. 'But it's not the same as having a mother to turn to. She was always here for me. We never ran out of things to talk about. We would have been proper companions as I grew older. Instead, I'm stuck here on my own a lot these days.'

'What was she like? I mean, to look at? I haven't seen any family photos around the place.'

'She was beautiful. I don't take after her. Father put all the family photos away after she died. He couldn't bear to be reminded of her.'

Cat couldn't understand that. Surely if you loved someone, you'd want to remember what they looked like? You'd want to go to the places they loved to remind yourself of them, wouldn't you? If he didn't love her garden refuge, how could he have loved her? The look on his face just then had been so grim – not the pained face of a lover deprived of the object of his affections. 'I suppose he has pictures of her in his room?'

Ellie shook her head. 'She sat for her portrait the year before she died. It was supposed to be hung in the drawing room but Father said it wasn't good enough. After she died, I found it wrapped up in sacking in the junk attic and I hung it in my bedroom. I love it and so does Henry. I'll show you, if you like.'

The rejected portrait was, in Cat's eyes, another proof of the General's disdain for his wife. And what would a vampire do to a wife he no longer loved? Would a disease of the blood be the perfect cover? Was she a vampire too? And could one vampire kill another from their family group? Was that allowed? And if not, where was Mrs Tilney now?

Cat had shifted from being uncomfortable and uneasy with the General to positively disliking him. How could he have taken against the woman that Ellie found so completely lovable? She'd read about people like that, people with hearts of stone and no compassion for others. Mr Allen used to tease her when she spoke of such things, saying they were exaggerated. But now she knew better than he.

Cat had just settled this point in her mind when the end of the lime-tree walk brought them face-to-face with the General.

She wanted to show her dislike, but her mother's voice lectured her on the obligations of a guest. So she swallowed her disdain and responded in monosyllables. His response was unexpected. 'I think we've given poor Catherine too much to take in at once,' he said, apparently solicitous. 'You girls should have a rest before lunch. And afterwards I'll show you round the abbey, Catherine.'

'There's no need for you to give up your time,' she said. 'I know you've got more important things to do than give me a guided tour. Ellie can show me around, and if there's anything she can't tell me about, I can always ask you later.'

But he was insistent. After a light lunch, he would gladly give up his time to share his home with her. It was almost as if he was afraid to let anyone else show her round the abbey. She couldn't help wondering whether he had something he desperately wanted to hide.

24

Back at the abbey, Cat went upstairs to change her shoes, followed by Ellie, who seemed to have overcome her reluctance to enter the guest room. The pair were deep in conversation but Ellie stopped in mid-sentence, staring at the bed. 'Where did you get that?' she demanded, pointing at the quilt.

Cat felt a blush rise up her throat. 'I was cold during the storm. I thought there might be blankets in that.' She pointed at the black japanned chest. 'I opened it and I found the quilt. Did I do something wrong?'

Ellie twisted her hand in her hair. 'That was the last quilt my mother made. I haven't seen it for years. I didn't know it was in here. Mrs Calman must have put it in the chest.' She drew in a ragged breath.

'I'm sorry.'

'No, you didn't do anything wrong.' Ellie managed a wan smile. 'I'm happy to see it being used. So many things of my mother's were put away after she died. It's good to see that again. I can remember her working on it.'

Again, Cat felt anger rising against the man who had

apparently turned so far against his wife that he didn't want her children to have any talismans to keep her memory fresh. If he could be so cruel to his children, how cruel had he been to his wife? 'Why don't you take it back to your room?' she said. 'Then it would be a constant reminder.'

Ellie's face lit up, then doubt chased the delight away. 'But what if you're cold in the night again?'

'I'll ask Mrs Calman for an extra blanket. I'm sure she's got whole bales of them tucked away somewhere.'

Ellie threw her arms round Cat and kissed her cheek. 'You're the best, Cat. I can't believe this has been right under my nose all the time.'

It would have been the perfect opportunity for Cat to ask about the other item that had been right under her nose, but something made her hold back. It was the only piece of evidence she had that all was not as it seemed with the Tilneys, and she'd read enough books and seen enough films to know she shouldn't relinquish it without good reason.

Just as she reached that conclusion, Ellie's eye was caught by the improperly closed cabinet. She crossed the room and went to shut it. 'I've got a confession to make,' Cat said. 'I searched the rest of the cabinet and that bottom drawer stuck when I was closing it.' She held her breath, expecting a horrified reaction.

Ellie just grinned. 'I'll get Calman to fix it. He's a good handyman. Don't worry about it.'

But Cat was not reassured. Either Calman was in on the secret, in which case he would be suspicious of what she had noticed. Or he wasn't, and then he'd wonder why she'd said nothing about a strange bloodstain. Mentally, Cat shook herself. There was nothing she could do to avert either possibility so there was no point in worrying. Better to concentrate on keeping things right between her and Ellie.

Until it was time for lunch, they sat cross-legged on Cat's bed and read to each other their favourite passages from the Hebridean Harpies books. In spite of the daylight streaming through the high windows, they managed to generate equal amounts of fear and laughter. On their way down to lunch, Ellie took the quilt to her room, then they girded their loins for the General again.

Lunch featured a lecture on the landscaping of the park and the creation of the walled garden. Just when Cat thought she would pass out with the tedium of it all, the General wiped his mouth with his napkin and stood up. 'Time for the house,' he said briskly, looking over his shoulder on his way to the door as if he expected them to fall in behind him in single file. Cat was not taken in. However grand his gait, however dignified his bearing, her reading had opened her eyes to the possibility that it was all a pretence.

They processed through the hall, through the drawing room they'd already used before and after meals, through a small room that had once been a smoking room but now lacked purpose, into a grand drawing room that was a match for the one in Ainslie Place. Again, the furniture was surprisingly modern, and although the General gave her a blow-by-blow account of each piece and its designer, Cat could not have been less interested. If he was trying to put her off the scent, he'd failed. She'd seen the Twilight films and she knew you could have the latest in designer clothes and furniture and still be a vampire. You didn't have to wear period costume and live in a museum.

The next room was the library, where Cat's interest was genuinely aroused. As the General boasted his way round the shelves, she hung back and tried to gain a sense of what was stored in this warehouse of knowledge. History, natural history, political economy, travel writing and scientific treatises were what caught her eye, but as they progressed, she was inevitably drawn to fiction shelves that contained dozens of leather-bound editions of the great Scottish writers, from Burns and Henryson through Sir Walter Scott to more recent titles that had clearly come from the bespoke bookbinder. She didn't imagine for a moment that the novels of Muriel Spark and Ali Smith had been originally published in matching soft pale leather. 'These books are, like, wow,' she said to Ellie, robbed of her articulacy by their desirability.

'I've never begrudged a penny spent on books,' the General said. 'A book is the means by which a man can better himself.'

'Or a woman,' Cat said.

He gave her a condescending smile. 'Indeed. But we have to press on, or we'll never get through the place. Feel free to come in here any time you want to borrow a book,' he added, magnanimous to the last.

To Cat's surprise, there was rather less of the abbey than she'd expected. The central courtyard, whose extent had been unsuspected until she'd seen the view from the hill above, constrained the available living quarters. They moved through a kitchen in a blur of modern appliances, where Ellie paused only to ask Mrs Calman to provide Cat with another blanket. The rest of the third side of the courtyard held more promise for Cat's fantasies. It was a maze of narrow passages and small rooms, dismissed by the General as storerooms, utility rooms, mud rooms, a gun room, and larders. 'This was the cloister, you see,' he informed her. 'These small rooms were the monks' cells. We've never needed them for accommodation, so they're the closest thing to original you'll find here in the abbey.'

The fourth side of the cloister was a surprise. Inside the ancient exterior stone walls, almost everything had been demolished, leaving a vast billiard room, a fully equipped gym and the General's office. Cat barely had time to glance inside the room, stuffed with state-of-the-art technology, before he closed it, the lock clicking firmly into place. 'The interior was a disgrace,' the General said. 'The best thing for it was to knock it down and start again.' Cat regretted the loss of mysterious antiquity, but even she had to admit the rooms had been well constructed.

Back in the hall, they climbed the stairs and the General led the way down the guest wing. There were three other suites of rooms apart from her lodgings. They had all been handsomely fitted out, with no expense spared in furnishings, décor or bathrooms. Cat could imagine nothing that would improve the rooms and she said so. The General took this as his cue to list the distinguished visitors they had entertained at the abbey. When it came to the dropping of names, Cat recalled Shakespeare's description of mercy dropping like the gentle rain from above. Though there was nothing gentle about the persistence of the General's listing of notable visitors. Politicians, generals, political commentators, Lord This and the Earl of That. They had all been made welcome at Northanger. 'And of course,' he added magnanimously, 'we look forward to receiving our new friends, the Allens, before too long.' It was a generous invitation, and Cat almost regretted the impossibility of thinking well of this cruel man who seemed better disposed towards her and her friends than his own family.

They returned to the main landing and the General nodded down the central corridor. Ellie had gone ahead of them and threw wide the modern–looking double doors that closed off the far part of the hallway. 'What are you doing?' the General shouted at her. 'There's nothing to be shown off down there.' Mortified, Ellie pulled the doors closed, but not before Cat caught a tantalising glimpse of what lay beyond.

'Catherine, I'm sure you must be ready for some tea now? Let's go downstairs and see what Mrs Calman can rustle up.' The General hustled her downstairs. Once he had them settled in the small drawing room, he strode off towards the kitchens.

Eagerly, Cat drew close to Ellie on the sofa. She'd caught sight of more doorways and, in the distance, a stone stairway climbing and descending one of the massive stone turrets that sat at each corner of the abbey. She was desperate to know what it was that the General wanted kept from her. At that moment, she would rather have been allowed to examine that half–corridor than everything else the General had shown her. 'Is that where you keep the prisoners?' she asked Ellie, hiding her curiosity in frivolity.

'No, they're all in the dungeons,' Ellie joked back. 'It's more soundproof down there. No, I was going to take you into what was my mother's room. Where she . . . where she died. Not that there's any sign of that,' she added quickly.

No wonder the General had reacted so fiercely. He wouldn't want to confront his part in the death of his wife, whatever that might have been. Neglect, cruelty or even murder, it didn't matter in the aftermath. She imagined he'd never been able to re-enter the room since the dreadful scene which released the suffering woman and left him to the stings of his conscience. Unless, of course, there had been no such scene and he'd simply made a prisoner of her elsewhere in the abbey. An even more chilling prospect, somehow.

'Maybe you could show me another time? Just the two of us?'

Ellie nodded uncertainly. 'We'll do it when Father's out of the house. And Mrs Calman's busy in the kitchen.'

'I suppose it's a kind of shrine to your mother's memory? Where your father can go to think about her?' Cat was fishing now, but she didn't think Ellie would take offence if she noticed.

'It's exactly as it was. But I don't think Father ever goes in. It has such painful memories.'

'You were with her till the very end, then? All of you?'

'No,' Ellie sighed. 'None of us realised the end was so close. Henry and I were both away at school and Freddie was at Sandhurst. Father sent for us, but by the time we got here, it was all over.'

Cat's suspicions hardened into certainties. There were only two possibilities. Could it be? Could General Tilney, vampire, also be General Tilney, murderer? Or kidnapper? He was Henry's father. Could she love a man who was the son of a killer? Could she have a murderer's daughter for her best friend? It was a terrible thought, but it made complete sense of everything she had observed in his behaviour. She put an arm round her friend and patted Ellie's knee sympathetically.

The door opened and Mrs Calman wheeled in a trolley loaded with tea and home baking. The two girls moved swiftly apart.

The housekeeper was followed by the General, who seemed preoccupied. While the girls drank tea and made short work of scones and pancakes, he paced up and down, holding his teacup and saucer delicately as he walked.

Eventually, he paused and gave Cat a rueful smile. 'You must think me the rudest host,' he said. 'But Mrs Calman has just passed on a message that has given me a great deal to consider. I'm going to leave you girls to it and get to work. I've got papers to read and a response to prepare for the ministry. I'll have supper in my office, so you might want to have a dinner tray up in your own sitting room? I'll organise it with Mrs Calman.' And abruptly he left them.

'Wow,' Cat said. 'Is he usually so intense?'

Ellie nodded. 'God, yes. He stays up till all hours in his office, reading whatever top secret stuff they send him and writing reports.'

It didn't feel very likely to Cat. Why would a retired general be in so much demand? Surely there were plenty of guys still running around in uniform who were up to speed on present-day conditions and weapons? What was so special about somebody whose war had been thirty years ago? But what if Mrs Tilney was indeed a prisoner in one of the towers? His supposed work for the ministry would be the perfect cover. What if the General waited till everyone was asleep and the Calmans in their own house, then crept up the stairs to feed his supposedly dead wife and enact his terrible cruelties on her? Now, more than ever, she wanted to explore the corridor that stretched behind those double doors. Because, now she thought about it, the forbidden gallery must turn a corner and stretch above the General's very office. Perhaps there was a secret passage. A house like Northanger should be riddled with them.

Cat wanted to leap to her feet and uncover the truth of the hidden rooms at once, but she had the good sense to know she must be patient. She would wait till Ellie had taken her to see Mrs Tilney's room, using that as a sort of reconnaissance trip for her own secret exploration. She could wait, couldn't she?

The young women passed a pleasant evening in their sitting room. When Ellie discovered at tea that Cat had never seen *Sex and the City*, she insisted her friend couldn't live another day without it. And as she predicted, Cat was gripped from the first episode. They watched the whole six hours of the first series, finishing practically on the stroke of midnight.

Revved up by the delights of the TV series, Cat's mind was still active as she prepared for bed. What if Mrs Tilney really was a prisoner? Cat might have been within feet of the poor woman's cell as the General showed her round the house. Those massive stone walls would muffle any sound of captivity. She recalled those arched passages of the maze of small rooms beyond the kitchen. Who knew what was going on there?

Her imagination conjured up a vision of the General carrying his unconscious wife through concealed doors and secret stairways to her new lodging, away from the eyes of her children, where he could use her as he pleased. Perhaps she was his secret source of blood, the one he could slake his thirst on so he was able to be safe around other humans.

Her father had often told Cat that she allowed her imagination to carry her away. But how else was she supposed to react when such powerful evidence was laid out before her? Something odd was going on at Northanger Abbey, and she was determined to find out what it was. Tomorrow, her quest would continue.

25

Cat's eagerness to turn detective next morning was unintentionally thwarted by the General. At breakfast, he informed the young women that he would be unavailable to escort them anywhere since he was hosting an important meeting of key strategists. 'We will be using the main drawing room all day, I'm afraid.' He glanced out of the window, where the sun was vainly trying to make its way through thin cloud. 'The forecast is for a cool day without rain. I suggest you have Mrs Calman make you up a packed lunch, Eleanor, and take Catherine on a hike up the Devil's Hump.'

'The Devil's Hump?' Cat was startled and it showed. The General grinned as widely as she'd ever seen, his teeth glittering.

'The hill you can see from the grounds,' Ellie explained. 'There's a local legend. Apparently the Devil came down to Kelso to steal some cattle. But a brave young cowherd raised the alarm and they chased him back to the cleft of hell he'd carved into the hillside. Just as he was about to disappear, the brave young cowherd jumped on his back. And the cleft closed behind the Devil, leaving his hump and the cowherd behind.'

'Pretty standard nonsense,' the General said. 'People will make up any old rubbish when they come across things they can't explain, from a peculiarly shaped hill to a meteor shower.'

Whether it was nothing more than legend, the story of the Devil's Hump was sufficiently exciting for Cat to be more sanguine about not having the chance to explore the abbey's mysteries. She had no walking boots with her, but she and Ellie had the same size feet and her host was able to kit her out with an old pair of hiking shoes. 'There's not much ankle support,' she apologised. 'But they'll protect your feet better than trainers.'

They hung around the kitchen while Mrs Calman packed substantial picnics, and Cat marvelled at the array of appliances. There was everything from a breadmaker to an ice-cream machine, including three different coffee makers. Some of the devices were incomprehensible to her and she was too shy of Mrs Calman to ask their purpose. It was hard to believe this temple to the preparation of food sheltered under the same label as Annie Morland's domain back in Dorset. Cat couldn't imagine sitting round the table here with a tumbler of squash, talking about the latest book she'd read.

With the picnics stowed in a couple of daypacks, the two young women set out, leaving by the kitchen door. Cat couldn't resist looking over her shoulder at the turret with the stair she'd glimpsed the day before. 'Do you ever go up the turrets?'

'Three of them are sealed off because the stairs aren't safe and Father says there's no point in spending what it would cost to repair or replace them. It's not as if there are lots of rooms you could use. They only ever had one proper room, right at the top.' Ellie struck off across the park at a steady pace.

'What about the fourth one?'

'You can only climb up another twenty feet or so, then it's closed off with a gate. We used to play up there when we were kids, but Father had the gate put in because he thought the stairs were too dodgy and he didn't want some visitor falling down and killing themselves.'

Her words only fuelled Cat's curiosity. But there was nothing to be gained until she could see the secret corridor for herself. Instead, she concentrated on enjoying the scenery as they climbed steadily through the park. Soon they entered a dark stand of conifers that scarcely let through enough light to trace their path. It was strange and even spooky; when they occasionally emerged into a clearing, Cat couldn't help wondering what macabre rituals it might have seen. At length they cleared the trees and reached a deer fence. Cat paused to catch her breath while Ellie undid the combination lock that held the tall gate fast.

Once through the gate, they were in open moorland. Ellie led the way along a faint path which climbed the Devil's Hump in a gentle spiral. As they rounded the hill, Cat caught sight of a pitched roof. 'What's that?' she asked.

'You'll see soon enough,' Ellie said, turning into a narrow cleft in the hillside. Cat followed her and found herself staring at a tiny red sandstone church surrounded by weathered gravestones.

'What is it?' she asked again.

'It's the Tilney family chapel. The path we've just been walking on, it's called a lyke-wake walk. It's the route the coffin is carried from the house to the chapel so it can be laid to rest here in the graveyard.'

'You're using the present tense,' Cat said.

'That's because we still do it. This is where we brought my mother. Father and Henry and Freddie and Calman carried the coffin.'

'Doesn't it freak you out, coming here?' Cat hung back as Ellie set off for the chapel.

Ellie looked back. 'Why should it? It's where we come to remember our dead. You're a vicar's daughter, you should understand the importance of memorials.' She gestured for Cat to follow. Reluctantly, she caught up and entered the chapel just behind Ellie.

It was a small, plain place with narrow wooden pews and frosted-glass windows. On the wall were several memorial plaques to various Tilney ancestors, dating back to the fifteenth century. Ellie was right, it wasn't freaking her out at all. Cat approached the freshest-looking plaque, an ornately carved memorial to Margaret Johanna Tilney. It gave her dates and beneath them, a single line of chiselled lettering: *Taken from us too soon.*

No wonder General Tilney had wanted Ellie to bring her here without him. This was no proof of his wife's demise, but being in the presence of her memorial would surely provoke a guilty reaction, whether he had had a hand in her death or her continued captivity. No man could fail to react in such circumstances. 'It's very moving,' she said.

'I like to come up here and remember her,' Ellie said. She gave her shoulders a little shake and said, 'Come on, let's carry on to the summit. We'll have our picnic up there.'

As they left the graveyard, Ellie casually pointed out her mother's headstone. Beneath her name and dates, it read,

Beloved wife of General Henry Tilney, mother to Frederick, Henry and Eleanor. We miss you every day.

They clambered up the hill and enjoyed the view while they worked their way through the minor feast that Mrs Calman had packed for them. Cat lay back on the warm grass and groaned. 'Thank God it's downhill all the way, because you're going to have to roll me down. How come you're not as fat as a barrel, living on Mrs C's cooking all the time?'

'It's tough,' Ellie said. 'I'm making the most of it while I'm home this time. I'm still holding out hope that Father will change his mind and let me go to art school in Edinburgh.'

'That would be so cool. You're lucky to have qualifications to do something like that. I've got a bunch of GCSEs but I didn't even bother sitting A-levels. You couldn't call what Mum taught me a curriculum.'

'What do you want to do?'

'Mum thinks I should train as a nanny, but I'd quite like to be a writer,' she said. 'Not for grown-ups, for kids. I'm really good at making up stories for the kids in the village. And I do the storytelling at Junior Church. Hey, you could be my illustrator!'

'That'd be fun. Maybe we could try to start one while you're here?'

'Yes, why not?'

Buoyed up with the idea of a joint project, Cat and Ellie made it back to Northanger Abbey in record time. Judging by the four substantial black cars parked outside, the meeting was still going strong, so they ran straight upstairs. 'I want a quick shower before we begin,' Ellie said as they reached the top of the stairs.

'Me too. But before we do that – your dad's obviously still tied up with his buddies. Why don't we take our chance? You could show me your mother's room.'

Ellie looked uncertain. 'I suppose. Look, why don't you come to my room first, then I can show you her portrait.' Clearly, she hoped this would be enough to assuage Cat's curiosity. Equally clearly, she did not know her friend as well as she thought.

They scuttled along the landing and turned into the kids' corridor, as Cat had come to think of it. Ellie's room was the second on the right and Cat was enchanted by it. The colours were different tones of lavender and cream, everything blending like a Pantone chart. Watercolours were pinned all over the walls; some landscapes, some seascapes and some of buildings and cities Cat didn't recognise. Oddly for the room of a teenage girl, there was no mirror on display for Cat to check whether her hostess had a reflection. But at the heart of the room, impossible to avoid, was a large oil painting of a woman. She had a mild and pensive face, fine featured with large blue eyes and a sweep of honey-blonde hair. 'She's lovely,' Cat said.

'Yes. I wish I looked like her.'

Cat couldn't help recalling what she'd learned from her reading about vampire 'families'. They were often loose-knit groups who had chosen to live together over the centuries because they were less visible in a family group. So Margaret Tilney wasn't necessarily the biological mother of any of the children. Given that she had a separate bedroom from her husband, they may not have been married. Perhaps she wasn't even his lover; perhaps that was the bone of contention that had led to her imprisonment.

The major flaw in this imaginative view of the Tilneys, which

Cat appeared to have mislaid in all her imaginings, was that vampire families had to keep moving because eventually their neighbours and colleagues noticed that nobody in the family seemed to age at the normal rate. Every dozen years or so, they had to disappear and start again. But the Tilneys had been in one place for a very long time and although the men retired from public life at a relatively youthful age, it would still have been hard to fool the whole of the Scottish Borders indefinitely. But no young woman has ever allowed reality to stand in the way of her romantic fantasies, and in this respect, Cat was no exception to the rule.

'You're beautiful too, Ellie. Just in a different way.' Cat put her arm round Ellie's shoulders and squeezed. 'And now I can picture what she looked like, why don't you show me her room so I have her really fixed in my mind's eye.'

Ellie let herself be steered out of the room and down the gallery. They turned into the middle corridor and passed the General's room. Ellie paused at the double doors and Cat feared she'd have to make the unthinkable bad-guest-move and open them herself. Then all at once, they were outside Mrs Tilney's door. Ellie took an audible breath and reached for the handle, while Cat, hardly able to breathe at all, turned back to shut the gallery doors behind them.

In that instant, the dreaded figure of the General appeared outlined against the light from the gallery. Before Cat could even groan a warning, the General barked, 'Eleanor,' in his best parade-ground voice. It bounced off the stone walls, tiny echoes ringing in Cat's ears. For a split second she hoped she might have escaped his notice, but knew at once it was a forlorn hope.

'Fuck,' Ellie muttered and took off at top speed down the hall. Father and daughter disappeared and Cat took the opportunity to sprint back to her own room, relieved not to see another soul. She didn't know whether she'd ever dare to leave her room again. But at least she would be clean if she had to leave in disgrace.

Standing in the shower as the water cascaded over her head, Cat resolved that she'd have to get into that room tonight, in case it occurred to the General to lock it up. For all she knew, he'd already done that.

She couldn't stay in the shower for ever, and when she finally returned to her bedroom, she'd scarcely rubbed a towel over her hair when there was a timid knock at the door. Making sure the towel was firmly wrapped around her, Cat cautiously inched the door open. Ellie stood there, looking on the verge of tears. 'Can I come in?' she said.

'Course you can.' Cat threw the door wide and welcomed her with a hug. 'Are we in deep shit?'

'Not as much as I thought. He's so distracted with his meeting he hardly told me off at all. He just wanted to make sure I was spruced up and changed—' She gestured at her little black dress. 'They're having cocktails before dinner. You're required too, I'm sorry.'

Cat looked at her in dismay. 'I haven't got anything like that to wear.'

'I did wonder. It's not really your style. Look, we're about the same size. Well, you're bigger in the bust than me, but we can get round that with the right fabric. I'll lend you something of mine.'

Half an hour later, Cat was squeezed into a ruby velvet dress.

The ruched material hid the fact that it was styled for a different shape and although she felt incredibly self-conscious, none of the four middle-aged men drinking cocktails seemed to pay her much attention. She and Ellie were clearly there for decorative purposes only, and they were able to escape when the men went into dinner. They retreated upstairs to more *Sex and the City*, but that night it was closer to eleven when they separated, worn out by emotion and exercise in the open air.

As she walked back to her room, Cat heard hearty male voices in the hall below and from her window she saw the headlights of four cars disappear down the drive. In the light of an almost full moon, the park looked eerie but empty. Would the General go straight to bed or would he go to his office? She'd have been willing to bet he wouldn't be ready for bed yet. He had the habit of working late, she knew, and she imagined he would want to make his notes on the lengthy conversations of the day immediately, while they were fresh in his mind. She cracked open her door and listened hard. For once, there were none of the sounds of the building creaking and settling that she'd grown accustomed to in the short time she'd been at Northanger.

Cat slipped off her shoes and moved cautiously down the hall. At the dog-leg she paused, holding her breath, and peered round the corner. The gallery was empty, and the silence persisted. She seized her courage in both hands and raced to the double doors as fast as she could. She opened them, slipped through and gently closed them behind her. She leaned against them for a moment, heart hammering. Was there any sign of pursuit? The only thing she could hear was the beating of blood in her ears.

She inched forward in the dark, feeling for the door handle.

After a few seconds, her hand closed round the knob and she twisted it open. The door swung silently back and in an instant she was inside. Moonlight illuminated the chamber through an array of arched windows that looked vaguely ecclesiastical and reminded Cat of the origins of the building. Although it bled most of the colour out of carpets, curtains and other soft furnishings, it was clear to Cat that this was no punishment cell. It looked like any other bedroom she'd seen in the abbey, except that it contained the small traces of individual habitation that were absent from the guest rooms – a hairbrush on the dressing table, a book and a pair of glasses at the bedside, a bottle of perfume beside them.

There were two other doors in the room. One led to a bathroom that had been stripped of toiletries and medication, the other to a dressing room bereft of clothing. It seemed that all but a few traces of Mrs Tilney had been removed from the room, either to save the General from painful reminders or else to cover his tracks. Then Cat thought of a third possibility. If Mrs Tilney were indeed a prisoner in the tower, she would need clothes and toiletries, no matter what the General's purpose for her.

Clearly there was nothing to learn here. There was nothing for it but to explore the turret. Luckily she had a spotlight app for her phone which would light her way up the stone spiral that rose inside the turret. Cat crept back to the door and pressed an ear to the wood. She could hear nothing, so she cracked it open and listened again. In the distance, she heard a faint noise that might have been a door closing but it was too far away for her to worry.

Cat edged the door open and slipped through. Darkness

again engulfed her as she silently pulled the door to and let the latch slip back into place. She tiptoed down the hall then turned on the bright screen of her phone app. It created an eerie glow, splashing shadows up the walls. But it provided a decent light to climb the stone stairs, so old and worn that each step had a depression in the middle.

Within a few seconds she had rounded the first turn in the spiral. She heard a scrabbling by her feet. Cat stifled a shriek and splashed the light downwards to reveal a tiny grey mouse paralysed with fear. Annoyed with herself, she shone the light upwards again. Ahead of her were more steps but now she could see the way ahead was blocked by a set of iron railings like an old fashioned prison cell, fastened with a heavy galvanised padlock. Cat crept closer, studying the padlock in the phone light. She didn't know whether to be relieved or disappointed at the cobwebs and dust that festooned the padlock and the nearby bars. It was clear that nobody had disturbed it in a very long time.

Then all at once noise and light seemed to fill the hallway. Swift footsteps clattered up stairs and a bright overhead light bathed her in its brilliance. Even if she'd had time to make her escape, Cat was frozen with fear. The General was coming. The General would not, could not let her get away.

She had never known such paralysing horror. Her legs trembled beneath her and somehow she managed to turn her head. The long shadow of a man was cast into the stairwell ahead of the person himself and she felt her throat close in panic. No weapon, no escape. She was entirely at his mercy.

26

The man who appeared in the stairway looked almost as shaken as Cat herself. 'What the hell are you playing at?' he demanded.

'Henry!' Cat yelped, her legs giving way.

He covered the steps between them in no time, pulling her unceremoniously to her feet. 'What are you doing, Cat?'

'How did you get here? How come you came up those stairs?'

'How come I came up those stairs? The lower flight is the quickest way from the back door to my room. Then I saw the light up here. Plus, I live here. Why shouldn't I come up any stair I want to?' He sounded angry, but he took a deep breath and managed to cool his temper a little. 'But you still haven't told me what the hell you think you're up to, prowling round my home in the dark like Harriet the bloody spy.'

Cat had never blushed so deeply. She was glad of the dimness of the light so he could not see how guilty she looked. He stared intently at her, as if her face held the answer. 'Come on,' he said. 'Let's get out of here before you get yourself in even more trouble.' He stopped to listen for a moment, then hustled her down the stairs and back along the hallway. He opened the double doors and let go her wrist. 'Run along to our sitting room and I'll join you in a minute.'

She didn't need to be told twice. Her feet barely touched the ground as she sprinted for safety and she didn't stop till she was curled in a corner of the sofa. Henry followed soon after. He threw his briefcase on the floor and crossed the room to stand in front of her. She couldn't avoid the inappropriate thought that he looked ridiculously handsome. He was wearing a charcoal pin-striped suit that seemed designed to make him look impossibly fit. His white shirt was still crisp. Even as she watched, he loosened his burgundy tie and undid the top button of his shirt. Cat thought it was possibly the sexiest thing she'd ever seen; and she knew that was the last thing she should be thinking.

'So, what were you up to, Cat?' Henry did not look pleased.

Cat studied the carpet. 'I've been to see your mother's room,' she mumbled.

'If I was in court, I'd ask the witness to speak up,' he said sternly. She flicked a quick look upwards to see if his face showed any lightening. It did not.

'I said, I've been to see your mother's room.'

'My mother's room? What in the name of God did you think you'd see there? And why were you sneaking around in the turret afterwards?'

'I wanted to picture her in her own room, not just as a portrait on Ellie's wall.' It was the best she could manage at short notice.

'You could have asked Ellie to show you.' He threw his hands up in a gesture of frustration. 'It's not nice, skulking around in other people's houses in the middle of the night.'

'I was trying not to disturb anyone,' she said, gaining a little confidence.

'And the turret? What did you think you were going to find there?'

'I was curious,' Cat mumbled. Torture would not have dragged the humiliating truth from her at that point. Realising she needed to get off the back foot, she raised her eyes to meet his dark stare. 'And why are you here, anyway? I thought you were going straight to Glasgow to try a case.'

He tutted impatiently and threw himself into a chair. She couldn't help admiring the sprawl of his long legs. 'The case was postponed for a day. I thought if I worked late and got all the papers ready, I could come back to Northanger and have a day with you and Ellie tomorrow.'

Her spirits lifted a fraction – he'd come back to see her! – then sank again. Because she'd blown it, comprehensively. 'That would be cool,' she said in a small voice. Then she remembered his dislike of the word. 'I mean, delightful. Fun. A nice surprise.'

He burst out laughing. 'Cat, you're impossible. So, did you like my mother's room? I've always thought it the best bedroom in the house. I've suggested to Ellie that she should move into it, but she just shudders and looks at me like I've said something disgusting. I suppose she sent you to give it the once-over?'

'Not exactly. She was going to show me, but the General called her away before we could go inside.'

'Still, I'm surprised by your fascination for my mother's room. It's not as if you knew her. We know how special she was, but it's touching that a complete stranger is so fascinated by her. I suppose it's Ellie. She doesn't have much chance to make close friends round here, with being away at school and then this place being so isolated. So she doesn't get much chance to talk about Mother. Has she been going on about her?'

'A bit. But what she did say made me wish I'd known your mother. And with her death being so quick, and none of her children with her . . . Such a sad story, Henry. And your father is so brusque about her . . .'

The lawyer in him sprang to the fore again and he leaned forward, pinning her with his gaze. 'And from these fragments of information, you've made up a whole story, haven't you? A woman scorned in her final illness, or worse? Is that the way your mind's going?' She gave him a look of mute appeal, but his blood was up and his opening speech to the jury was under way. 'It's true that my mother's death happened more suddenly than any of us anticipated. But the underlying cancer, the leukaemia, was terminal. My father took her to several leading specialists and they all said the same thing. We all saw her deterioration and her bravery. And she wanted for nothing in her final days. Nobody could have been more devoted or more devastated than my father.'

'I didn't see any signs of that in him,' Cat said, snatching at any straw of defence.

'Of course you didn't. He's a soldier. He's trained to put his feelings to one side and get on with things. But to those of us who know him, his pain is as visible as a scar. It's why he's so brusque. So overbearing. He needs to control everything because the prospect of his life running out of control again is too terrible. I've never had a moment's doubt that he loved her. Even though he was as shouty with her as he is with the rest of us, and sometimes he drove her to despair with his bloody-minded stubbornness. But he adored her. Don't you dare doubt that, Cat.'

'Believe me, Henry, nobody could be happier than me to hear it. Anything else would have been awful.'

'You say awful, but that's what you were thinking, isn't it? Jeez, Cat, is this how you generally behave when you're invited into people's homes? Just think for a minute what you've been fantasising about. What kind of people do you think we are here? We're not the kind of low-life heathens I find myself defending in court every week. I don't know what life's like in Dorset, but here in the Borders we don't deal in the kind of atrocity you've been imagining. Besides, how do you think my father could get away with murder? Or, what? Keeping my mother locked up like a princess in a tower? We've got the Calmans following our lives as closely as the shadows on the walls. Do you really think they'd cover up murder out of a sense of loyalty to my father? Two hundred years ago, maybe, but not these days.' He shook his head, reverting to the 'more in sorrow than in anger' mode. 'I can't believe you even considered such a thing. I'm disappointed, Cat. I'm really disappointed.'

She could barely swallow the lump in her throat. With tears pricking her eyes, she jumped to her feet, choked out, 'I'm so, so sorry,' and ran from the room, not pausing till she threw herself on the bed and began to sob.

The visions of romance were over. Henry's words, brief though they had been, had such an impact that all she could see was the absurd extravagance of her recent imaginings. She had humiliated herself, shamed herself, abused her hosts. Sobs shook her shoulders; it wasn't only that she despised herself. Henry too must hold her in total contempt now. Her terrible folly was laid bare before him. He tried really hard to treat it like a joke, but it had become clear to her that he was wounded at the notion she should think so badly of his father. She hated herself more than she could express.

Her imagination had taken liberties, and now she would have to pay the price. It was over with Henry. Nobody could forgive the absurdity of her curiosity and suspicions. Thank God she hadn't said anything about her vampire convictions.

That thought brought her up short. However fanciful some of her thoughts had been since she came to Northanger, there was no escaping the hard fact of the family Bible with the bullet hole. That was not the sort of family heirloom that most people had, secreted away in a hiding place where casual eyes would not see it. For all Henry's outrage, there were still secrets in Northanger Abbey.

But that was little consolation for a broken heart. Cat stripped off for bed, throwing her clothes on a chair. Not even bothering to clean her teeth, she curled up under the covers – including the tartan blanket Mrs Calman had delivered – and clutched her misery to her chest, certain she would never sleep again.

But although it was restless and her dreams confused, sleep she did and when she woke, it was to another bright morning, the sun pouring in through curtains she had forgotten to close in her state of desolation. Her heart was still heavy with shame and self-disgust, but her stomach rumbled complaint that all this high-octane emotion had stripped her of available calories. Cat glanced at her watch, surprised to see it was just after seven.

If she was quick, perhaps she could get in and out of breakfast before Henry appeared. She knew she couldn't avoid him for ever, but she wanted to put it off for as long as possible.

She scrambled into clean clothes and ran downstairs, apparently the only inmate of the house stirring. But as soon as she crossed the threshold of the dining room, she realised her error. There, hollow-eyed and sipping a cup of tea, was Henry. He looked as if he'd barely slept. Unshaven and tousled, he was almost more attractive than ever, Cat thought hopelessly.

He gave her a wan smile. 'Good morning.'

Cat nodded. 'Morning, Henry.' She turned her back and moved to the sideboard to pour herself some coffee.

He cleared his throat. 'I think I was a bit rough on you last night,' he said. 'I should know by now how you girls love to dramatise every little incident in your lives. I know from Ellie how little it means in reality.'

Cat couldn't quite believe her ears. Her heart soared in her chest. She turned to him, her face radiant. 'I can't believe you said that. Thank you, Henry. Thank you so much. You have no idea how crap I've been feeling.'

He shrugged. 'Let's just draw a line under it and move on. We don't want one silly indiscretion to ruin your time here with us.'

Cat piled a bowl with cereal and sat down with him. 'I won't forget or defend what I did. But I am sorry. And I don't want it to spoil things between the three of us.' She knew she was remarkably lucky to have achieved this measure of clemency, given the alarming and insulting nature of her suspicions. Slowly, it was beginning to dawn on her that the books she had read and the dramas she had watched had brought her to

Northanger Abbey determined to discover dark secrets, set on scaring herself silly.

She recalled the feelings she'd harboured before she even arrived. She'd been infatuated with the idea of Northanger, regardless of what the reality might be. Engrossing and enthralling though the Hebridean Harpies were, horrifying and heart-stopping though the fictional world of vampires was, they were not source books on the life and habits of the Scottish landed classes. There might be distant and exotic places where such things were commonplace, but here in the Borders, the chances were slim that life was going to imitate art.

It was time to let it go. Cat had to start seeing the world as it was, not as she dreamed it. People were not angels or devils. Even in her darkest imaginings, she had still been forced to consider the General's magnanimity. And she must acknowledge to herself that, even with such paragons as Henry and Ellie, some slight imperfection might eventually appear. Everyone had shades of grey between the black and the white of their extreme characteristics. It was just that some, like the General, were less amiable than others.

Having now made her mind up on these points, Cat felt much less tremulous about the prospects for the rest of her stay. There was one point, however, on which she still sought reassurance. 'You won't tell them, will you? You won't tell Ellie or your father what an ass I made of myself?'

Henry shook his head. 'I think you've suffered enough, being lectured in the middle of the night by me. I won't say a word, Cat. Now, since I'm here all day, what shall we do? Do you fancy a run out to Kelso? Or Coldstream? See some civilisation and check out your Facebook and Twitter? See what's been happening in the world?'

Distracted by his mention of social media, she said, 'Did you see anyone in Edinburgh? The Allens? Bella? My brother?'

Henry got up to fetch some food. With his back to her, he said, 'I was working. Life still goes on for some of us, even during the festivals.'

'So, no news? You didn't even see your brother?'

He flashed a quick glance over his shoulder. 'No. Nothing to report.' He returned to the table just as Ellie came in. They soon hatched a plan to drive up to Kelso and on to Coldstream for lunch so Cat could see something of the small Borders towns whose identity had been forged generations before, when they were at the heart of the Debatable Lands constantly fought over by the English and the Scots. It was a prospect of far more delight than Cat could have imagined possible on waking. She was determined to make the most of it.

27

Cat was entirely charmed by the cobbled square at the heart of Kelso. 'It's the largest town square in Scotland,' Henry said as he eased into a parking space on a side street. The three of them walked back to the square with its array of Victorian and Georgian buildings. Cat felt like the luckiest person in town to be walking the streets in such company. Henry looked every inch the country gentleman, complete with tweed cap and matching jacket, while Ellie lacked only a Labrador to complete her county set image.

'There's a café with free wifi on the square itself,' Ellie said. 'Do you want to do that first, or have a walk around?'

'Let's go to the café first. Then we'll have something to gossip about, I feel sure.'

Henry groaned. 'What have I let myself in for?'

'Oh, shut up,' Ellie said. 'You know you love knowing every-thing that's going on. I never met a man who loved a good gossip more than you.'

They entered the café and sat at the three points of a triangle round a table. They restrained themselves until they'd ordered their drinks, then they each whipped out their smartphones, piggybacked on to the free wifi and lost all sense of where and with whom they were.

Cat logged on to her Facebook account first of all and was amazed to see there were no messages from Bella. A quick trip to her friend's page revealed only a couple of anodyne messages about a comedy event and a Book Festival reading she'd been to. Even more surprising was that there were no new photographs in any of her albums. It was odd, for a woman whose evening was not complete until she'd taken at least half a dozen photographs, and not all of them selfies. The only explanation Cat could think of was that her brother had returned and the two lovebirds had no time for anyone but themselves. She gave a little shrug and went back to her own Facebook page so she could let her sisters and Susie Allen know what a wonderful time she was having.

Once she had completed her updates, she went to Twitter, where she quickly responded to a handful of tweets from her few followers and the many writers, comedians and broadcasters she followed. She had barely finished when she spotted the alert that indicated she had a Direct Message waiting.

Wondering who was sending her a private communication, Cat clicked through to the appropriate page. To her surprise, the message was from her brother. James had written:

Where have u been? Been trying to get hold of u for 2 days.

Soz. No wifi or 3g at Northanger. Had to come into Kelso with H&E to get a signal. U ok?

Feel like shit. Finished with Bella. Left her & Edinbro y'day. Never want 2c either again.

'Oh my God!' Cat gasped.
Ellie looked up. 'What's the matter?'
'Later,' Cat said, thumbs darting over the keypad.

WTF? What hap?

I'm stupid, that's what hap. I trusted Bella, big mistake. Feel total fuckwit, esp after talking to M&D about getting wed. I'm gutted . . .

. . . Only u kno what she's like. How she can be all charm & fun & that's all u can c. Just hope ur gone from NA b4 tt bastard Tilney announces . . .

. . . their engagement. Cuz I know u will want to slap him till his ears bleed

'Oh my good God,' Cat exclaimed again, waving away Henry's questioning expression. 'In a minute.' He carried on watching her, clearly seeing that whatever she was reading was not improving as it continued.

Freddie Tilney? Engaged to BELLA? Tell me this is a wind-up, I thought he was just flirting 4 something 2 do.

U saw him flirting and u didn't say anything 2 me?

Henry sd he was just bored and playing silly games. So i never sd anything. My bad, bro, so sorry

Johnny T will be gutted 2. And M&D. Have emailed all of them. What's worst, she kept pretending she still loved me, rt to bitter end . . .

. . . then finally she dumped me in a txt. A fucking txt. Can u imagine how I felt? She totally played me. Sucker that I am . . .

. . . She sd, "this has been a terrible mistake, I see that now Freddie has proposed to me" . . .

. . . Be very careful round that Tilney family. I don't want them wrecking ur life like they wrecked mine. L8rs, sis. Tk cr.

Cat's eyes filled with tears. 'My poor sweet James,' she said, her voice shaky.

'Whatever has happened?' Ellie said, reaching out for Cat's hand. 'Trouble at home?'

'I think I can hazard a guess,' Henry said bitterly. 'Our brother.'

'Is he ill?' Ellie asked.

'Not physically. Just heartsick.' Cat looked at her friends. Her rapprochement with Henry was so recent, it still felt fragile. She didn't want to risk it by launching into the stream of invective she wanted to hurl at his brother.

'Cat's trying to spare our feelings,' Henry said. 'Bloody

Freddie has had his way with the lovely Bella Thorpe, and I'm guessing that James found out.' He shook his head and sighed. 'He just doesn't give a shit about anyone but himself. Is that what happened, Cat?'

'Not exactly, no. Bella dumped James, not the other way round. She dumped him because she's got engaged to your brother instead.' She couldn't keep the anger out of her voice, which was why she'd been reluctant to talk about it.

'Oh my God,' Ellie groaned. 'What an utter bastard Freddie is.'

'I'm so sorry about this,' Henry said. 'It never crossed my mind that she'd fall for his bullshit. I thought she was having as much of a laugh as him. I'd no idea—'

'Never mind that,' Cat said. 'I need to ask a favour.'

'Anything. After this, anything.' Ellie gripped her hand tightly.

'I want you to take me back to Northanger so I can pack up and head off to Edinburgh. The Allens are there till tomorrow. I'll go back to Dorset with them.'

'But why? Surely you don't blame us for Freddie's shitty behaviour?' Henry protested.

'No, of course not. But if he's getting engaged to Bella, surely he's going to have to talk to your father? He'll have to come home to Northanger. He'll probably bring Bella with him to meet your father properly, as a future daughter-in-law. And I can't trust myself under the same roof as them. I swear, I'd want to scratch her eyes out. Honestly, who'd have believed she could treat poor James like that? From being the loveliest man in the world to the poor sod who gets dumped in no time flat. It sucks.'

'Duped and dumped, by the sound of it,' Henry said. 'But I can't believe she's engaged to Freddie. I think there must be some mistake about that. I'm really sorry that Bella has chucked your brother, but it's just not credible that Freddie's actually going to marry the girl.'

'It's true. She texted James that it was all over, that Freddie had proposed to her. Look—' She proffered her phone and Ellie shuffled round the table so she could read it too. 'Sorry about the bit at the end, but he's just upset. He doesn't mean it. He hardly knows you two.'

The Tilneys said nothing as they read the DMs. Henry handed back the phone and sighed. 'Well, if it's true, God help us all. What a disaster that would be. Freddie wouldn't be the first man who has chosen a wife with less sense than his family expected.'

'It's awful,' Ellie said. 'Can you imagine Bella Thorpe running Northanger? And that mother of hers with her interior designs? I think I want to kill myself.'

'I almost feel sorry for Freddie,' Henry said. 'Both as husband and son. He's going to spend the next few years getting it in the neck from both sides. Cat, you know them better than we do. What sort of family are they? What's the mother like?'

'Apart from her terrible taste,' Ellie said darkly. 'I've seen the pics she's always shoving under people's noses with her iPad.'

'I don't believe there's any harm in her,' Cat said. 'She thinks her family are the brightest and the best looking and the most talented in the country, but she's not the only mother who's that misguided about her kids. I expect my mum's quite nice about me when I'm not there.'

'What was Bella's father?' Henry asked.

'A solicitor, I believe. They live in Crouch End. Though Bella has her eye on Chelsea,' Cat added with a trace of malice.

'Are they loaded?' Ellie asked.

'Don't think so. Bella's always going on about being skint. And the flat they're in for the festival is pretty poky and on the edge of the centre. They only come so Mrs Thorpe can pick up potential clients. But that won't matter in your family, surely? Your father said the other day money only mattered because it allowed him to promote the happiness of his children.' Cat made the quotation mark sign in the air.

'But would it be promoting Freddie's happiness, to support him marrying an empty-headed gold-digger like Bella Thorpe? I know she was your friend, Cat, but I assumed that was just because her mum is Susie's old pal and you were thrown together.'

'She can be good fun.' Cat felt a little uncomfortable at the wholesale trashing of someone whose company she had enjoyed, even though she clearly hadn't understood what Bella was really like.

'Fun's not enough. You think she's a gold-digger?' Henry said.

Cat thought for a moment. 'Now I think about it, she did seem pretty put out that my parents weren't about to set them up in a nice little house in London, with a cushy number for James in a London set of chambers. I don't know where she got that idea from, but she wasn't thrilled at the thought of York and a mortgage. So maybe Ellie's right and she saw Freddie as a better prospect.'

'In fairness to Freddie,' Ellie said, 'he's not the sort to go around busting up other people's engagements. It's not like he has any trouble finding girlfriends. He's just not met the right one before.'

Henry gave her a condescending smile. 'You're much too indulgent of our brother, Ellie. When he's in the mood, he'll chase anything with a pulse. But if Bella Thorpe's really got her hooks into him, his days on the town are numbered. It's all over for him. He's a dead man, and not just brain dead.' He gave Ellie a gentle punch. 'Just the kind of soul mate sister-in-law you've always craved, Ellie. Open, candid, artless, loyal, unpretentious and not in the least devious.'

'The very qualities that would delight me if they were for real, dear Henry. I'll have to leave that up to you to supply me with.'

Henry looked quickly away and grunted.

'Poor James,' Cat said. 'He's never going to get over this.'

Henry swigged his coffee, realised it had gone cold and pulled a face. 'It's tough for him right now. But I think it's hard on you too, Cat. Bella was your friend. You did everything together in Edinburgh. You'll miss that intimacy too.'

Cat shook her head. 'No,' she said firmly. 'I only saw in Bella what I wanted to see. I was desperate for a friend and I thought she was the one. I'm hurt, yes, but I'm not grieving like James is. If I never hear from her or see her again, I won't lose sleep over it.' She turned to Ellie and smiled. 'Besides, I've got a better friend now.'

Henry looked fondly on the two girls. 'Ah, Cat. You've got a gift for always finding the positive. We should all learn from that.'

'And the positive is that Father will never accept Bella

Thorpe as a suitable chatelaine for Northanger,' Ellie said firmly. 'She might think she's engaged to Freddie, but five minutes with Father and it'll be all over. There's no way he'd support Freddie marrying someone with nothing to bring to the party.'

'Surely your father doesn't expect Freddie to marry for money?' This was as monstrous a notion to Cat as any she'd attributed to the General.

'It's not quite that simple,' Henry said. 'It's always good to bring more money into an estate like Northanger, to build for the future. But it's not about greed. It's more to do with understanding the power and obligation that goes with great wealth and great property. It's the reason why you seldom get divorces among the dukes and earls and landowners, unless the estate is entailed. Divorce means splitting the land and the money, which ultimately makes life very hard for your children. So the landed classes put up and shut up and send the wife to live in the dower house or the cadet branch property. Thank God I'm a younger son and don't have to bother about all that crap.'

'And you don't have to bother about leaving,' Ellie added. 'Northanger is the last place you'll find Freddie right now. If he really is engaged to Bella, he won't dare come near Father. And if he's not? Well, he's due to rejoin his regiment very soon and he'll be desperate to make the most of every minute of freedom. So you're safer with us than anywhere else.'

Reassured by this, Cat found herself able to rediscover some pleasure in the day. Since Henry was departing that evening for Glasgow, they made the most of their time, visiting Coldstream and Jedburgh as well before returning to Northanger. But before Henry left, they extracted a promise from him that he would have them to Woodston for lunch on Saturday. The General insisted he'd drive them over himself. 'Always good to see the place,' he said. 'Besides, if I'm coming, Henry will have to make sure to lay on a decent spread. I'm doing this for your sake, ladies.'

It was, Cat thought, a small price to pay. What counted was that she would be in Henry's company once more. She would have another opportunity to demonstrate that she had moved on from her disastrous adventure. An opportunity, in short, to demonstrate how much more amenable she was than Bella Thorpe.

28

Cat was convinced that the rain had started the moment Henry left. All through Friday, there was a slow, steady drizzle that turned every vista misty. Cat and Ellie made the most of their confinement, however, by starting to investigate whether it really would be practical for them to work together on some books for children. Before too long, they had discovered their ideas were remarkably similar and by the time they went to bed on Friday evening, they were delighted and confident that together they could make something that children would enjoy.

Saturday was no brighter when they left Northanger. The General gloomily predicted that the further west they went, the heavier the rain would become. He even cracked a joke about Glasgow and rain, which stunned Cat into silence.

The young women were in the back of the Mercedes together, and as soon as they climbed out of the valley and into the land of 3G, they were both engrossed in their phones. Momentarily, Cat let out a yelp of surprise. There, in her inbox was an email from the woman she hoped never to hear from again.

Hi Cat ☺

Susie said she didn't think you had wifi at Northanger Abbey
but I told her that's totally incredible. I meant to write before but
you know how it is in Edinburgh, not a minute's peace, right?
I've been on the point of emailing you every day since you left,
but always got interrupted by something or other. Anyway, here
I am now, so get back to me soon as you can, ok, gf? ☺

Honestly, Cat, since you took off for NA, it's been a drag.
Everybody worth talking to has left town, I swear. But if you
were here, it would be primo, like before. The thing is, I
haven't heard from Jamie since he went back to Newcastle
and I'm worried in case he's got hold of the wrong end of the
stick, you know how dim men are when it comes to emotional
stuff. So I need you to put in a good word for me with your
bro because he is totes the only man for me. Totes.

You have missed out on some seriously bad
wardrobe malfunctions round Charlotte Sq Gdns. Fat
middle-aged women in jeggings, FFS. And honestly, some
of the men have no clue about colour-coding. I wish you
were here to take the piss with me. But I bet you're so busy
having a totes lush time that you never think of your friend
Bella. I could tell you things about that family you're hanging
out with that would make your hair stand on end, swear
down. Thank goodness that nightmare Freddie Tilney has
left Edinburgh to go back and kill some more innocent
women and children.

You remember how he was always chasing me? Giving
out the innuendoes and totes gagging for it? After you went
off with the rest of his family, he just got worse. It was like,

every time I turned round, there he was, making out I
wanted him. Yeah, right, I wanted him like HepC. I know lots
of girls like that sort of thing, but you know me better, Cat. I
never met a man with a higher opinion of himself, and he
was desperate for me to share it. He even took me to that
mausoleum on Ainslie Place to try and impress me, can you
believe that? And when I made it clear that I was totes not
into him and I was engaged to Jamie, he started flirting with
that dog Charlotte Davis. Can you believe the man?

But here's the thing. He was really pissed off with me and
I think he got hold of my phone at a party the other night.
When I checked my phone, I could see there had been
messages sent to Jamie that I didn't send but, like, the text
was erased so I couldn't see what they said.☹ And now he
won't answer his phone to me and I'm really unhappy about
the situation. So I thought you could, like, tell him about
Freddie getting hold of my phone and saying god knows what
to Jamie. Because you know how sensitive Jamie is, right?
And sometimes, when I couldn't escape Freddie and I had to
dance with him or whatever, Jamie looked really hurt, like it
was my fault some idiot had attached himself to me.

Anyway. I'm miserable without you, I have the most
miserable face in Edinburgh. Last night Susie Allen said I
looked like an advert for misery. Help me out, Cat. We're
going to be sisters, remember? If we can just get over this
bump in the road. Please, please help me sort things out
with your lovely bro.

Love you, miss you. ☹

Bella

Even Cat, with her propensity to see the best in everyone, saw right through the artifice of the message. She read it through again and couldn't credit the inconsistencies, contradictions and downright lies. She was ashamed of Bella and ashamed of herself for having taken so long to see through her. Her pathetic pretence of friendship was as disgusting as her excuses were empty and her demands brazen. Did she think Cat was so thick she'd actually plead with Jamie to take her back? Unbelievable.

She dug Ellie in the ribs and handed her the phone, scrolling up to the start of the message. 'Can you believe this?' she said softly. The General was listening to Radio 4, but Cat knew all about the enhanced hearing of vampires. As soon as she had the thought, she scolded herself. She had drawn a line. She was moving forward.

'She's unreal,' Ellie murmured. 'I think both our brothers have had a lucky escape. What a devious cow!'

'I thought she was my friend. But she clearly thinks I'm an idiot, and nobody chooses to be friends with an idiot. More fool me for not seeing that she was using me to get closer to James. I swear I don't think she ever gave a damn for either of us.' She sighed. 'I chose really badly there.'

Ellie leaned into her. 'It's like Henry said, you were thrown together and she just dazzled you with her fancy clothes and her smart London talk. You're worth so much more than her.'

'You're very sweet. You and Henry both.'

'That's because we like you, numbskull. Wait till Henry sees this email, though. He'll totally crack up.'

In spite of the General's forecast, the rain cleared as they skirted Glasgow and approached Loch Lomond. It was still far from a sunny day, but at least it was dry and clear as they drove up the lochside road to emerge at a substantial two-storey stone villa that sat a little distance back from the edge of the loch in its own grounds. 'Here we are,' the General said as they turned into the driveway. 'Clearly it's not on the scale of Northanger Abbey. Doubtless it's a mere cottage by comparison with Andrew Allen's pile. But it's a decent size and it's perfectly habitable. And it's convenient for Henry when he has to try cases in Glasgow. Who knows, he may even end up making it his home in the long run. It's only been in the family fifty years or so, Frederick could hardly object to my cutting it out of his estate.'

Cat wasn't listening because Henry had appeared in the porch at the sound of the car. Her spirit quickened at the sight of him and she felt a curious yearning sensation in her stomach. He waved as they approached, then hurried over to open the back door. 'You made it,' he said cheerfully.

'Of course we made it,' the General said, stepping out of the car and squaring his shoulders.

'Come on in, the coffee's on,' Henry said, bowing low and gesturing towards the house.

A small but well-proportioned hallway led into a pleasant sitting room with views of the garden to the rear and the side, which disappointed Cat, who was longing for a vista of the loch itself. 'We'll just have some coffee and then I'll show you around,' Henry said.

'Have the decorators not completed the drawing room?' the General called after Henry as he left the room.

'Yes. But the furniture hasn't come yet,' he called back.

Until he returned, the General prowled up and down,

checking the mantelpiece for dust and the crystal decanters for smears. The coffee was served as the General liked it, in china cups, and it came with an assortment of tiny pastries that Cat felt she could have eaten all day. But her impatience to see the rest of the house restrained her appetite and she was finished ahead of the others.

Seeing this, Henry jumped to his feet, saying, 'Come on, Cat, let me give you the tour.' She hardly dared let herself believe it, but it was almost as if he was as keen to be alone with her as she with him.

He waved her ahead into the hall then showed her into the kitchen opposite. It was nothing like Mrs Calman's domain – it was a country kitchen that resembled her home in Dorset, except that everything in it was at least twenty years newer. There was even a small table in the side bay window where it would be possible to take a more modest breakfast than the General ever laid on in his other homes. 'It feels very welcoming,' she said.

'I like it here,' Henry said. 'Northanger is fabulous and I'm lucky to be part of it, but Woodston is built on a more human scale. I could imagine living somewhere like this very comfortably.'

'I understand why,' Cat said, following him into a dining room whose view made her exclaim, 'Henry, this is glorious!' Before her the loch shimmered in the pearly light. A handful of small boats skimmed the water and, in the distance, she could see the rounded humps of foothills giving way to mountains behind.

'It's a pretty stunning way to start and end the day, sitting in here taking one's meals,' he admitted.

She dragged her eyes from the view and took in the elegant Georgian dining set that occupied the centre of the room. Table, eight chairs, a long sideboard. And beyond, an elegant marble fireplace with, she was pleased to see, a modern gas fire with its arrangement of fake coal and logs. It would actually be possible to live here without servants!

A second door led from the dining room into a substantial drawing room which shared the dramatic view of the loch. Its walls were a pale muted green and the room smelled faintly of fresh paint. It was completely empty of furniture. 'Father decided this room needed to be redone. As you can see, the decorators just finished. There won't be furniture for a couple of weeks yet. But you get the idea?'

'It's the perfect room, Henry. I wouldn't care if I had to sit on the floor in a room like this.' Cat whirled around like a ballerina, twirling easily on the polished oak boards.

'Let me show you the garden,' Henry said, opening the French windows that led outside. They strolled down towards the loch, with her host pointing out items of interest in a faintly desultory way. 'Any more news from your brother?' he asked as they skirted a small fountain with a pond stocked with koi carp.

'Oh, I must show you this. It completely slipped my mind, I've been enjoying this so much.' Cat waved a generous arm at the garden while she fished out her phone with the other hand. 'This will totally blow your socks off.' She opened Bella's email and handed Henry the phone.

He read it carefully, his expression tightening as he reached the end. 'What do you make of that?' he said.

'That I was a fool ever to be taken in by her. That she is everything I would hate to be. What do you think?'

'I think it's to your credit that you see her so clearly now. Anyone can be fooled for some of the time by the likes of Bella Thorpe.'

She had never seen such an expression of distaste on his face, not even when he'd found her creeping around the turret in the night.

'But here's what I don't get,' she said. 'I get that she was trying to get her hooks into Freddie and that somehow he escaped her clutches. What I don't get is what Freddie thought he was doing? You told me yourself he knew she was engaged to James. Why couldn't he have chased after some unattached girl? Why flatter Bella so much that she ditched James, and then leave her in the lurch? That seems incredibly cruel to me.'

Henry made a rueful face. 'All Freddie will have seen was the challenge of the forbidden fruit. He's not deliberately cruel. Just immensely self-centred and depressingly vain. I think he's never been properly in love with anyone but himself, so he has no notion of how much hurt he causes.'

'What you're saying is he never really gave a toss for Bella?'

'Pretty much, yes. All he was looking for was a bit of fun to occupy his leave.'

'So he led her on? Just for what he could get out of it?' Now Cat was the one displaying disgust.

Henry nodded. 'That's my shitty big brother.'

'I'd have to agree with that. I don't think I'm ever going to like your brother, Henry. Even though he's done my family a favour in a roundabout way. And I suppose Bella will survive because she's not got much of a heart to break.'

'And if she'd had a heart to break, she'd never have got tangled up with Freddie in the first place because she would have been too tender-hearted to dump James like that. I am sorry that Freddie is such a pig, though.'

'You turned out very differently.'

Henry smiled. 'Some people say I was my mother's son, while Freddie takes after my father. I couldn't possibly comment.'

Before Cat could pursue this, their colloquy was interrupted by the arrival of Ellie and the General, who kindly insisted on walking Cat down to the landing stage and giving her a lecture on the names and heights of all the hills that could be seen from that vantage point. By the time he had finished, it was time for lunch, a delicious collation of cold meats, salads, cheeses and assorted items from a local delicatessen whose produce the General particularly recommended to Cat. She imagined it would be extremely unlikely if she were ever to have the opportunity to patronise it, since it was almost five hundred miles from her home.

After lunch the General decided he needed a nap before driving back to Northanger, so the others walked out on the lawn once again, settling in a little gazebo with a view north up the loch.

'So, Cat,' Henry said, leaning back on the bench and stretching his legs out. 'What are you going to do with your life?'

Cat was nonplussed. This question was normally the domain of her parents' generation. 'I don't know,' she said. 'I was homeschooled so I don't have any of the qualifications that get you to university. I'm not academic like James. He breezed through A-levels and Oxford entrance, but just reading the exam papers made my head swim.'

'But you're clearly not stupid,' Henry said.

'She's just not academic,' Ellie said firmly. 'She's a brilliant story-teller, Henry. Wait till you see the ideas she's come up with for kids' books. I'm going to illustrate them and we're going to publish them online if we can't get a proper publisher.'

Henry grinned. 'I'll shut up, then. You've clearly got it all worked out.'

'I'm good with kids,' Cat said. 'I thought about becoming a nanny. But you need qualifications for that too. And I'm not sure how much I want to live in somebody else's house.'

'I guess we'll just have to become the next Julia Donaldson and Axel Scheffler,' Ellie said. 'To save you from the fate worse than death of other people's kids.'

'So I suppose you'll have to come back and visit us again?' Henry said, looking pleased. 'If you two are serious.'

'Oh, we're serious all right,' Ellie said. 'This might just be what it takes to persuade Father to let me go to art school.'

'Good luck with that one,' Henry said drily. 'Now, who wants to walk down the shore to the ice-cream van?'

By the time they'd returned from their walk, the General was up and about and making a list for Henry of things that needed to be attended to at Woodston. 'Are you not coming back with us?' Cat asked. Fond as she was of Ellie, Northanger without Henry lacked a certain sparkle. And without him to keep her imagination in check, a certain menace.

'My case resumes on Monday. Tomorrow, I have to visit my client in prison, so it's not possible. But if we finish on Tuesday, as we're supposed to, I'll come back to Northanger for dinner.'

Before any further plans could be made, the General

announced it was time to set off. 'Your brother has returned to his regiment, I hear,' he said as they strolled back to the car. 'Cheeky boy should have stopped off to say goodbye.'

'He was probably looking for more fun than Northanger could provide,' Henry remarked. His father gave him a shrewd look but said nothing. And so, without further discussion, the visit was concluded and the young women settled down to enjoy their Internet access for as long as it took to reach the black spot that was Northanger Abbey.

29

Sunday turned out to offer more entertainment than Cat had expected. The General announced that they were invited to lunch by friends with a castle near Melrose. 'There's some sort of open-air drama in the grounds later that we have to stay for,' he grumbled. 'I hope I can sneak away and play billiards.'

The friends turned out to be a large extended family with plenty of conversation; the drama a double bill of Tom Stoppard plays hot from the Fringe. Cat's only knowledge of his work had been the screenplay of *Shakespeare in Love*, so the evening turned out to be surprising in every respect.

It was late when they got back, the General grumbling even more because he had to be up early in the morning to catch a train to London. 'Bloody MOD,' he complained. 'Why can't they start meetings at a civilised time of day? I had enough of getting up in the middle of the night when I was in the army.'

'Will you be gone long?' Ellie asked.

'I'll stay at the club tomorrow night. See some old friends on Tuesday and head back in the evening.'

With the General gone, Cat's pleasure in Northanger

increased dramatically. She and Ellie did some work on their story ideas, then went for a walk, then sprawled on the sofas in the drawing room talking about the relative merits of Brad Pitt and Ryan Gosling. 'This is such bliss,' Ellie said when Mrs Calman brought them a trifle for afternoon tea. 'Never leave, Cat. Stay here for ever and be my partner in crime.' Mrs Calman harrumphed on her way out the door.

'You're so sweet. But I don't want to overstay my welcome. I should probably think about going home.' There was some truth in what Cat said; but there was also some underhandedness for, by testing the water, she hoped to win Ellie's approval for a longer stay.

'No way,' Ellie protested. 'Life here is so dull on my own. You have to keep me company a bit longer. Besides, it's the Northanger Common Riding next Sunday. You've got to stay for that.'

'Like in the photograph you showed me?'

'Exactly. You Southerners have nothing to compare.'

'Explain it to me properly.'

'All the Borders towns and villages have something similar. Basically, all the local men get on horseback and ride the parish boundaries, or ride out to the nearby villages and raise a standard and have a drink then ride back. And then the whole town has a party. It's sort of like a Spanish fiesta but with more drink and worse dancing. Our Common Riding starts off and finishes up here, so there's lots of socialising and stuff. And if you go up to the top of the drive, you can see the riders all strung out across the landscape below. It's quite a sight.'

'Sounds like it. And it'll be OK with your father if I stay on?'

'Of course. He thinks you're the bee's knees. And Henry will be really chuffed too. Someone to show off his pretty riding to. Boss, in his world.'

Later, as they were leaving the upstairs sitting room to head for bed, they saw twin beams cut the darkness of the window, then heard the unmistakable sound of tyres on gravel. 'Who can it be at this time of night?' Ellie wondered. 'Unless it's Freddie. He's always turning up at ridiculous times of the day or night.'

'I thought he'd gone back to his regiment?'

'Yes, but if they're shipping out right away, he might have a twenty-four-hour leave. Oh, look, off you go to bed, I'll sort him out.'

And so they parted on the landing, Ellie running downstairs and Cat hurrying to her room. The last thing she wanted was a midnight confrontation with Freddie Tilney. If he was here for a day, she didn't see how she could avoid an encounter, and if they did meet, she didn't see how she could avoid telling him what she thought of his behaviour. At least the General would not be there to witness her indulging in behaviour so inappropriate for a guest of the family.

Such were her thoughts as she got ready for bed and climbed beneath the covers. But Cat had barely picked up her book when she thought she heard a footstep in the corridor outside. Her heart leapt with anxiety. Was she imagining things? But no, for as she stared at the door, she saw the handle move a little. The idea of someone approaching so covertly made her pulse race. Was this the point where her wildest fears became a reality?

Telling herself not to be ridiculous, Cat slipped out of bed and tiptoed to the door. She gripped the handle, turned it swiftly and yanked the door open. To her amazement, Ellie was standing there, pale-faced and clearly agitated. 'What's the matter? Come in, tell me what's wrong!'

But Ellie stood mute, shaking her head. 'I can't,' she said, her voice tremulous.

Cat put a hand on her arm. 'Why not? Don't be silly, Ellie, come inside and sit down before you fall down.'

'Stop being so kind, Cat. I can't bear it, not with what I've got to say to you.'

Cat's mouth fell open. Surely it could not be bad news about Henry? 'Has something happened at Woodston?'

'Woodston? No. It's my father. He's come back from London.' She looked away and Cat could see tears glistening in her eyes. 'I don't know how to say this. After everything I said to you today. I thought we'd be together for at least another week. I was counting on it.'

'Me too. What's gone wrong?'

Ellie gave an angry shrug. 'My father has just come home and announced that first thing on Tuesday we are flying off to Nice to stay with our cousins there for two weeks. Apparently it's been in the diary but he forgot all about it. I don't know when this was decided or why, but I have no choice in the matter, apparently.'

Cat stared in shock. 'You're a grown woman. He can't make you go where you don't want to go.'

Ellie smacked her fist into the door jamb. 'You've seen what he's like. He won't stand for defiance. At least, not from me.'

There was no possibility of argument. 'I've seen that. Look, I don't blame you. Don't get yourself in such a state. I'm sorry we can't stick together longer, but that's just how it is. I'm not offended. I know you can't help it. We'll get together again when you get back from France. You could come down to Dorset, if you don't mind chaos.'

'I can't make any promises.' Ellie looked at the ground.

'We'll just have to make the most of tomorrow, then. Maybe when Calman takes you to the airport on Tuesday morning he can drop me off at the station in Newcastle?'

Ellie shook her head. 'I wish that was possible. But Father's already made the arrangements. There's an express coach from Newcastle to London at seven thirty tomorrow morning. He's reserved you a seat on it. Calman will pick you up at the front door at six.'

Cat was so shocked she staggered backwards till the bed caught the back of her knees and she sat down abruptly. 'You're kidding.'

'I know, I could hardly believe it when he told me,' Ellie said, anger replacing sorrow in her voice. 'Believe me, you can't be more pissed off than I am right now. Jeez. What will your parents think of us? No way they'll want me anywhere near your place. They'll hate me for taking you away from the Allens, your real friends, then treating you like this. Driving you out of the house in the middle of the night without warning. I can't believe my father's manners. Please, please don't tar me with the same brush.' She grasped her hair and twisted it in her hands. 'Something like this, it's so awful. It makes me see that I have to break free.'

'But not tonight, Ellie. Let him have his way. It's not worth it.' Cat could hardly assemble her words into sentences. 'Have I done something to offend him, is that it?'

'If you have, I've no idea how. He's really wound up about something, though. I know he always seems bad-tempered, but mostly I can talk him round and calm him down. Not tonight, though. Something has got under his skin, but I don't see how it can have anything to do with you.'

'If it is, whatever it is, I'm really sorry. Don't fret about me, Ellie. I'm just sorry I couldn't get in touch with Mum and Dad to let them know. Or James. He would have come for me, if your father wasn't so eager to see the back of me.'

'I'm sorry. I suppose it's too late to phone him now. But Calman won't mind taking you, I know that.'

Now Cat snapped. 'It's not the journey that bothers me. It's being thrown out in the middle of the night like a disgraced Victorian housemaid. And there's nothing you can do about that, Ellie, so you'd better leave me to my packing.' Her voice cracked on the final word and she felt tears blocking her throat. So she got to her feet and closed the door in her friend's face.

For the second time in a few days, she threw herself down on the bed and sobbed. How had it come to this? She'd made two friends since she'd left the Piddle Valley and in their different ways, they'd both totally let her down. How could the General treat her so cruelly? Without any reason that could justify such behaviour? No apology from him, either. And she wouldn't even have the chance to say goodbye to Henry. At this thought, the tears rose again to choke her. She'd thought he was showing signs of returning her feelings, but that would never happen now. Who knew if they'd ever meet again, living at opposite ends of the country, in such different social circles.

How had this happened? Cat had somehow gone from being the bee's knees to the shit on his shoe in the space of a day.

It was as incomprehensible as it was mortifying. What would her parents think she'd done to cause this abrupt departure? How would she explain it to the Allens, who thought so highly of the Tilneys?

And the way the General had arranged things, without any consultation. She'd never heard of anything so high-handed, not in any of her father's four parishes. Who did he think he was?

Then something struck her. Something she had done which, if it had been discovered, might have given offence. Not offence of the order of throwing her out in the middle of the night, but some umbrage. She dragged herself off the bed and opened her bag. She rummaged among her clothes, but the Bible with the bullet hole was exactly where she had left it, tucked under a pair of sweaters. So her single transgression had not been discovered. Cat debated whether to leave the book lying on the bed when she went, so they would know what she had discovered. Then she thought better of it. She would take it with her and perhaps ask her father what he thought it might mean.

The night passed heavily. She tried to go to sleep but she was too agitated and her mind refused to rest. She'd been frightened of imagined horrors in this room, but those shadows were meaningless compared to the abject misery that now held her captive. The strange noises of the wind and the sinister creaking of the old building no longer held any fear for her. Cat had real pain to blot them out.

Eventually, she gave up on sleep. She took a long shower, hoping in spite of the General's obsession with good plumbing that the running water might keep him awake. Then she dressed and packed her bag. She sat on the edge of the bed, mute and miserable.

At half past five, there was a tap at the door. When Cat opened it, Ellie stood there with a tray. 'I brought you some coffee and brioches,' she said abjectly.

'I'm not hungry,' Cat said. She gave one last look round the room, picked up her bag and marched down the hall to the gallery. She humped her bag downstairs, glancing in at the dining room as she passed. It was hard to believe that less than twenty-four hours ago, she and Ellie had been laughing over breakfast, delighting in the General's absence.

Ellie trailed behind her. 'Email me, Cat. As soon as you get home. Let me hear from you as soon as you can, please? I won't be able to settle till I know you're back home safe. We can still be friends, Cat. We can still do the books together.'

Cat sighed. 'Will your father allow you to be in touch with me?'

'Oh, please. I'm not his prisoner. Look, I know I need to make changes. But it's not easy. Be my friend. Help me.'

Before Cat could say more, Mrs Calman emerged from the kitchen. 'Some sandwiches,' she said briskly, handing Cat a carrier bag laden with food.

'Thank you,' Cat said, as dignified as she could manage.

'Have you got enough money?' Ellie asked desperately as Cat opened the front door. 'Only, you've been gone from home a while, and I just thought . . .'

Cat closed her eyes momentarily. She hadn't even thought about money. 'Can you lend me some?'

'Wait there.' Ellie ran upstairs like the wind. Mrs Calman stood silent as a pillar while they both waited for her return.

Ellie thrust a bundle of notes into Cat's hand. 'There's a hundred.'

'That's more than I need.'

'Just take it.'

'I'll pay you back,' Cat said. Another black mark against the General, who had never even considered how she might pay her way home.

'No hurry,' Ellie said. 'Be in touch, yeah?'

Cat nodded and walked out the front door. Calman stood at ease by the car. She'd slipped so far down the pecking order that he wasn't even wearing a tie. Calman's cravat told her all she needed to know about her new position apropos the Tilney family. Loading her own bag into the boot, Cat pressed her lips firmly together. She wouldn't give them the satisfaction of seeing her tears. However hard it might be, she was done with Northanger Abbey.

30

Calman spoke not a word during the journey, which Cat was grateful for, since she didn't think she could open her mouth without howling like a baby. At that hour of the morning, they made good time and he pulled up in an unattractive side street near the railway station at a few minutes after seven. It didn't look like a promising location for a coach station, but the bus for London was sitting in the morning sunshine with its door open.

Cat took her bag from the boot and hurried to collect her ticket. To her surprise, when she approached the coach, Calman was standing a few feet away, hands in his trouser pockets, looking more like a nightclub bouncer than the general factotum of a great house. Clearly he was waiting to make sure she boarded the coach. It added a whole new level of insult to being seen off the premises. What did he think she was going to do? Sneak back to Northanger and burn the place to the ground? Not that they didn't deserve it, after the way they'd treated her. But she would show she was better than them. She gave Calman a little wave. 'Do thank your wife for taking such good care of me,' she said in her most gracious tones as she climbed aboard.

Her seat was halfway up the coach, by the window. Her hopes of being left alone to wallow in her misery were dashed when a black youth around her own age dropped into the seat next to her. 'All right, pet?' he greeted her. She gave him a pained smile and he laughed. 'Don't look so worried, I'm not going to bother you.' He plugged in his earphones and took a tablet computer out of his backpack. Inside a minute he was lost in a world of his own.

Cat was grateful for his disengagement. Seven and a half hours of being dragged into someone else's concerns would have left her feeling even more murderous towards General Tilney, hard though that might be to credit. The journey itself had no terrors for her. She had plenty to think about and plenty of Hebridean Harpies to amuse her on her e-reader. The hard part was dragging her mind clear of Northanger Abbey.

She glanced at her watch. On the other side of the country, Henry would be sitting in the dining room at Woodston with his morning coffee and his bowl of cereal. She couldn't believe he knew anything of what had happened, for he would surely have been in touch. Which reminded her, she hadn't checked her phone to see if there were any messages. Not to mention the necessity of letting her parents know she was on her way home.

Cat rummaged in her daypack and fished out her phone. She thumbed the button to wake it up and nothing happened. She repeated her action, with no result. She pressed the power button but again there was no response. Realising the extent of her misfortune, Cat groaned out loud. She'd run the battery down during their car journey back from Woodston and she'd forgotten to charge it up again; the lack of signal at Northanger had broken her regular habit of plugging it in every night. And the charger was in her big bag, which was in the luggage locker somewhere under the coach. She was trapped in her isolation, unable to vent her feelings to anyone but herself.

The dead phone reminded her of how buoyant she'd felt on the journey back from Woodston. She'd posted photos of the house and the loch views to her Facebook page and tweeted her delight to the world. She'd even emailed a few pics to her parents, to let them see what a great time she was having. It had been a magical day. In spite of her terrible gaffe at Northanger, Henry was clearly pleased to see her and eager to spirit her off on her own. She couldn't have wished for a better reaction to Bella's ridiculous email. And he'd cared enough to ask about her future, as if it might concern him. She didn't think she was imagining the undercurrent of affection that was building between them. This hollow feeling in her stomach when she thought of him was, she believed, a barometer of love.

And that day at Woodston, the General had been as genial as she'd ever seen him. Even Ellie had commented on his high opinion of her. So what could have happened to throw the switch from regard to contempt – for only contempt could have led to her abrupt dismissal. Surely Henry hadn't told him about her night-time prowling and embarrassing suspicions? She couldn't believe that of Henry, for what positive motive could he possibly have harboured for such a revelation? It wasn't as if it was the sort of thing you could make a joke about – 'Hey, Dad, Cat thinks you murdered my mother. Did you ever hear anything so funny?' No, that one wouldn't work, not even on the Fringe.

What would Henry think when he turned up at Northanger tomorrow evening to find them all gone? She was sure one of the Calmans would bring him up to speed. The question was whether they knew the true reason she'd been banished, which was more than she did herself. Cat wondered what they'd been told, because their behaviour had been at odds. Calman could not have been colder, while Mrs Calman, although she had said nothing, had provided her with enough food for a long weekend. So how would Henry react? Would he, like Ellie, acquiesce without protest in his father's actions? Or would he be filled with regret and resentment? Would he be sufficiently moved to stand up to his father?

She doubted this last point. It was, she knew, hard to break the habit of a lifetime. And the General had so drilled his younger children in obedience that they struggled even to doubt his certainties. No, Henry would let her go. It was over before it had started. Over before he'd even kissed her properly – social air-kissing didn't count, obviously.

Cat was so bound up in her thoughts and regrets that she barely noticed the passing of time or landscape. She almost welcomed the length and tedium of the journey, for once she had completed the second stage, another four hours on the coach from Victoria to Dorchester, she would be plunged into the necessity of explaining her precipitate return to her family and friends.

Although she longed to be back in their company after a month's absence, Cat had no relish for an explanation that could only reflect badly on her. Even though she knew herself to be blameless, her mother and father, like all parents, would inevitably suspect their child had committed some sin so heinous or shaming she dared not admit to it. They might not go so far as to voice their views, but she knew that's what they'd be thinking.

At that point, she was so depressed that she started on the sandwiches. Her last taste of Northanger, she thought as she bit into the rare roast beef, horseradish and lamb's lettuce roll. Cat closed her eyes and savoured it. At least there were still some simple pleasures left to her.

Seven hours and fifty-three minutes after they'd left Newcastle, they pulled into the grimy terminal at Victoria. The exhaust-laden fumes were a shock to Cat's lungs after the clear Borders atmosphere and the air-conditioning of the coach. She collected her bag and found the stand where the Dorchester service would leave from.

There were fewer travellers heading west that afternoon, so she had a double seat to herself. As they headed into the evening sun and the landscape grew increasingly familiar, Cat began to feel nostalgic for home. She'd dreamed of a very different return, the sort of triumph that featured in so many of the fictions she loved. She'd imagined Henry driving her back from Northanger; introducing him to the family; walking through the orchard to the Allens' house, where he would declare undying love on the banks of the river. But her dreams were shattered now, revealed for the foolishness they had always been.

At least she'd been able to charge up her phone on this coach. But now that it was possible to text or phone home, Cat found herself increasingly reluctant to do so. Eventually, when they were less than an hour from Dorchester and the sun was starting to sink in the distance, she composed the necessary text.

On coach 2 Dorch. Due 9.17. Can u pick me up pse? Cat x

She despatched it to her father, and within five minutes the reply came.

??? Of course I can. Are you OK? Dad

How could she even begin to answer that question?

I'm OK. Fone ws dead b4. Looking 4ward 2 seeing u. Mist u all. C u soon. X

She could imagine them all, agog in the kitchen, wondering what on earth had brought her back so abruptly. They wouldn't understand, any more than she had.

When she stepped off the coach at Dorchester, the sight of her father was almost more than she could bear. Cat threw herself into his hug, a bittersweet mixture of joy and pain twisting her heart. Now she was finally where she knew she was unconditionally loved, she could let go. Tears dripped down her cheeks as her father gently patted her back, bemused but professionally accustomed to offering comfort.

When Cat could at last let go, Mr Morland slung an arm round her shoulders and picked up her bag. 'You don't have to say anything now unless you want to get it off your chest before we get home,' he said. 'Otherwise, wait so you don't have to go through it all twice.'

Cat swallowed and nodded. 'OK. I love you, Dad.'

'I know,' he said. 'And we love you too. No matter what. You know that.'

The last few miles of the journey were the hardest. But by the time they arrived at the vicarage, Cat had herself under control so that when they pulled up in the drive and her mother and sisters fell upon her with delight, she was able to contain her tears and enjoy the pleasure of being back in the bosom of a loving family again, rather than one that was ruled by a heartless tyrant.

Her mother bustled around the kitchen, heating soup and opening tins of baking while her sisters quizzed her about the excitements of Edinburgh and the shocking behaviour of Bella Thorpe. Eventually, though, those subjects were temporarily exhausted and Richard Morland shooed his younger daughters upstairs, citing the lateness of the hour.

Then at last, Cat was able to tell her story. She could tell from the looks her parents exchanged that they were shocked by a father who would throw a young woman out of doors with no notice to travel the length and breadth of the country alone. 'And all this was decided in the middle of the night?' Annie said, indignant.

'It was after midnight when Ellie told me.'

'I can hardly credit it,' Richard said. 'At the very least he should have phoned us to let us know Cat was on her way home. We could have been out, or away.'

Cat managed a feeble giggle. 'You're never away.'

'Yes, but General Tilney wasn't to know that. I'm astonished. Susie Allen spoke so highly of him. And you've no idea what provoked this?'

'No idea at all. Truly, Dad, I'm not trying to cover up anything I did wrong. He seemed to quite like me. Ellie said he thought I was the bee's knees. And then he just turned.'

'Well, it sounds like you're well out of that house,' Annie said with finality. 'From what you say, he's a real control freak. Those poor children of his.' She shook her head.

'It's like they're scared of what will happen if they stand up to him,' Cat said. 'Which is weird, because Henry is totally not a wimp. If you spent any time with him, you'd know he's got opinions of his own. But when it comes to his father, he just gives in. It's like their father has some terrible hold on them.'

Her father rolled his eyes. 'Spare us the melodrama, Cat. You're still pretending you're the heroine in one of those books of yours. The Tilneys are just another screwed-up family who need to find some grace.' And so they left it, seeing exhaustion had caught up with Cat, who was more than glad to fall into her own bed, where to her surprise she slept like the dead.

Of course, the whole story had to be retold when Susie Allen came round for coffee in the morning. 'OK,' Susie said. 'Let me run this past you again. He came back from London with some cock-and-bull story about a trip to rellies in the South of France that he'd completely forgotten?'

'That's what Ellie said. I never actually spoke to him after he came back.'

'Extraordinary. I can just about see how you might forget you were going to Nice, but that's no excuse to throw Cat out of the house before dawn. Thank heavens you're home safe, Cat. With a man like that, you could have had a lucky escape.'

'Don't encourage her,' Richard said as he passed through the kitchen on his way to conduct a funeral.

'He was always very keen on you and Mr Allen,' Cat said. 'He talked about inviting you to Northanger.'

Susie snorted, 'He can whistle for that. I wouldn't set foot within a mile of any house of his.'

'What did he want with Susie and Andrew?' Annie wondered.

'I don't know. But he talks about money a lot. I think he spends a lot of time working out how much people are worth. In cash, I mean, not what they're really worth,' Cat said sadly. 'Maybe he realised how skint we are, and that's why he was so keen to get rid of me.'

'That's incredibly depressing,' Susie said.

'All the more reason to be glad you won't have to have anything to do with the Tilneys from hereon.' Annie's voice was firm. But as she stood up to make more tea, she missed the fleeting look of regret that crossed her daughter's face.

The support of family and friends surrounded Cat and supported her over the coming days. But in spite of their love and concern, she remained pale and drawn and more prone to long walks alone than she had been before her trip to Edinburgh. It wasn't her treatment at the hands of the General that bothered her; she had accepted that as incomprehensible and of little use in the imaginative fantasies she liked to engage in and she had put it behind her. But she could not manage that feat when it came to Henry.

What wounded her heart and bruised her self-esteem was that she had heard nothing from him. Surely he must have heard what had happened by now? How could he turn his back on all that had started to blossom between them? If he was really incapable of standing up for what he wanted, it was probably as well to find that out now, she supposed. But still. No excuse or explanation could ease her pain.

Cat had sat down to email Ellie several times, but she couldn't find a place to start. In the end, she used the excuse of returning her hundred pounds to write a brief note thanking her for her hospitality at Northanger and hoping they could find a way to continue their collaboration, whether digitally or face-to-face. She considered every word carefully, mindful that his sister might show it to Henry. Cat was not hopeful of a response, however.

Seeing what she was about, her mother sighed. 'You and James have both had a pretty torrid summer of it. Strange relationships, made and ended so soon. But that's part of being young, I suppose. Better luck next time for both of you.'

'Maybe Ellie and I can still be friends.' She licked the envelope and closed it. 'She's really lovely, Mum.'

'I wouldn't bank on it, not unless her father falls under a bus. I wish you had something to take your mind off all this. At least poor James has his work. It's about time you started thinking about your future, Cat. You'll be eighteen before you know it and your child benefit will run out. We're not loaded like your Edinburgh pals. You'll either have to go to college or get a job. Have you given it any thought?'

Cat sighed. Like she could think about the future when her life was in ruins. 'Me and Ellie have a plan. We're going to do children's books. She's a really brilliant illustrator, and you know how good I am at making up stories for the kids.'

She was too busy staring out of the window to catch her mother's look of gentle compassion. 'That's probably not on the cards now, sweetheart.'

'I know.'

'Do you remember a while back we talked about you training as a nanny?'

Listlessly, Cat nodded. 'Yeah, but I don't have the right qualifications.'

'That might not be such a problem,' Annie said. 'While you were gone, I made some enquiries. And there's a college in the North East where they train girls with non-traditional educational backgrounds. You come out of it with a proper childcare qualification. And if you got in, you could stay with James. What do you think?'

'Whatever,' Cat said. 'I probably wouldn't get in.'

'Let me go and get the bumf. I put it upstairs somewhere.'

Cat watched her mother leave the room with indulgent affection. Annie always wanted to make it better, even if she didn't understand what the problem really was. Cat filled the kettle and leaned against the worktop while she waited for it to boil. Vaguely, she heard the gravel in the drive crunch in the background. Her father was back sooner than she'd expected. Maybe she could get him to give her a driving lesson. She'd need to be able to drive if she was going to be a nanny.

But the back door didn't open. Instead, there was a tentative knock which was not followed by a friend or parishioner walking straight in. Perhaps it was a parcel. Cat pushed off from the worktop and crossed to the door.

It wasn't a delivery of any kind. Standing on the kitchen doorstep was the last person she'd expected to see. Cat's hand flew to her mouth. 'You!' she exclaimed.

31

Henry pushed his thick blond hair back from his forehead and gazed intently at Cat, an anxious expression on his face. He looked crumpled, like a man who has spent too long without a break in the driver's seat. A faint shadow of stubble shaded his jawline. A poor attempt at a smile lifted one corner of his mouth. 'Hi, Cat,' he said.

For a moment, she thought her heart would explode in an incendiary mix of shock and delight. 'Henry.' The single word was all she could manage.

'I've come to apologise. Will you talk to me?'

She stepped back and waved him into the kitchen. Henry walked in, giving the room a keen appraisal and smiling at what he saw. He turned to face her. 'The way my family has treated you – and your brother too, indirectly – appals me. I'm ashamed to be a Tilney right now.'

Before either could say another word, Annie bounced back into the room waving a thin bundle of papers. 'I found it. Heaven knows why, but I put it in with the Mothers' Union agenda.' She stopped in her tracks and surveyed the young people in the kitchen. 'Who's this, Cat?'

Henry stepped forward and offered his hand, more hesitantly than Cat had ever seen before. 'Mrs Morland? I'm Henry Tilney. I've come to apologise for the terrible way my father treated your daughter. I wanted to do it in person so you would be in no doubt how serious I am. And of course, I wanted to be sure that Cat had got home safe and well.'

Annie, open-hearted as her daughter, shook his hand. 'Take your coat off and sit down. If you've driven from Scotland you'll be desperate for a decent cup of tea. You get nothing but sweepings in those motorway café cuppas. Cat, fetch down the tins. Henry won't say no to some home baking, will you?'

Looking somewhat taken aback, Henry shrugged off his creased suit jacket and sat down at the kitchen table. Cat set down the cake tins and pulled out a chair to face him. 'Thank you,' he said. 'Your generosity makes me even more ashamed.'

Annie poured boiling water into three mugs. 'You're not your father, though, are you? What kind of person blames the child for the sins of the father?'

'That's kind of you to say so.'

'Our children's friends are always welcome here, Henry. Perhaps one day we'll get to meet your sister?'

'I'm sure she'd be delighted.'

'How was your drive?' Annie asked, handing out the mugs of tea and offering milk from the plastic bottle. And still Cat said nothing, apparently struck dumb by the arrival of the son of her persecutor.

'Tedious,' Henry said. 'But I came as soon as I heard what had happened.' He looked at Cat. 'I didn't get back on Tuesday night as I'd hoped. I had to go straight back to Edinburgh to pick up some case papers for the next day. So I only found out what had happened when I got back last night. As soon as I heard, I phoned my father in Nice and got some answers from him. Then I got straight in the car and set off.' He sipped his tea and gave a little smile. 'Slept in the car, I'm afraid. Sorry I look like a vagrant.' They sat in silence for a moment while Henry drank tea and wolfed cake.

Cat – anxious, agitated, pink-cheeked and bright-eyed – was so changed from the apathetic creature of a few minutes before that a far less astute judge than her mother would have suspected she was more than pleased to see Henry. When he drained his cup and beamed his thanks at Annie, she said, 'Cat, why don't you and Henry walk over to the Allens'? I'm sure Susie would be thrilled to see him.'

'That would be splendid,' Henry said. He grabbed his jacket and waited for Cat to rise so he could follow her out. They walked down the drive to the garden, where a path led across the meadows and through the orchard to the rear of the Allens' property. No sooner were they out of sight of the kitchen windows than Henry grabbed Cat's hand and pulled her round to face him. 'Are you ever going to speak to me again?' he asked, his tone a plea.

'I don't know what to say. One minute I'm an outcast, the next minute you turn up here being charming to my mother. What am I supposed to think?'

'That I'm desperately sorry and ashamed about what happened to you. That whatever the truth of the situation, my father dealt with it in an atrocious way.'

'The truth of the situation? The truth of the situation is that your father threw me out of Northanger Abbey in the middle of the night and didn't even ask whether I had enough money to get home. If it hadn't been for Ellie—'

He gave a bitter laugh. '"If it hadn't been for Ellie." So it's true, then?'

'Henry, I have no idea what you're talking about.'

'Because it's all right with me, if that's how it is. I just wish you'd told me instead of letting me make a complete fool of myself.'

'Told you *what?* What am I supposed to have been keeping secret?'

'You know perfectly well.'

'What? Tell me. What?'

'That you're a lesbian. That you're in love with Ellie.'

Cat stared at him, thunderstruck. 'A *lesbian?* Me? What are you talking about?'

'That's why Father threw you out. Because he discovered that it wasn't me you were interested in, it was Ellie.' He let go her hand and turned away. 'Really, Cat, I wish you'd felt able to be honest with me.'

'I'm not a lesbian, Henry. I swear. I don't even know any lesbians. Well, apart from the women who run the Post Office, and they don't count because they're older than God. Where did your father get this mad idea?'

Henry stuck his hands in his trouser pockets and began to pace back and forth, as if he were in court. 'He was in London for a meeting, then he went to play poker. He ran into Johnny Thorpe—'

'That pig?' Cat was immediately wary. What fresh harm were the Thorpes intent on wreaking on her family?

'My father likes him for some reason I've never been able to fathom. Anyway, they got talking and Father said you were staying with us and he rather thought you and I might end up as an item.'

Cat flushed. 'Jeez! Talk about presumptuous.'

Henry looked discomfited. 'Whatever. According to my father, Johnny burst out laughing and said he was barking up the wrong tree. Johnny said he'd been sniffing around — his words, not mine, before you slap me — but then he'd found out from his sister that you're a lesbian.'

Furious, Cat turned on him. 'And your father — and now you — believed it, of course. You men are so vain. All this because I told Bella I wasn't interested in her tedious brother. If a woman doesn't fall over herself to go out with one of you — because you're a pig, or you're a drunk, or you're a bore — then she must be a lesbian? How dare you, Henry Tilney. How dare you come here and say these things to me?'

He held his hands up in a gesture of surrender. 'Don't shoot the messenger. I came to try and put things right.'

'But you started off assuming this shit was the truth. Like you could trust Johnny Thorpe ahead of me, just because he's one of the boys.'

'My father said it made sense to him. You have to admit, Cat, you and Ellie are very affectionate with each other. Always hugging and stuff.'

'That's just how girls are, Henry. I don't have any guilty secrets. The people with the guilty secrets are your family.' The words were out before she could stop herself. She had never been so angry, and her judgement had disappeared with her equilibrium.

He gave her a look of contempt. 'You're not still banging on about my father being the secret slayer of the west wing?'

'You know what, Henry? For the longest time I thought you were vampires. The way you all avoid the sunlight. The way you all look young for your years. The fact that none of you looks like the woman you call your mother. The food you eat – rare steaks and liver, all that blood. But you Tilneys are a different kind of bloodsucker. It's money you're interested in, not blood.'

Henry stopped in his tracks, his mouth open, his expression bewildered. 'Vampires? You mean, like in those books and films? With all that misogyny and oppression and werewolves and shit?'

'Exactly. Because what is your father if he's not oppressive and misogynist? Treating me like dirt, and all because he believed Johnny Thorpe. Even if he'd been telling the truth, what sort of excuse is that for throwing somebody out of your house in the middle of the night? So what if I was a lesbian – which, by the way, I am definitely not. So what if Ellie is a lesbian? Though God help her if she is. So yes, I think your family is riddled with secrets. I found the Bible, Henry. I found the Bible.'

Henry cast around histrionically, as if looking for an escape route from this madwoman. 'You found the Bible?' he said in tones of exaggerated calm. 'What is that supposed to mean?'

'The family Bible. With the births and marriages, but not many deaths. Where all the boys called Henry Tilney seem to live to adulthood, which is unheard of back when loads and loads of babies and young children died.'

'We're not a family that has ever celebrated death, Cat. It's a tradition.'

'Oh, bollocks, Henry. You're a family that has your own chapel and graveyard. You're not exactly, "death where is thy sting", are you? But more than that—'

'Wait a minute, is this the Bible with the bullet hole?'

Cat was taken aback at his willingness to own something of her argument. 'Yes.'

'And that proves what, exactly?'

Cat hesitated. She hadn't taken the opportunity to ask her father what he thought about the Bible with the bullet hole. 'Well, only a creature steeped in evil would shoot a Bible.' She was floundering and she knew it, but she wasn't giving ground.

'That's a bit racist, Cat.' He couldn't restrain a wry smile, and she felt her resistance challenged.

'What do you mean, racist?'

'That bullet came from a German gun. And that Bible is the reason I'm here today.'

She frowned. 'I don't understand.'

'My great-great grandfather was an officer in the First World War. He carried his Bible inside his tunic and it took a bullet for him on the Somme. If not for the Bible, he would have been killed, and I wouldn't have been born. Cat, we're not vampires. That's crazy. Vampires don't exist in the real world. Any more than the zombie apocalypse is just round the corner.'

Hands on hips, she stared him down. 'Prove it.'

He burst out laughing. 'You can't prove a negative. I can't prove there are no such things as vampires any more than you can prove you're not a lesbian. You're a vicar's daughter, Cat – surely you of all people understand there's a point where you have to have faith? Take people on trust?'

They stood staring at each other, neither willing to capitulate. Then Henry made an impatient gesture. 'This is stupid, Cat. I came here to apologise for my father, that's true. But that's only part of the reason. I came because ever since I met you at Fiona Alexander's dance class I've been falling in love with you.'

Her mouth suddenly dry, Cat took a step backwards. 'No.'

He looked stricken. 'You don't feel the same?'

At last, Cat composed herself and spoke sense. 'Oh, Henry, I'm completely crazy about you.' And she threw her arms round the startled young man, who quickly recovered himself and gathered her into a warm embrace. Finally, Cat knew the kiss she'd dreamed of since that first dance. They stood locked together in the orchard, oblivious to anything but each other, as young lovers are inclined to be.

It was some time before they reached the Allens' house and afterwards, neither would have been able to give any sort of account of the conversation that took place there. By the time they returned to the vicarage, the matter was sealed. Henry explained to the Morlands that he had argued so fiercely with his father that he feared there could be no reconciliation. 'But I have a profession,' he said. 'I'll be fully qualified by the end of the year. I can support myself without taking a penny from him. I'll be fine. Straightening things out with Cat has been worth much more than any amount of money.'

The two young lovers looked at each other. 'Vampire,' she said.

'Lesbian,' he replied.

And to the astonishment of the Morlands, they burst into helpless laughter.

Epilogue

Four years later

Henry had never looked more handsome, Cat thought as she walked down the aisle of the parish church at Farleigh Piddle on her father's arm. Her husband-to-be had the perfect figure for full morning dress, and the pearl grey of his cut-away coat emphasised the golden glow of his tanned skin and the sun-bleached highlights in his dark blond hair. There wasn't a more handsome man in the church. Probably not in the whole Piddle Valley, she reckoned.

In the four years that had passed since her enforced flight from Northanger Abbey, our cast of characters had undergone a bewildering kaleidoscope of changes. Cat herself had pursued her mother's suggestion of training as a nanny. Once qualified, Henry had found her part-time work with one of his colleagues, so their two-year commute between Newcastle and Edinburgh was finally ended. They'd lived together quite happily in the little flat in the Lawnmarket, but Henry's growing success meant they were considering a move to something more spacious. 'Something with a nursery,' Cat had confided to her mother the night before the wedding. 'Not right away. Don't get the wrong idea. But down the line.'

Spurred on by Henry's confrontation with her father, Ellie had also taken her life into her own hands. She accepted a place at the Edinburgh School of Art to pursue a course in design, funding herself by selling some of the jewellery her mother had left her. 'I only sold the ugly pieces,' she told Cat. 'Big stones in clumsy settings. I've kept the antiques. But my father really does have dreadful taste in jewellery. I'm not sorry to see the back of most of it.' Of her romantic life, she never spoke, perhaps with good reason.

Ellie and Cat had continued with their children's book project. They'd collected a raft of rejections, but finally an indie publisher in Edinburgh had bought the first two books in a series of comedy vampire stories. 'Because of our family experience,' Ellie had said with a giggle when they finally met their editor. Cat kicked her under the table. Not everyone could be expected to share their sense of humour.

Freddie's tour of duty in Afghanistan being over, he had resigned his commission and taken up a lucrative position with an armament company. He was unable to attend the wedding because of a sales trip to a Gulf emirate. Nobody minded.

James Morland had carved out a niche in immigration and human rights law in his chambers in York. He'd fallen in love with one of his clients, a Somali woman who had just opened a restaurant near the university that was already winning rave reviews. James had gained both happiness and half a stone in the process.

Bella Thorpe had featured briefly in a reality TV show but had been eliminated in the first public vote of the season. Her brother Johnny had been fired by his bank after a series of dubious transactions came to light. Susie Allen took great delight in reporting their misfortunes to the Morlands, and even the vicar could not avoid the sin of *schadenfreude*.

And what of General Tilney? His first reaction to the rebellion of his younger children was to cut off their allowances and bar them from Northanger Abbey. His capacity for cutting off his nose was remarkable, but he had reckoned without the compassion their mother had installed in Henry and Ellie. A year after the terrible night when he had cast Cat out of the abbey, his younger son arrived there, having colluded with Mrs Calman to ensure the General was home alone.

Henry never revealed what had passed between them, but although there was never much subsequent warmth between father and son, neither was there the bitterness there had been previously. Ellie too had been welcomed back into the fold; now she had completed her degree, she was to take up residence at Woodston, where her father had promised to build a studio at the water's edge.

The moral or message of this story is hard to discern. And that is as it should be, for as Catherine Morland found out to her cost, it is not the function of fiction to offer lessons in life.